Your brother was always nice to me in middle school," I say. "He even gave me a flower once."

"He did?" Julia says.

"Yeah. Your parents had brought you a bouquet, because of the show, and I was standing next to you after the performance and I guess I looked lonely or something because Alex pulled out a flower from your bouquet and handed it to me."

"That is so sweet," Vanessa says.

"I should get the credit," Julia says. "It was *my* flower he stole. I'm going to have to yell at him for that."

"No, don't!"

She laughs at my panic. "I'm just teasing. I'm glad he did it." She glances up. "What's that sound?"

"Lunch bell," Vanessa says. "Let's go."

As we walk out the building, I'm feeling very optimistic about this summer for the first time since Mom committed me to coming here. I already have people to hang out with, and even more important . . .

Alex Braverman is here. And I'm about to see him.

As we cross the courtyard, I pull out my hair elastic and shake my hair so it falls around my face, then rake my fingers through the waves.

Alex Braverman is here. And I'm about to see him. A ponytail isn't going to cut it.

Funded by LSTA
BOOKS4U PRO.
2013

Also by Claire LaZebnik

Epic Fail

If You Lived Here, You'd Be Home Now

The Smart One and the Pretty One

Knitting Under the Influence

Same As It Never Was

Claire LaZebnik

the trouble with flirting

HARPER TEEN

An Imprint of HarperCollinsPublishers

HarperTeen is an imprint of HarperCollins Publishers.

The Trouble with Flirting
Copyright © 2013 by Claire LaZebnik

www.epicreads.com

Library of Congress Cataloging-in-Publication Data
LaZebnik, Claire Scovell.
The trouble with flirting / Claire LaZebnik. — 1st ed.
p. cm.
Summary: Loosely based on Jane Austen's *Mansfield Park*,
relates high school junior Franny's summer at Mansfield
College in Portland, Oregon, where she helps her aunt sew
costumes for an acting program and gets caught between the
boy she likes and the one who likes her.
ISBN 978-0-06-192127-8 (pbk bdg)
[1. Interpersonal relations—Fiction. 2. Theater—Fiction.
3. Actors and actresses—Fiction. 4. Flirting—Fiction.
5. Universities and colleges—Fiction. 6. Portland (Or.)—
Fiction.] I. Title.
PZ7.L4496Tro 2013   2012030300
[Fic]—dc23   CIP
                                                             AC

13 14 15 16 17   CG/RRDH   10 9 8 7 6 5 4 3 2 1
❖
First Edition

For Johnny, who taught me everything I know about summer acting programs and who makes me laugh more than anyone else in the world.

act 1

scene one

When Jasper Snowden's parents divorced, Jasper got to stay in his bedroom in the big house he'd always lived in, while his parents took turns living there with him. They said they didn't want him to have to bounce around from one bed to another. To make the arrangement work smoothly, Mr. Snowden (who, my mother said, "is in real estate—and that's where the real money is, you know") bought two other houses in the same neighborhood, one for him and one for his ex-wife.

That's how the rich get divorced, I guess: they just stash every member of the family in his or her own comfortable home. If the Snowdens had had a dog, he'd probably have gotten his own little dog-sized house with a lovely view of the fire station.

Yeah, my parents' divorce was a little different from that.

Mom and William and I stayed in the three-bedroom

apartment we'd been living in for the past five years, and my dad got a one-room studio in a building about twenty minutes away. "It's ugly and it looks out on a parking lot, but at least it's small" is his big joke about it. The one he's repeated every time I've come over.

He feels bad there's no real guest bed at his place, and has told William and me we can have the futon whenever we want and he'll sleep on the floor. But that just seems weird, so we never sleep over.

Whenever he feels glum about our housing situation, Dad cheers himself up by reminding us all that at least he's close to us and both apartments are in the same good school district.

But sometimes I wonder if going to school in a wealthy neighborhood is such a great thing for us anyway. No one's about to ostracize us because we're not rich, but there are times when it's just awkward. Like when you all go out to dinner and everyone's going to split the check, but you have to point out that all you got was some soup because you can't afford to chip in for everyone else's thirty-dollar entrées. Or when the kids at lunch are all comparing what they got for Christmas that year and you can only really listen, because what are you going to say? *I got three new books and a shirt?* William and I have this shorthand where he'll say to me something like *Clayton Walstaff got a vintage Gibson guitar for Christmas,* and I'll say something like *Yeah, well, Georgia Olstead got a BMW,* and then we just laugh because it's all so ridiculous.

And then there's the whole *what are you doing this summer?* conversation, which starts early in the spring, and this year—my junior year—is more intense than ever before, because everyone knows this is the summer to do something to impress colleges. And impressive summers don't come cheap.

A lot of money can buy you a "community service" trip, like the one my friend Kiana is going on: she'll travel to Costa Rica, where she'll carry water or something for the first week and then party with other Americans at a beach resort for another week. She's already decided that her college essay is going to be about how great it is to "help our brothers and sisters in our global village." She's just waiting to plug in some firsthand specifics.

Money can also buy you a summer term at Oxford or some other fantastic European university. My friend Chloe is going to the Sorbonne, where she'll sit in on fiction classes during the day and hang out in Paris at night. *Her* college essay? Probably something like "how I stopped being a tourist and became a citizen of the world."

Wait—maybe I'm wrong. An impressive summer isn't necessarily all about money.

Sometimes it's about connections.

Zelda Moreno's mom knows a doctor who's taking Zelda in as a research assistant ("I spent my summer curing cancer!"), and Drew Desanti's dad got him a gig in an architecture firm ("building a better, greener future"), and Natalie Nowak's uncle Joe got her an internship with a magazine-editor friend of his ("the written word *can* change the world").

My parents may not have money, but at least they don't have any connections, either. (Sorry. I inherited Dad's sense of humor.)

Not that it matters. I can't apply for any cool unpaid internships or traveling programs anyway: I have to earn money this summer for college. My mother made that clear long ago. She also said, "Jobs teach discipline and the value of hard work and the importance of not taking anything for granted. And that's the gift I'm giving to you."

"I'd rather have a laptop," I said.

"A job can get you one of those, too. And don't be a wiseass, Franny."

William is no help at all. *He* started working the summer he was fourteen, walking people's dogs and washing cars, and then, when he was older, scooping ice cream and ripping tickets at the movie theater. Now that he's in college, he's moved up in the world and is going to be working at an investment bank in New York City (and sharing a sublet with his longtime girlfriend).

If it weren't for William, I might have been able to wriggle out of a summer job for one more year, but he's always been one of those good, responsible oldest sons, which means I have to be good too or be forever cast as the family screwup.

Also? I really do need a new laptop. The one I'm currently using is a hand-me-down from Dad, and he bought it more than five years ago. Do you know what five years *is* in the laptop universe? Like a hundred human years.

"I don't want to scoop ice cream all summer long," I said to Mom as we discussed my job prospects at the kitchen table.

"Don't worry—it's not an option anyway. I walked by there last night and they're fully staffed for the summer already. The Shoe Zone is hiring, though."

I shuddered. "Great. I can touch people's feet all summer. And here I was envying Sarah Gabrielle because she's going on an African safari."

"Sarah Gabrielle's mother has a nanny for each kid so she never has to interact with any of them, and she sends them far away whenever she can. Is that really what you want? A mother who'd rather not have you around?"

Mom said it jokingly, but I knew she wanted some real reassurance that I didn't feel like I was having a deprived childhood. My mom is tough about rules, but deep down she's a big pile of insecure mush who needs her kids to tell her that, in spite of getting a divorce and having to say no to us about almost everything due to lack of funds, she's done right by us. Which I guess she has.

So I swallowed the sarcastic comment I was tempted to make and instead squeezed her shoulder and said lightly, "Nah, I'll take the interfering, overbearing mom I've got."

"And we'll both keep thinking about the summer," she said, patting my hand. "We'll find you something good."

Remember how I said my parents have no connections? That wasn't entirely accurate. They have no powerful or rich or interesting connections, but they do have relatives out in the workforce, which is how Mom scored me a summer job.

"I found the perfect thing for you!" she told me when she picked me up after school one afternoon in late May. She had come straight from her job teaching English at a middle school that's two towns over from us.

"The perfect thing?" I repeated as I closed my car door.

"The job," she said impatiently. "The summer job. And you're going to love it."

"Really? What is it?" I'd been looking but hadn't had any luck yet. There were too many out-of-work adults who were willing to take anything that paid, and a lot of college students had already come back home for the summer and were also looking for jobs. So I was mildly excited to hear what she'd been able to find.

I was less excited when she told me. "Sewing costumes?" I repeated dubiously. "With Aunt Amelia?"

"Doesn't that sound fun? You love the theater!"

"I know," I said. "And you were the one who said it was a waste of my time, remember?" I acted some in middle school, usually in lead roles, but right before high school Mom and Dad sat me down—presenting a united front even though they were already divorced—and told me that I had to figure out what really mattered to me and focus on that.

Then of course they *told* me what really mattered to me, which according to them was maintaining a high GPA and pitching for the softball team—two things that could potentially score me a college scholarship. So I stopped acting and focused on schoolwork, which is why my GPA is currently somewhere around 4.1, and on my pitching, which is why my rotator cuff is a mess and I'm not playing *any* sports at all anymore.

Mom waved her hand dismissively. "I never said theater was a waste of time, exactly, just that it shouldn't be your biggest priority, since you're good at so many other things. Anyway, the point is, this is at Mansfield College! Remember? Lucinda's kid told us the program changed his life, and you said you wanted to apply."

"Right—and *you* said I had to work, remember?"

"So this is the best of both worlds: you get to be there *and* you get to earn money!"

"But I don't get to act," I said. "Which is kind of the point of an acting program."

"You'll still be in that atmosphere, right? You'll see all the shows and be around kids your own age."

"Where would I live?"

"With Aunt Amelia."

"Bleah."

She shot me a reproving look. "Aunt Amelia means well."

"She complains all the time about everything. And if I'm working for her—"

"First of all, it's only for six weeks."

"Only!"

"Second of all, she said you can eat meals in the dining hall with the campers or students or whatever they're called. Doesn't that sound like fun? But you'll *also* be earning a paycheck. Win-win!"

"You already told her I'd do it, didn't you?" I said.

And that's how I found out that yes, I *was* already committed to sewing costumes with my aunt Amelia at the Mansfield College High School Theater Program in a suburb of Portland, Oregon, the summer before my senior year of high school.

What a fascinating college essay I'm going to get out of *that*. "Changing the world one stitch at a time . . ."

scene two

Aunt Amelia wants me to arrive at Mansfield the day before the enrolled students move in, so she can show me around before things get too crazy. The session begins in late June, so after school ends I have two blissful weeks of sitting around other people's pools and catching up on all the TV I missed during finals.

My flight from Phoenix to Portland is short, which is too bad. I haven't flown much on my own—okay, the truth is I've *never* flown on my own; I've barely ever flown at all—and I get a little thrill looking out the window when we take off and land and smiling mysteriously at the middle-aged man sitting next to me. I wonder if he thinks I'm cute and is glad he's sitting next to me and not someone old and fat. We don't ever talk, other than "excuse me" when our elbows bump, so I never find out.

Amelia greets me at the airport with a brusque kiss

on the cheek and a "you've gotten tall," then drives us to the campus, which is very leafy-green and pretty.

I know a lot of kids who are planning to apply to Mansfield College, but it's too small and low-key for me. Some people want that. I want something a little more exciting if I'm going to be spending four years of my life there. NYU would be perfect—I'm desperate to get in.

Mansfield seems especially sleepy now, with all the students gone for the summer. It's a total ghost town, but Amelia says unenthusiastically that that will change once the high-school seniors arrive.

She trots me quickly past some buildings. "That's the dining hall, that's the dorm, that's the administrative building; that's the little forest where I've seen some of the students smoking and I expect you to stay away from there. Speaking of which, you'd better not smoke. Or drink. Or do anything even worse. I'll send you home in a second if I catch you doing anything like that—and don't think, *She wouldn't really,* because I promise you I would."

The tour ends at the theater building, where Amelia has her workroom. She leads me inside and says it's time to see how good I am at sewing.

My mom taught me a long time ago. Their mother—hers and Amelia's—was a professional seamstress, which is why they're both so good at it. Mom only ever used her skill to make Halloween costumes for me and William. But because Mom thinks it's important for people to be able to do things for themselves like cook and sew and clean, she's made sure William and I have all the basics down.

I think I'm competent, but after Amelia tests me with a few seams, she informs me that my hand stitches should be smaller and tighter and that I have a "lead foot" on the machine.

"I'm not surprised," she adds. "Your mother was like that too—more interested in finishing quickly than in the quality of the work. It's no wonder she's not a professional."

"I don't think she was ever trying to be one," I say.

"Well, of course that's what she says *now*."

I decide not to argue the point and glance around the workroom. It's a small space, with two machines side by side and several windows. It's super hot, and it's not even July yet, so I've got to figure it's only going to get hotter over the next five weeks. The one square fan is useless against the flood of sunshine coming in, but Amelia tells me we can't pull the shades down because she needs the light.

"My eyes," she says, "aren't what they used to be," which is probably true, since there are pairs of reading glasses scattered all over the office, within easy reach no matter where she might be sitting or standing.

"So how does this all work?" I ask, resigning myself to a lot of future sweating. "What costumes will we be making?"

"We have five weeks to design and create costumes for four different casts," she says with a weird mixture of gloom and pride. "I've already spoken to the directors and have some sense of what they'll be wanting, but we can't really move forward until the kids are cast and we can measure them, which always takes a few days. Until then we'll be hunting up sources, checking through the archives, and figuring out fabrics."

"How many cast members altogether?"

"Forty-eight. Twelve to a play."

"That's a lot of costumes," I say.

Amelia throws her hands up in the air. "It's an ungodly amount of work! Hundreds of costumes—most cast members play multiple roles—and they all have to be ready by the same time."

I drop down onto the stool. "And there's only the two of us?"

"I've done it every summer for fifteen years," she says, tossing her head. "With only one assistant, just like now. It's never easy, but it always gets done. Just be prepared for a lot of long hours and hard work."

"Do you make everything from scratch?"

"Not everything. I buy some pieces and use what I can from the school's archives."

"Oh," I say, relieved. "That's not so bad, then."

"It's still bad," she says. "We'll have to alter everything. Teenage girls today are either too fat or too thin. There's no such thing as a normal body anymore."

"I beg your pardon," I say with mock indignation.

I'm just joking, but she narrows her eyes at me and tilts her head back so she can survey me over her long, thin nose. "Don't fish for compliments. You may discover that no one feels like giving you one."

"I wasn't," I say—which, by the way, is *true*.

"Your body is fine now, but give it twenty, thirty years. Gravity and time do horrible things to a woman. I had your body once."

"How'd I end up with it, then?" I say jovially.

She just sighs. "Time and gravity get us all in the end," she says darkly. "Time and gravity."

Amelia shows me the costume and prop archives under the theater, and then she takes me to her apartment. We drive, since she picked me up at the airport, but she says she usually walks, because her apartment is so close to campus. She works there year-round, running the costume part of the theater department (she also teaches a course on costume design and one on costume history), and rents the place from a building Mansfield owns. It's in a beautiful, expensive neighborhood—she tells me she couldn't afford to live there if the college didn't subsidize it. There are several entryways into her building, and a fenced-off area with a postage-stamp-sized pool and a cheap aboveground hot tub that Amelia tells me she's sure is a breeding ground for dangerous bacteria.

The actual apartment is small but clean and neat. Her furniture is simple and generic, but every window has some kind of gorgeous curtain on it—all handmade by her, of course—and the sofa and chair pillows are wildly luxurious, covered with tassels, fringe, and buttons, like something out of a harem.

Makes me wonder if somewhere inside Amelia there's a romantic soul. You certainly wouldn't know it to look at her in her white oxford shirt and cotton khakis.

"You have your own room to sleep in, but there's only one bathroom," she tells me as she leads me around. "Please wipe down the sink after you use it. I can't stand finding hairs lying around."

"I'll try to remember," I say. "It's nice of you to let me stay here."

"I'm looking forward to the company."

She sounds as stiff as I do, and I wonder if she means it or not. My mom claimed this whole thing was Amelia's idea, but now that I'm here, my presence seems to be making her uncomfortable.

I unpack in the guest bedroom, which is small and

clean like the rest of the apartment, while Amelia boils some penne pasta for dinner. She mixes it with some pesto from a jar, and heats up a box of frozen brussels sprouts to serve on the side. "Tomorrow the dining hall will be open, and you can eat as many meals there as you like," she says as we sit down at her small table. "I'm sure you'd rather be with kids your own age."

"This is nice too," I say, but of course she's right. Plus . . . frozen brussels sprouts? On my first night there? Really?

After dinner she turns on the TV and settles down with a cup of chamomile tea to watch *House Hunters International.*

"I'd like to live in Europe for a while," she says during a commercial break.

"Why don't you?" I ask.

"Because life doesn't work that way."

I really don't know all that much about my aunt, other than that she's older than my mother, and thinner and crabbier. Whenever she used to come visit us, William and I would try to keep our distance, because if we got too close, she would grab us by the arm and interrogate us about our studies and extracurriculars, an activity that would end with her shaking her head and pursing her lips in a way that suggested we weren't performing up to her expectations.

I know she was married once, a long time ago, before

I was even born, but all Mom ever said about that was a flat "It didn't work out." As far as I know, Amelia hasn't had a boyfriend since then. Of course, it's possible she leads a much more exciting personal life than we're aware of, but after spending today with her, I kind of doubt it.

Which makes me feel tender toward her. Poor Aunt Amelia. Stuck in this small, plain apartment, sewing costumes for other people to wear all day long.

So I say, "Hey, maybe someday you and I could take a trip to Europe together."

"And who do you think would pay for that?" she snaps in response. "Your mother? Me? We're both barely getting by. Dreams are easy, Franny, but you can't live on them."

"Or not," I say, and we wait in silence for the commercials to end.

When we walk to campus the next morning, I can *feel* a difference in the air: it's like the school has come alive in the last twelve hours. The dining hall is pumping out bready, coffee-ish smells, which make me glad Amelia scored me a meal card.

"We'll have lunch there today, right?" I say hopefully.

"*I* won't be eating in the dining hall," Amelia replies. "I ate there once, and that was enough for me. I found five hairs in one plate of food. I'm amazed they don't get cited by the health department. But I'm sure it'll be fine for you. Kids have stomachs of steel."

We go to her office, and she puts me to work for the next few hours mending a splitting seam on an enormous stage curtain. The actual sewing isn't difficult, since I can do it on the machine, but wrestling huge armfuls of velvet into submission is hot, exhausting work, and time passes slowly. The all-female seventies folk music Amelia plays at a low wail only increases my restlessness.

All morning long I can hear happy voices outside in the courtyard and cars pulling up and doors banging. The students are definitely arriving. When Amelia finally says, "You might as well go—you're obviously not focusing on your work anyway," she doesn't need to tell me twice. I'm on my feet and out the door in seconds.

I stop outside and blink, dazed for a moment by the bright sunshine.

Dozens of kids my age are milling around, greeting one another with squeals of excitement, rolling and hauling luggage across the courtyard, and running in and out of the dorm across the way and the dining hall next to it.

I see a girl grab a guy by the arm a few yards away from me. "You *have* to be Jorey!" she cries. "I recognize you from your profile pic!"

"Carson?" he says. "Carson Bailey?"

"Oh, my God, I can't believe we're actually meeting after all those endless IM sessions!" She's screaming and he's screaming and they're both jumping up and down. "You're like the male equivalent of me! I totally love you!"

"I totally love *you*!"

More screaming, more jumping.

I move through the throng, with no particular destination in mind. I'm thinking that if I can just connect with someone who seems nice, then maybe she'll introduce me around and I'll have people to eat meals with. I'm not going to spend my entire summer hanging out with Amelia.

I feel funny, though: I'm not one of them. But I'm *sort of* one of them. But I'm not one of them.

Like that.

I spot a girl who's struggling to get through the dorm door with two large bags. I race ahead to grab it and hold it for her. "Thanks," she says as she moves through. "That is *so* nice of you."

Some other kids are coming out of the dorm, and because I'm already holding the door open, I'm stuck there holding it for them, too. Everyone thanks me, but no one stops to talk.

There's finally a break in the traffic, so I let go of the door. I step back without looking and almost collide with a slim boy with large brown eyes who instantly says, "Sorry!"

"My fault," I say.

He shakes his head in friendly disagreement and slips around me to get into the dorm. I decide to follow him in and see what it's like inside.

I step into a big lobby that's dominated by an industrial-looking stairwell. There are bulletin boards running at eye level along all the walls, which are already filled with notices, most of them of the ONLY GIRLS ARE ALLOWED ON THE THIRD FLOOR AFTER 9 P.M. variety. I wander past them and then through an archway into an enormous common room with a bunch of sofas and armchairs, a row of vending machines, a piano, and a TV.

No one's hanging out in there: kids stick their heads in and say "Nice!" or "Ugh," depending on what they think of it, but they all move on, eager to unpack or explore more, I assume.

I head back out toward the stairs, thinking maybe I'll sneak up and see what the actual rooms look like. I get to the bottom of the stairs at the same time as two girls with lots of luggage, and I move aside to let them go up first.

"Thanks," one says, with a distracted glance my way. She's tall and skinny, with light brown skin, wildly corkscrewing black hair with gold glints that's currently being held off her face by a wide headband, and enormous dark eyes framed by chunky glasses. She's wearing black lace-up work boots, denim shorts, and a narrow tank top.

"No worries," I say.

The taller girl at her side halts. "Franny? Franny Pearson?"

I whip around to get a better look at her. She's pretty, with thick, dark layered hair and big blue eyes. And I totally know her. "Julia? Oh, my God!"

Turns out I can squeal with the best of them.

I know someone here!

Or at least I *knew* her, back in eighth grade. I haven't seen her since then.

"I can't believe it!" She drops the bag she's carrying and lets go of the handle of her rolling suitcase so she can throw her arms around me. "Why didn't I see your name anywhere? You didn't join the Mansfield Facebook group!"

I hug her back. "Yeah, that's because—"

But before I can explain, the other girl is asking, "How do you guys know each other?"

Julia releases me. "We went to middle school together, but then we went to different high schools and kind of lost touch. But I should have guessed you'd be here, Franny. You were always one of the best actors."

"So were you," I say. "But I'm not actually here."

The other girl raises her eyebrows. "You a ghost?"

"I mean, I'm not in the acting program. I'm working here this summer—helping my aunt. She's the costume designer."

"Oh." There's an awkward moment of silence. Then Julia says, "Cool. Wish I could sew."

"Yeah," the other girl says. "Me too." She nods up the stairs. "Where are you staying? Here in the dorm?"

"I wish. No, I have a room in my aunt's apartment."

"My name's Vanessa, by the way."

I introduce myself and say, "Can I help you guys carry your stuff up?"

"Yes, *please*." Julia instantly hands me a bag. It's covered in Burberry plaid. "Have you seen the dorm rooms yet?"

I shake my head.

"Julia and I started talking outside and then realized we were in the same room," Vanessa explains as we all struggle our way up the stairs, their rolling trunks making a *thunk, thunk, thunk* sound on each step. "We don't know if it's just the two of us or not."

We reach the second floor. There's a locked door to get onto the hallway and a sign on it that says, ONLY BOYS ARE ALLOWED ON THE SECOND FLOOR AFTER 9 P.M.!

"What do you think they think changes after nine o'clock at night?" I ask, nodding toward the sign. You can hear voices from behind the door and see some blurry movement through its smoky glass panes.

"Sex," Julia says. "I mean, I assume."

"I've heard you can have sex as early as seven p.m.," I say. "But never before five on a Sunday."

Vanessa laughs as we head up the second flight. "You know what's really funny? This is an *acting* program—most of the guys are gay. So if they think telling girls to stay away is going to keep anyone nice and innocent, they're nuts."

"I'm glad we're on separate floors, though," Julia says as we reach the second landing and stop in front of another smoked-glass-paned door. "I have a twin brother, and believe me, you don't want to share a bathroom with a seventeen-year-old boy. They're pigs."

"Your brother—" I start to say, but Vanessa's already speaking: "Hold on, we need a key." She juggles her stuff so she can slip the card out of her back pocket; then she unlocks the door and we step through. The hallway runs the length of the building, with doors on both sides.

"Room 307," Julia murmurs, scanning the numbers as we move along. A lot of the doors are open, and you can hear girls discussing who should sleep where and which side of the closet they want.

"There it is—307!" I spot it first. It's about halfway down, on the right.

Vanessa is still holding her key card in her hand, and it opens this door too.

The carded lock is the only modern touch. Otherwise, it's your basic unadorned dorm room, probably unchanged for decades: white walls, bunk beds, scratched-up wooden desks and chests of drawers. There are plain plastic shades on the windows.

"Looks like there'll be four of us," Julia says, since there are two sets of bunk beds and four dressers.

"That could just be during the year," I say. "Maybe it's different for the summer students."

"Well, there are at least three of us—someone's already left her stuff," Vanessa says. There's a duffel bag on one of the bottom mattresses, and an enormous rolling trunk pulled right up next to it, which is open. A pair of jeans dangles out the top, and one fancy high-heeled jeweled sandal has fallen on the floor next to the bed. The label says Prada.

Of course.

Julia and Vanessa are discussing which beds they should take.

"The thing is," Julia says, screwing her pretty mouth up uncertainly, "I get really freaked out on a top bunk. When I was little, my friend's brother fell off and broke his arm, and that's all I can think about."

"Go ahead and take the other bottom then," Vanessa says. "I'm happy to take one of the tops. See, I figure that if the whole thing crashes down, it's not the girl who's on top who's in trouble—it's the girl on the bottom."

"Oh, God, don't say that. Now *that's* all I'm going to think about."

"You want me to sleep over the other girl? In case we don't have a fourth?"

"It's up to you," Julia says, but she doesn't say, *No, don't, it'll be more fun to share with you,* the way I would have.

I'm beginning to remember what Julia's like.

"The other one's closer to the window anyway," Vanessa says diplomatically. "I'm going to go ahead and make the bed now in case we don't have much time later." She climbs halfway up the bunk-bed ladder and starts unfolding the sheets that have been left in a pile on top of the bed for the students to use.

Julia removes the folded sheets from her own mattress and puts them on top of one of the dressers. "Don't laugh at me, guys. I brought my own from home." She kneels in front of her brand-new-looking wheeled suitcase, unzips it, and digs through until she pulls out a pile of neatly folded snow-white sheets. The scent of lavender wafts toward me as she stands up with them.

"That was smart," Vanessa says. She's perched on the bunk-bed ladder, trying to arrange the bottom sheet without losing her balance. "Why didn't I think of that?"

"I learned the hard way," Julia says. "Last summer I went to this language-immersion program, and their sheets were so rough I felt like I was sleeping on sandpaper. I was red all over for months afterward."

"You're like the princess and the pea," Vanessa says with an amused glance over her shoulder.

"I'm very delicate," Julia says, fluttering her eyelids. "Hey, Franny, what does 'the princess and the pea' make you think of?"

"*Once Upon a Mattress!*"

"Exactly. We both had lead roles in it in middle school," she explains to Vanessa.

"It was a lot of fun," I say.

Here's what I remember about being in a show with Julia Braverman:

The Good: She seemed genuinely pleased that we both got good roles in the school musical and happy to hang out with me at rehearsals. Even though her family was über-rich—everyone knew it, even back in middle school—and she wore expensive clothing and was always traveling to places like Belize and Thailand, she wasn't snobbish. We had come from different elementary schools and had different groups of friends that didn't overlap much, but we got along fine.

The Bad: I don't think Julia ever once asked me about myself or my family. At rehearsals I heard a *lot* about her life. Like I knew that she got so nervous before every performance that she had diarrhea (not exactly the kind of thing you want to remember about someone you haven't seen in almost four years, but I don't seem to be able to forget that little detail), and I knew that she had a crush on Steven Segelman even though it was pretty obvious that he was obsessed with Rachel Goldman. But she never bothered to learn anything personal about me.

The Ugly: She was always going through some kind of emotional crisis, always grabbing on to me and moaning about how scared/tired/overwhelmed/anxious/miserable she was, even though (as far as I could tell) her life was pretty good. I endured it because I didn't know anyone else in the cast very well—my friends were mostly athletes, not performers—and she always seemed happy to see me.

Actually, things aren't that different now. When you're away from home, any familiar face looks pretty good.

Any familiar face that's not your annoying aunt's, I mean.

"Hey, Julia?" I ask casually as I reach up to tug on Vanessa's sheet from my end, to help smooth it out. "How's your brother doing?"

She's pulling something big and white out of her bag—ah, a pillow. She fluffs it up a bit. "Alex?" she says absently. "He's good, I guess. Same as always. He's here too, you know."

I turn around to look at her. "Wait, *really*?"

"Uh-huh. Room 203."

"I met him outside," Vanessa puts in. She clambers down the ladder and surveys her handiwork, then reaches up to tuck in an uneven bit of sheet hem. "He's pretty cute."

"I totally had a crush on him back in middle school." I say it lightly, which makes me feel like I'm betraying my thirteen-year-old self. Back then I wouldn't have called it a crush. I was seriously and totally in *love* with Alex Braverman.

"Oh, God, everyone did. They still do." Julia places the pillow at the top of her bed. "At least you never tried to wangle an invitation to the house just to meet him. Do you remember Cara Sackeroff?"

"The one who always wore glittery eye shadow?"

She shakes her head. "That was the other Cara. Piecrust."

"Cara Piecrust?" Vanessa repeats incredulously.

"That was what we always called her—I think her last name was really Pietz. Something like that."

I nodded along, but I didn't recognize the nickname. Must have been something Julia's circle called her, not mine.

"Anyway, she begged me to do this English project with her and then said we had to do it at *my* house because her younger sister was a total pain in the butt, and so I said fine and then she spent the entire time following Alex around. She even went into his *room* after he'd gone in there and shut the door just to get away from her. I wasn't allowed to invite her over ever again. Not that I wanted to."

"He was really nice to me," I say. "He even gave me a flower once."

"He did?"

"Yeah. Your parents had brought you a bouquet, because of the show, and I was standing next to you after the performance and my parents weren't there that night—they had just separated and everything was like this big deal with them and there had been some confusion about which one was going when—and anyway, I guess I looked lonely or something because Alex pulled out a flower from your bouquet and handed it to me."

"That is so sweet," Vanessa says.

"I should get the credit," Julia says. "It was *my* flower he stole. I'm going to have to yell at him for that."

"No, don't!"

She laughs at my panic. "I'm just teasing. I'm glad he did it." She glances up. "What's that sound?"

"Lunch bell," Vanessa says. "Let's go."

"Let me just change my shoes." As she slips off her sneakers and puts on some flip-flops, Julia glances at me. "Oh, wait . . . can you eat there?"

"Yeah, I have a meal card." As we walk down the stairs and out the building, I'm feeling very optimistic about this summer for the first time since Mom committed me to coming here. I already have people to hang out with, and even more important . . .

Alex Braverman is here. And I'm about to see him.

As we cross the courtyard, I pull out my hair elastic and shake my hair so it falls around my face, then rake my fingers through the waves.

Alex Braverman is here. And I'm about to see him. A ponytail isn't going to cut it.

scene three

I follow Julia and Vanessa into the dining hall, a large open room with a snaking buffet line at one end, a salad bar in the middle, and about a dozen large round tables filling up the rest of the space.

We get in line together. I grab a slice of pizza and a brownie; Vanessa grabs a slice of pizza and a dish of vanilla pudding; Julia doesn't grab anything until we reach the salad bar, and then she piles lettuce on her plate and douses it with balsamic vinegar.

We get drinks, then look around for a place to sit. "This way," Julia says, and leads us over to a table.

She drops her tray down in front of an empty chair that's next to an extremely good-looking guy. She says to him, "You remember Franny? She went to our middle school."

He smiles up at me. "Hey, Franny! Nice to see you again."

"Hey, Alex," I say. Even if I hadn't recognized him—which I had—I would have figured out pretty quickly that he was Julia's brother: they have the same straight nose, same unusually light blue eyes, same thick dark hair. They're beautiful specimens, both of them, a persuasive argument for genetic engineering.

"Can you believe it?" Julia says, plopping down on the seat next to him. "I'm so relieved to actually know someone already. I was freaking out all yesterday about being with strangers," she tells me and Vanessa.

"She really was," Alex says. "But she freaks out easily."

"True. And now I know Vanessa, too. She's my roommate and she's from New York and she's way cooler than we are."

"Way cooler than you'll *ever* be," Vanessa adds with a laugh. We both sit down at the table. "Who are you?" she asks the thin, brown-eyed guy on Alex's other side.

"Lawrence." He squints at me. "You look really familiar."

"Probably because I knocked into you at the entrance to the dorm half an hour ago," I say. "Sorry about that."

"Oh, right. Yeah, that's it. Totally my fault."

"Nope, mine." We grin at each other.

"You were Lady Larken!" Alex says suddenly.

"I was?" Lawrence says with mock surprise.

"No, *I* was," I say. "In *Once Upon a Mattress*."

"I totally remember you," Alex says.

"You acted like you already did!"

"I knew you looked familiar. But it just clicked: You were Lady Larken, and you wore a big pouffy dress. And you sang a couple of songs. You have a great voice."

"Thanks, but I don't really—I'm just good at faking it."

"And we had a class together, right?"

"Chemistry."

"Ms. Adanasio."

"Except she disappeared three-quarters of the way through the year, remember? And they hired that other guy to take her place?"

"Oh, right," he says. "The guy who never showered."

"I wonder if we'll get to do any singing in the shows here," Vanessa says. "I mean, I know it's not specifically musical theater, but there'll be some singing, right?"

The others start discussing that, which leaves me out of the conversation, so I pick at my slice of pizza without much interest. Hunger fled at the sight of Alex Braverman. Stomachs are like that—there isn't room for both swooning-on-the-inside and digesting.

A guy and a girl approach our table. They obviously know each other already, since their arms are entwined.

"Can we sit here?" asks the girl.

Everyone at our table nods frantically, not just to be friendly but also because the two newcomers are like *comically* good-looking. As they sit down and introduce themselves—Isabella Zevallos, Harry Cartwright—the rest of us stare at them unabashedly.

Harry's got gray-green eyes and thick dark blond hair that he runs his fingers through impatiently whenever it falls forward into his eyes, which it keeps doing, because, as far as I can tell, it's been cut to do just that. His features aren't perfect—his nose is a little crooked, like maybe it's been broken, and his eyes are almost too far apart and his lips are so full they're verging on feminine—but somehow it all kind of works together. When our eyes accidentally meet at one point, I quickly glance away, embarrassed to be caught studying him so openly, but then I realize that every other girl at the table is doing the same thing, except for Isabella, who's watching the rest of us with amusement and leaning her head in toward Harry's to exchange a whisper.

So they're definitely a couple.

No wonder: they belong together. Isabella is so beautiful that if she's even a halfway decent actress, she'll be a star one day. The girl is gorgeous, but not in the way that the prettiest girl at my high school is gorgeous (long blond hair, long blond legs, long blond personality)—no, Isabella looks more like an adult than a teenager. She has elegantly angular cheekbones and slightly tilted dark eyes that swiftly examine all of us from under a thick fringe of eyelash. Even her hairstyle is grown-up: it's pinned in a narrow coil at the back of her head. It makes her look like an old-fashioned movie star. She's wearing a silky white tank top over tight blue jeans, and her bare shoulders are elegantly square above her slender arms.

After all the introductions, she and Harry quickly and confidently take charge of the conversation.

"You wouldn't believe all the ways we've traveled today!" Isabella says, leaning back in her chair and arching her flawless neck in a luxurious stretch. "First by plane—"

"No," Harry corrects her. "Car to the airport first."

"Oh, right, *then* the plane, then the tram to the shuttle bus, the bus to the camp van, then on foot from the dorm—"

"The only thing we didn't take today was a horse-drawn carriage."

"Or a ride on a camel."

"You know, I *should* get a camel—it'd be faster than a car in L.A. traffic. Plus I could name it Lumpy."

"Lumpy would be a good name for a camel," she agrees.

"You're from L.A.?" Julia leans forward. "Both of you?"

Harry grins at her. It's a charming grin but veers toward overkill, what with the too-cute dimples under his green eyes. "Yep. From the same part of L.A.—Brentwood."

"So you two already know each other?" Julia's eyes

dart back and forth, assessing the situation. I remember her crush on Steven Segelman, and I can kind of see how Harry is a similar type to S-squared. Pretty boys, both of them. Steven didn't have a brain in his head. I wonder about Harry.

"Best friends since ninth grade."

Best friends? Really? That would imply they're not a couple. . . . Oh, wait: Absurdly gorgeous guy with a close friend who's a girl? Who loves theater?

So he's gay. Sorry, Julia. And then I notice that Lawrence is gaping at Harry too.

Clearly, I'd be wise to assume *every* guy here is gay until proven otherwise.

"Not the *beginning* of ninth grade," Isabella says. "It was during *The Music Man*, and you were dating what's her name, the girl with the enormous . . ." She curves her fingers into round shapes.

"Nose?" he suggests mischievously.

She laughs. "That too. Anyway, she hated me ever since Jackson Trent kissed me in seventh grade, and every time I tried to talk to you she'd get between us, blocking me with her enormous—"

"Nose."

"That too. . . . She made it clear I wasn't welcome. It wasn't until you broke up with her—"

He grimaces. "And what fun *that* was, what with the tears and the screams and the begging—"

"Yes, you *did* get emotional, didn't you? But at least I was finally permitted to talk to you, and *that's* when we became friends. And you learned to date less clingy girls."

Girls. Okay, so he's *not* gay. Then why aren't they a couple?

I give up. Sooner or later we'll know all about one another. I don't have to figure it all out in the first hour.

"Were you also in *The Music Man*?" Julia asks Harry.

"Of course he was," Isabella says. "He was Harold Hill. Harry always gets the lead."

"It helps to be a guy," he says. "There are always more girls than guys trying out for roles. You don't even have to be talented, just willing to make a fool of yourself." He jerks his chin at Lawrence and Alex. "Right?"

"I take voice lessons," Lawrence says seriously. "And acting classes. And dance."

Harry shrugs cheerfully. "Well, of course it doesn't *hurt* to be hardworking and talented. I'm just saying you don't have to be. I mean, look at how the girls outnumber the guys here." He waves a hand at the students, and I look around. He's right. There are probably four girls for each boy. "All we men have to do is show up."

"Whose phone is that?" Isabella asks, because there's an unmistakable buzzing sound of a phone set on vibrate. She glances around the table. "Didn't they say we weren't allowed to use our phones except in our rooms at night?"

"It's mine," I say, and pull it out of my pocket and read: *Lunchtime is over.* Thanks, Amelia.

"It's the first day," says Alex. "I don't think they're going to really come down on us yet. But you should still probably hide it, Franny."

"It's okay," I say, texting back a quick *BRB*—I doubt she'll know what that means, but let her spend time figuring it out—before sticking my phone back in my pocket. "I'm allowed to use mine."

"Why's that?" asks Lawrence. "You special?"

"My mommy always said I was." I flutter my eyelids. "But, that's not why—it's because I'm not actually a student here."

"What do you mean?" Isabella asks.

"She's doing an internship with the costume director," Julia cuts in.

"It's not exactly an internship." I get to my feet. "More what you'd call a job—I'm working for the costume mistress. Who's also my aunt. Not coincidentally."

"What's it like?" asks Vanessa.

"You know those nineteenth-century sweatshops where it was always incredibly hot and people had to work long hours under brutal conditions? Basically like that. Only with folk music."

"Sounds rough," says Harry. "Especially the folk-music part."

"Yeah, that stuff'll kill you. Anyway, I really do have to go back now."

"You'll come to dinner here, though, right?" Julia says.

"That's my plan."

"We'll save you a seat if we get here first."

"Thanks," I say, oddly touched.

"Oh, and one more thing," Harry says. "If you're going to be working on my costume, I feel it's important you know ahead of time that I dress to the left. And that I need a *lot* of extra room over there."

I stare at him blankly. I have no idea what he means, but Isabella is laughing. I look to Julia, who's equally confused. "What does that even mean?" She turns to her brother. "Alex?"

He shifts uncomfortably. "I only know because Dad's tailor asked me once, and Dad had to explain it to me. It has to do with the way guys' pants fit . . ." He trails off.

"How they fit?" Julia repeats.

But Vanessa gets it. "He means which side they put their junk on when they get dressed," she says calmly.

"Oh," I say. Then I wrinkle my nose. "Ew. TMI, Harry."

He smiles like a cat that's pleased with itself. "Just felt someone should know."

"Yeah, you should ignore that feeling in the future. Bye, guys."

As I walk away, I hear Isabella saying in a low voice, "So, wait—she's really not in the program?" I can't hear the response.

I leave the dining hall and pause out front, adjusting to the hot muggy air. Everyone else is inside. It's just me out there.

It's kind of an icky feeling, like I've been exiled from all the fun. I know that's not how it is. No one's kicking me out. No one's treating me like some kind of outsider. They were all actually really nice to me. But it still *feels* that way.

I start to cross the courtyard to the theater but have to jump back when a car comes zooming up the gravel drive. It's not a through street or anything—there's a sign at the entrance that says only college-owned vehicles are allowed to come down this way, but this car is a small silver Porsche convertible.

The car brakes near me in an abrupt spray of gravel, and a guy gets out of the driver's seat. He's got flat brown hair and a round head and appears to be somewhat challenged in the chin department. He's wearing sunglasses, so I can't see his eyes, but he looks college-aged. "Hey, there," he says, amiably hailing me. "Where is everyone?"

"The dining hall." I jerk my thumb in that direction.

He leans down to the car window. "She says they're all in the dining hall."

A girl gets out of the passenger seat. She looks a little bit younger than he does—roughly my age—and pretty, with honey-colored hair, large hazel eyes, and a heart-shaped face. She's wearing very short denim cut-offs and a tight blue T-shirt. Perfect body: small, compact, curvy. "That's why it's so quiet. I was wondering if I had the day wrong," she tells me. "I was here earlier to drop my stuff off, and then we went out to lunch. I figured I should have one last good meal before I have to eat dining-hall food all summer."

"It's actually not too bad," I say. "The pizza's decent."

"Really? I'm dubious." There's a pause.

"I'm Franny," I say, since we're just standing there.

"Oh, hi. I'm Marie."

She doesn't bother to introduce the guy, so he says to me, "I'm James," before turning back to her. "Well, I guess this is good-bye for now."

"Don't you think we should get my purse out of the car before you take off?"

"Oh, right." He scuttles around to the passenger side and gets out a large quilted leather purse.

"*Now* we can say good-bye," she says as he hands it to her. She offers her cheek to his lips and he plants a solid one there, making an appreciative smacking sound that seems to cause her pain, since she winces.

But she recovers and says, "I'll let you know when

you can come see me. There are all these rules about visitors and going off campus, but I am *not* going to be a prisoner here for the next six weeks, so expect to hear from me soon."

"I'll break any rules for you," he says with awkward gallantry.

Her lip curls. "But you wouldn't be the one breaking them; I would."

"Right. Text me," he says, and gets in his Porsche and continues driving down the sloping road—which means he has to drive past us again a few seconds later, because the gravel road only leads to an area that lets you turn a car around. He gives us a little wave as he goes by.

"He's nice," I say.

She shrugs. "Uh-huh. Let's go in. I don't want to miss the meeting."

"I'm going this way," I say, indicating the theater.

"I thought you said we were supposed to be in the dining hall."

"*You* are. All the acting students are. I'm working on costumes."

"Oh," she says, her eyes darting away. "That's great." She turns toward the dining room, then stops. "Hey, since you don't have to make the meeting, would you mind doing me a huge favor and just running my purse up to my room?" She holds it out toward me. "It's really heavy. I don't want to have to lug it around all afternoon, but I'm already late. It would be so incred-ibly nice of you—"

"I can't get in there," I say, glad I have an easy excuse. I'm not about to be turned into anyone's personal bell-hop. "No key. Sorry."

"I could give you mine and you could just run it back to me." A pause. I don't jump at the offer. She threads the bag back on her arm. "Guess I'll have to be even later than I already am."

"Sorry," I say again. "Bye."

"There you are. Finally," Aunt Amelia says when I walk into her workroom. The Sweatshop.

"I was meeting people."

"Were they nice?"

"Some of them," I say, and for some reason it's Alex's blue eyes and slow smile that I'm seeing as I say that.

A couple of hours later I think maybe I'm hallu-cinating—the heat's gotten to me—because the guy himself is suddenly standing right there in the door-way, trying to get our attention with a cheerfully uncertain "Um . . . hello?"

Before I can process that he's maybe actually really there, Amelia looks up and says coldly, "How can we help you?"

"Sorry to bother you, but Ted—my director—he said maybe we could borrow a few hats for the rest of the afternoon? Hey, Franny."

"So you two have met," Amelia says with an annoying little smile.

"We went to school together." I stand up. "I can show him where the hats are, if you want." I hope I don't sound *too* eager.

She's back to working at the machine, material bunched up all around her, so she just nods absently. "Don't give him anything that looks new or expensive. Not if they're just using them for goofing around."

"We're playing an improv game," Alex says.

"Nothing new or expensive," she repeats. "And I want them back before dinner, clean and brushed. The key's in the top drawer of my desk, Franny."

I get the key and lead Alex out of the Sweatshop and down the hallway to the back of the theater, then outside and along the building to the separate entrance for the basement storage area, which I open with the key. We go inside and head down the narrow stairs. The switch I flick on the way down only connects to one small hanging bulb, but at the bottom I turn on the real lights and we stop and take in the rows and rows of racks and shelves.

Alex gives a low whistle. "Wow. Impressive."

"I know, right? I totally want to explore. Are you in a hurry?"

"Nah. Your aunt was right—we're really just goofing around up there."

"What do you think of the program so far?" I

ask as we start walking again.

"The first two hours have been magnificent," he says with a laugh. "Well, there were about three minutes that were kind of boring, but I got through them."

"Sorry. Lame question."

"No," he says. "It wasn't. I was just teasing." And he smiles his nice smile at me, and my momentary insecurity is gone.

"Can I show you my favorite costumes?" I ask. "The Restoration ones? They're incredible."

"Definitely."

As we walk in the narrow aisle between the racks of labeled clothing, I run my hand lightly along the plastic-covered costumes and say, "So how'd you and your sister both end up here this summer?"

"Partially through shared interests and partially through nepotism. My uncle is the head of the program." He gives me a sideways look. "Do you think less of me now that you know I pulled strings to get in?"

"Hey, I'm only here because of my aunt. Nepotism rules. But are you actually into acting?"

"I guess. I was Tevye in our school production of *Fiddler on the Roof* last fall."

"That's a huge role!" My awe is genuine. He hadn't even tried out for the plays in middle school—I had no idea he could carry a whole show.

He shrugs dismissively. "I got lucky. I only tried out

because Julia said I should, and I wasn't playing a sport that season."

"But you wanted to go to acting camp?"

"'Wanted to' is a slight exaggeration. My parents kind of pushed me into it. They think a summer at Mansfield will help get me into college. I play baseball, so there's that . . . but so do a million other guys, and after I got the *Fiddler* thing, they thought maybe the combination of sports and theater would make me stand out from the crowd. It's all they can think about these days—my getting into college."

"Tell me about it. My mom actually snuck an SAT prep book into my suitcase." I grinned. "Not that I mind—it makes an excellent lap desk for my MacBook."

He nods. "Just once I wish one of my parents would say, 'No matter what happens with college, we have faith in you—we know you're going to be fine.' But they don't. Instead they keep saying, 'Where you go to school will determine the course of the rest of your life.' Oh, and sometimes they like to add, 'But, hey, we don't want you to feel like you're under too much pressure,' right after that."

"Right," I say. "Which of course makes it all okay."

"Of course. . . . The crazy thing is, my mother dropped out of college halfway through her junior year and my dad went to state school in Indiana. So why they think I can only have a good life if I get into the Ivy

League . . ." He shakes his head.

"I know. My mom *did* go to Penn—and now she's struggling to make ends meet as a middle-school English teacher, so you'd think she'd know that going to a good college doesn't solve all your problems. But she's just as bad as your parents. It's like mass hysteria or something." I stop in front of the rack I'd been looking for. "Here—these are the Restoration costumes. Cool, right? Look at this one." I pull out an elaborately ruffled man's outfit, with puffy pantaloons and a long striped overcoat.

"Wow. Amazing. Do you know what play that was for?"

"They're all tagged." I pull the paper tag out of the collar and squint at it. "*Tartuffe* in '02 and *The Country Wife* in '09."

"Wonder if we'll end up wearing something like this."

"You'd look good in it." I hold it up to him. "It brings out the stripes in your eyes." I hang it back up. "Do you know what play you're going to be in?"

"Not yet. Will you be here for the performances?"

"I hope so. Amelia will need me to pin hems and sew on buttons right up until the last minute, don't you think?"

"Definitely. We'll find a reason for you to stay."

I focus on rearranging the plastic cover so he won't

see the pleasure in my eyes at his *we*. "Come on—I'll show you the hats."

It seems relevant to mention at this point that I've had two fairly serious boyfriends since entering high school.

The first was Samuel Ellerstein. He was cute and fun, and I felt cute and fun when I was with him. He laughed at my jokes and he laughed at his jokes and he laughed at every one of life's little absurdities. He even laughed when I ran into him with his arm around Janet Rollins at a movie theater on the night he had told me he was having dinner with his grandmother. I liked that he was lighthearted and didn't take anything seriously, until it hit me that *anything* included me, his girlfriend. So we broke up. It wasn't too painful. He laughed and I shrugged.

Tyler Gustafson broke my heart a little bit more. Not in any permanent way, but my tears soaked a few pillowcases before I got over him.

The thing about Tyler is that, compared to Samuel, he was perfect—I mean, he took *everything* seriously. He was one of the most intense people I'd ever met: When he'd talk about global warming or the (wrong) direction our country was heading in, his eyes would glow with fervor. His skin radiated heat when he was discussing politics or a great book—I swear you could put your palm on his arm and actually *feel* his energy.

It was amazing to feel that intensity directed at me for a little while.

But it didn't take long for me to realize that on the list of things Tyler cared deeply about—a list that included world politics, his next history test, his GPA, the environment, and *The Daily Show*—girlfriend Franny Pearson fell nowhere near the top. Even the Eco Club at school came above me. I could sit at his side and admire him—silently because he needed to concentrate—while he studied and kept up with the ten million environmental and political blogs he read and/or contributed to, but if I wanted more from him, I had to wait my turn.

I didn't get a lot of turns.

It was bad luck that my birthday was the day before his AP English exam. I knew he'd beg off celebrating in order to study. What I didn't see coming was how deeply unhappy he'd be when I borrowed my mother's car and stopped by his house, just to say hi. On my *birthday*.

"Oh, no," he said when he opened the door. He didn't invite me in, just stood there, shaking his head. "Oh, no. You're great and all, Franny, but no relationship I'm going to have now is worth compromising my future for."

He really meant that: I could feel the heat of his sincerity burning through his shirtsleeve as he hugged me good-bye.

So now I just want someone who's capable of taking

me seriously and who's willing to shrug off the rest of the world when we're alone.

Of course, I've no objection to blue eyes and broad shoulders.

They'd be a nice bonus.

scene four

'm walking into the dining hall at six that evening when someone grabs my arm.

"Thank God you're here!" Julia says. "I so need to talk to someone I can trust!" She hauls me over to an empty corner. "Harry Cartwright! Oh, my God. Harry Cartwright!"

"That's the blond guy who was at our table today, right?"

"Oh, like you didn't notice him!"

I shrug. He hadn't made a huge impression on me. He was no Alex. But of course Alex's sister wouldn't feel that way.

"We talked so much this afternoon!" she says. "And he's amazing. He knows all these famous people—his dad is like this music producer in L.A. or something—but he's not pretentious. He's really funny. And don't you think he's super cute? I mean, look at him." She points across the room. Harry is lounging over by the drinks dispenser, and I do mean *lounging*: he's kind of leaning his hip on the counter as he's filling up his cup, like he's too cool to stand upright. I bet he practices that pose in his room at night.

Marie—the girl I met out front earlier with her boyfriend—comes up to Harry as we're watching and nudges him aside with her elbow so she can fill her own cup. He deliberately cuts back in front of her, and she shoves at him jokingly, and then they keep tussling for space in front of the machine, laughing and saying stuff we can't hear.

"Oh, God, it's *her*," Julia says. "Our third room-mate. She came early, grabbed the best bed in the room, and then left. It's too bad she came back—she's been all over Harry all day. Look at her now."

The flirting looks pretty mutual from where I'm standing. "She has a boyfriend, you know," I say.

"She does?"

"Yeah, I met him. So she's probably not actually interested in Harry."

She rolls her eyes. "Right. Because no one has ever cheated on a boyfriend or switched to a new one."

I ignore that. "Do you have a fourth roommate?" I ask.

"Yeah—apparently her name's Jillian something, but she still hasn't shown up."

Once we've filled our trays, we head over to join pretty much the same group that ate lunch together, with the addition of honey-haired Marie, who has followed Harry Cartwright over and is now sitting next to him.

Julia grabs the seat on Harry's other side and instantly goes to work on him, teasing him mercilessly and flirtatiously about anything and everything, including his black T-shirt and black jeans ("can you say *hipster*?"), his purple Converse, his way of talking, eating, breathing. He rolls his eyes and teases her back, asking her if those eyelashes are long enough (they *are* bordering on drag queen) and why girls think they can get away with eating other people's food (after she coyly sneaks a french fry off his plate).

I'm on her other side, and Julia pulls me into the conversation, but only as wingman to her flirting. "Real men don't wear purple shoes, am I right?" she says to me, but before I can even respond, her shoulder is back in my face and she's saying to Harry, "Don't get me wrong, I love a man who's so confident about his masculinity he can spend the summer at a theater camp wearing purple and *still* assume every girl will fall at his feet."

"Do I assume that?" Harry says. He appeals to his other neighbor. "Marie, help me out here. Do I act like I expect all the girls are going to fall at my feet?"

Marie has been poking at her food and casting annoyed glances their way during this exchange, but she quickly regains her interest in the conversation now that Harry's paying attention to her. "Absolutely. You're a total narcissist."

"Oh, hey, Marie," Julia says, like she just remembered. "Franny said something about meeting your boyfriend today? Who is he?"

Marie flicks at a crumb on the table. "He's just a guy I know. Who happens to have a really cool car and doesn't mind driving me around in it."

Harry looks interested. "What kind of car?"

"Porsche."

"Nice," he says, bobbing his head in a slow, appreciative nod. "My next car is going to be a Porsche."

"What do you have now?" Marie asks.

"A Porsche," he says with a cryptic smirk. I can't tell if he's joking or not.

"Guys and their cars." Julia tosses her head so her long dark hair flies around her face. "Franny, why do you think guys are so obsessed with cars? Doesn't Freud or someone have a theory about that?" She's supposedly talking to me. But she's not really.

"Freud or someone?" Harry repeats. "Am I supposed to be impressed by the depth of intellect you're revealing here?"

"Look who's talking!" she shoots back. "The guy

who carries a comic book around with him. I saw it, you know."

"It's a graphic novel. Marie, could you please explain to our friend here the difference between a graphic novel and the Archie comics *she* reads?"

Marie giggles and pushes at his arm. "You are so bad!"

I sigh and twirl some spaghetti on my fork. I'd prefer a conversation where I'm not just there to help other people flirt, but Vanessa and Lawrence are both off getting something at the buffet, and everyone else has paired off in conversation.

Sudden movement across the table grabs my attention. Alex is pushing his chair back and standing up. "That's it, I'm getting you a cookie all your own!"

"I didn't say I wanted one!" Isabella protests, laughing up at him.

"No, you just keep staring at mine—I know when someone's about to steal my food the second I look away. It's easier for me just to get you your own. What kind do you want?"

"Surprise me," she says. "Since you seem to be able to read my mind."

"Only when it comes to food."

"Really?" she asks archly. "You sure?"

"Yeah, girls are a total mystery to me."

"We don't actually have cooties," she says. "In case

you were stuck in that particular phase of development."

He grins down at her. "Good to know. I'll file that bit of information away for future reference." He looks around the table. "Anyone else need anything while I'm up?"

I scramble to my feet. "I want something to drink, but I'll go with you." We head across the dining hall together. "So did you get in trouble for taking too long with the hats today?"

"Nah. It was fine. How'd the rest of your afternoon go?"

"Great. I only pricked my finger fifteen times with the needle."

"Aw, poor Franny. Hey, I wanted to ask you—how come you even know how to sew?"

"How come you don't?" I say, and he smiles absently. He's studying the plates of dessert laid out under the sneeze guard.

"So what kind of cookie should I bring back for Isabella?" he asks. "Do girls have a favorite kind?"

"It's not like we vote on it."

"I'll get her one of each." He piles cookies up on a plate. One of the dining-hall workers squints suspiciously at him, but he doesn't seem to notice. "Can you grab an oatmeal raisin for me, Franny?"

"Sure," I say. "Anything for Isabella." He doesn't even hear me. He's heading back across the room, and

Isabella is raising her pretty face to smile her welcome and thanks at him.

She's let her hair down since lunchtime. It falls in a shining curtain down to her shoulders, dark and glossy, but as she looks up, she smooths it back, off her face, and you can see the delicate angles of her high cheekbones and perfectly sculpted chin.

I think, *I could hate her.*

After dinner, everyone races off to some big assembly with the graduate-student directors in the theater auditorium.

I walk back to Aunt Amelia's apartment, where I join her in watching reality TV shows, but after a couple of hours of listening to her complain about how tacky and rude all the people are, I'm ready to scream. "I'm going to walk over to the dorm," I say finally, rising to my feet and stretching. "See if anyone's around."

"All right," she says. "But don't stay out past ten. I don't want to be kept up waiting for you." Then she adds, as an afterthought, "Plus it might not be safe."

As I enter the courtyard area, I'm glad to see everyone's out of the meeting, some of them milling around outside, most of them going into the dorm. I follow a group inside and then head into the common room, where people are sprawled on every piece of furniture. Some guy is playing a Sondheim tune on the piano, and two girls have sandwiched him on the bench and are singing along.

I spot Vanessa and Julia talking together on one of the big sofas.

"We got put in casts!" Julia calls out as soon as I get close.

"Cool! Who are you both?"

"We don't have our roles yet," Vanessa says. "Just our plays. Lawrence and I are in *A Midsummer Night's Dream*, Julia and Harry are in *Twelfth Night*"—that explains why Julia's grinning like she won some kind of a prize: she's with Harry—"and Alex and Isabella are in *Measure for Measure*. Which is funny because the main character's name is Isabella. But maybe it's not a coincidence. Maybe they did that on purpose so she can play that role?"

"They wouldn't cast her in something because of her *name*," Julia says. "That wouldn't be fair. Anyway, they don't know who's going to be who yet—they're going to listen to us read for a few days first."

"I hope they cast gender-blind," Vanessa says.

"They'll definitely have to have some girls playing male roles," Julia says. "There are way more girls than boys here."

"I want to be Bottom."

"You're crazy," says Julia. "Wear a donkey's head for half of every performance?"

"It would be cool."

"It would be *hot*. And sweaty and hard to see or hear anything."

I sit down next to Julia. "Are they all Shakespeare plays?"

"Yeah," Vanessa says. "They're also doing *Winter's Tale*, so four plays altogether. I'm so glad I'm in *Midsummer*, though. That's the coolest."

"Do they always do all Shakespeare?"

"Nope. They just felt like it this year, I guess."

"The directors are changing the plays a lot," Julia says. "They're shortening them and combining roles and stuff to make them work for us. Oh, did I tell you, Vanessa, that Charles said that if he'd realized Alex and I looked so much alike, he'd have asked to have us both in *Twelfth Night*? You know—to play Viola and Sebastian."

"That would have totally rocked!"

"No kidding—I'd have definitely gotten the lead then. Charles is my director," Julia adds, turning to me. "He's a graduate student at NYU."

"I think all the directors are graduate students," Vanessa says. "And they all did this program back in high school."

"Jillian was supposed to be in my cast too," Julia says. "Our missing fourth roommate."

"She still hasn't shown up?" I say.

Julia shakes her head and lowers her voice. "Charles said there was a sudden death in her family—that's all he would tell me—and so she's not coming."

"That's so sad," I say.

"I know," Julia says, and Vanessa nods and we're all quiet for a moment because it feels like we should be.

Vanessa breaks the silence. "This may be a heartless question, but does it matter that your cast will be short an actor?"

"Charles said he'll figure it out. He said he'd have most of us doubling up on roles anyway—I guess he'll just have more of that. Oh, there's Alex." She waves at her brother, who's entering the common room side by side with Isabella.

"I'm so excited!" Isabella says when they reach us. "I love *Measure for Measure*! I feel like someone just handed me a gift. And it doesn't suck that Alex is in my cast." The two of them bump fists. "Oh—there's one of my roommates. I have to ask her something. Be right back." She slides away. Gracefully, of course.

"Hey, Franny," Alex says, noticing me now that Isabella's gone—or at least that's what it feels like. You only really notice the moon when the sun goes down, right? "What have you been up to?"

"Not much." I tilt my head back so I can look up at him. "So you're in *Measure for Measure* too? I don't know anything about it."

"It's an amazing play." Then he says to Julia, "Shove over." She makes a face at him, but she and I both slide down so he can squeeze in at the end. He turns back to me. "It's, like, the coolest Shakespeare play of all, and I'm not just saying that because I'm stuck with it. I wrote a paper on it last year for English."

"What's it about?"

He describes the story to me, and it's so noisy in the room now with everyone piling in there that I miss half of what he's saying, but I don't care because I'm just enjoying the fact that we're crammed tightly together on the sofa, our legs pressed against each other, and he's paying attention to me and me alone.

I know it's silly, my getting all swoony and ridiculous over a guy so quickly, but it's not really a sudden thing. You don't forget the first guy who gave you a flower (even if it was from his sister's bouquet and he never said a word about it, just handed it to you and walked away), especially if you already thought he was kind of sweet and dreamy.

You know those little ducks that imprint on the first thing they see walking by them after they're born and will just follow that animal around, whatever and whoever it is? I think maybe when I first started noticing boys, Alex was the one I noticed first, and I got a little imprinted on him. And now that I'm seeing him again all these years later, I have to say I had good taste back in eighth grade.

I realize I have no idea what he's been saying for the last couple of minutes—I've been too busy gazing dreamily into those handsome blue eyes—so I drag my attention back to his words. ". . . but the good characters do some really lousy things in the play and some of the supposedly bad characters are totally likable, so it's hard to know who to root for. At the end, someone says we should only be judged on our actions, not on our intentions or beliefs—but it's not clear whether Shakespeare actually believes that or not."

"I don't know," I say. "It seems like if you shoot at someone and miss, you're still guilty of *something*."

"Yeah, I agree. Our director, Ted, says he wants us to think about all this stuff the whole time we're working on the play and decide where we come down on it—whether we'd want to go through life being judged solely on our actions or on our intentions. Or whether both matter equally."

"I love thinking about stuff like that." I'm feeling a pang of envy. I wish I could be in a play. It's not just that the people around me are excited about the shows they're in and bonding over who's in which cast and talking about what roles they might get—it's also that it sounds so *cool*. I mean, I don't go around reading Shakespeare in my free time or anything, but the few shows I've read or seen have stayed with me, and everything Alex just told me is reminding me *why*. "But I don't see how we can ever really judge people by—"

"Well, look at *this* attractive group," someone interrupts loudly.

I look up to see Harry Cartwright sauntering toward us, hands in his pockets, shoulders slouched just so. He's probably studied every issue of *GQ* to get the right air of casual indifference. He waits a beat, making sure everyone's attention is focused on him.

"I mean, really—just *look* at you all," he says. He points to Vanessa. "*You* are like the epitome of hipster chic. And *you*"—to Julia—"are total classic gorgeousity, like a movie star, and *you*"—turning to me—"*you're* Miss Smith after she takes off her glasses and suddenly everyone realizes how pretty she is. And *you*"—to Alex—"well, you're just butt-ugly and should get up off this sofa and let someone sit here who's actually worthy of these lovely ladies."

"I have a suggestion where *you* can sit," Alex says.

"No need to be explicit about it." Harry suddenly throws himself across all our laps so he's lying on his back, his head resting on Julia's knees, his body and legs spread out on the rest of us.

"Get off!" Alex says, shoving at Harry's feet.

Harry raises them off Alex's lap and crosses his ankles on the arm of the sofa. "I'm comfortable, and there's nowhere else to sit." He folds his arms behind his head and flutters his eyes up at Julia. "You guys don't mind, right?"

"I am so close to dumping you off," she says, and bounces her knees a couple of times so he has to grab her leg to keep from falling.

"That's not nice," he says. "If you're not careful, I'm going to go in search of a more friendly lap."

"God forbid," she says, but I notice she also stops bouncing.

Not only has Harry's arrival put a stop to my private conversation with Alex, but he's also been followed over by the ever-attentive Marie.

"You are such a total loon," she says, gazing down adoringly at him. "That can't be comfortable."

He pats his flat stomach. "Come perch right here and find out."

"Don't you dare!" Julia says. "We'd be crushed."

"Thanks a lot," Marie says, crossing her arms tightly.

"That wasn't a *you're so fat* comment," Julia says. "It was a *my legs can't support another ounce* comment."

"Are you okay?" Alex asks me.

"Yeah." Harry's legs across my lap don't bother me—I just don't see why he always has to be the center of attention.

And apparently someone else thinks it's her turn there: Marie clears her throat and says loudly, "So you guys know how I was put in the *Winter's Tale* cast?"

"Were you?" Julia says indifferently. "Harry, get your elbow out of my stomach."

"Get your stomach out of my elbow," he replies.

"I hate that play, so I wanted to switch—" Marie says.

"You can't do that," Vanessa says. "Right? I mean that was the first thing they told us. No switching." I don't know where or how she got a pen, but she appears to be writing the word *Shakespeare* in big bubble letters on Harry's forearm.

"You get what you get and you don't get upset," Julia says with a giggle. "Remember that, Alex? Our nanny used to say that all the time."

"Didn't work," Alex says. "You still got upset."

"Which is why I always got the biggest piece of cake. Squeaky wheel."

Harry says to her, "When you talk I can feel the vibrations in your stomach."

"Anyway," Marie says, raising her voice even more, "I just wanted you guys to know that I'm going to be in *Twelfth Night* with you." She pokes Harry in the ribs. "Isn't that great?"

"Great." He curls his free hand into a fist and raises it up from his lying-down position. "Our cast totally rules! Power to the people."

Julia and Vanessa exchange a look. Vanessa bends back down over her artwork with a shrug, and Julia says, "They really let you switch?"

"Charles is so nice," Marie says. Her thick light hair is pulled back in a ponytail, which makes her amber eyes look enormous. I had an American Girl doll who looked like her. I can't remember which one. Nellie? Kit? Definitely not Josefina. "We're going to have a blast."

"It's just they said we absolutely couldn't switch, not under any condition." Julia's voice is suddenly unusually high and strained. "Are you sure they said you were going to be in our cast?"

"Yeah, totally. And some girl named Diane is going to take my place in *Winter's Tale*." Marie pokes Harry again. "Anyone want to grab a soda or something from the dining hall before curfew?"

"What time is it?" I ask. I can't get my cell phone out of my pocket to check because Harry's legs are pinning me down.

"They told us to always wear a watch," Marie says, then puts her hand to her mouth. "Oh, sorry—I forgot. You're not actually in the program. I'm such an idiot."

Alex says, "It's nine thirty. You don't have to go yet, do you, Franny?"

"Not yet," I say, because I don't care if I'm late and Amelia gets mad at me—not if Alex wants me to stay.

Isabella chooses that moment to come back to our sofa. I'm not particularly happy to see her, especially since Alex looks up eagerly as she approaches, but she's not here for him. She catches Harry's eye and makes a gesture: index and middle finger extended, pressed together, raised toward her mouth. He instantly rolls off our legs and onto his feet, eliciting a chorus of "ow"s from his human cushions. "So sorry," he says jauntily. "As you were, folks." He and Isabella head toward the front door.

"Wait for me, guys!" Vanessa jumps up and runs after them.

"What was that about?" asks Marie, watching them go, a little annoyed furrow between her eyebrows.

"Cigarette break," I guess.

Julia rises to her feet. "Brianna's in my cast," she says, nodding across the room toward a tiny redhead. "I'm going to go say hi."

"I'll come with you," Marie says instantly. "Now that I'm in your cast, I should meet everyone in it."

Julia gives a reluctant nod. I'm guessing the whole point of talking to Brianna was to discuss the unfairness of Marie's switching casts when they'd been told it was against the rules.

They leave. Alex and I are alone on the sofa. We're still sitting very close from being crammed in with the others, but neither of us shifts away.

"You don't smoke, do you?" he asks.

I shake my head. "My mother sniffs me whenever I walk through the door. She'd know in a second if I smoked a single cigarette, and she's already listed the things I would have to give up if she ever finds out I have, like the use of her car, my cell phone, my happiness and freedom . . . Plus my big brother told me that if I'm ever stupid enough to start smoking, he will never talk to me again."

"That's a threat?" Alex says. "If Julia said she'd never talk to me again, I'd be lighting up within seconds."

"I like my brother. He's a good guy." I'm hoping he'll ask me more questions about William, who's one of my favorite topics, but a graduate student appears at the entrance to the common room and calls for quiet. He's tall and thin, with thick black glasses (not unlike Vanessa's, come to think of it).

"Just a quick announcement, guys," he says, and Julia shouts, "Go, Charles!" He acknowledges her with a salute and continues: "I'm just reminding you that you all need to be in your rooms at eleven, with lights out at midnight. It may sound early to you right now, but, trust me, we're going to be working you so hard, you'll be grateful for every minute of sleep you get. One of us will flick the lights at ten fifty, so wrap up your conversations then and head up. Tea, cocoa, and soda are available in the dining hall until ten thirty every night, so feel free to wander over there and grab some—just get back in time." He glances around. "This is all very cozy. Glad to see you're making friends. Just remember:

sleep is also your friend." There's a collective groan at that, and Charles says, "Hey! This is my A material. It's not getting any better than this." He raps on the wall with his knuckles. "Eleven o'clock, guys. Don't make us come fetch you after that. You won't like us if we do, I promise." He walks back out of the room.

Alex stands up and extends his hand to me. "Want to go get something to drink in the dining hall?"

"Sure." I let him pull me to my feet. His hand is warm and dry and squeezes mine briefly before releasing it, which is nice, but I'd rather have stayed on the sofa with him a while longer.

I'm even more bummed when we get outside and see Isabella, Harry, and Vanessa heading toward us. Alex instantly invites them to come with us to the dining hall and somehow ends up walking next to Isabella, while I fall back between Vanessa and Harry, both of whom now smell like dirty ashtrays.

It's getting late anyway, and there no longer seems to be a good reason to risk pissing off Amelia, so I say a general good night and move off.

Alex is too busy listening to something Isabella's saying to do more than raise his hand in a distracted farewell.

scene five

"This isn't awkward at all," says Lawrence as I measure his inseam.

"I prefer to think of it as friendly. Really friendly." I write down the measurement and then thread the tape measure around his waist. Short as he is, I'm still a couple of inches shorter. I blame my mother for that—she barely makes five feet. I'm a couple of inches taller than her and a lot thinner. She says that's because I take after my father's side of the family ("they're all crazy skinny"), but I've seen photos of her at my age, and her body was just like mine. The problem is, she eats when she's not happy.

These days she eats a lot.

That reminds me: I should call her tonight. I text her pretty regularly, several times a day, just stuff about what I'm doing and eating—nothing too exciting since there's nothing too exciting to report—but I know she likes to hear my voice from time to time too.

"So what's my costume going to look like?" Lawrence asks.

I gather up the measuring tape. "Can't tell you."

"Why not?"

"Because I don't know."

"Tell me as soon as you do. Don't let them make me look stupid, okay?"

"No problem," I say. "I'll take care of it, because it's all up to me. Everyone here listens to what I say. I'm pretty much the girl in charge. No one has more power than the costume assistant, you know."

"Shut up," he says, and cuffs my shoulder affectionately. Lawrence and I have hung out together a lot over the last few days, and he gets me.

I'm starting to get him, too, and so, since we're alone in the little dressing room in the Sweatshop, I lean closer and whisper, "How are things going with you-know-who?"

"We talked until one last night," he whispers back.

I raise my eyebrows. "Just talked?"

"Just talked. It would be too weird to do anything else. I mean, we're *roommates*."

"Yeah, I guess so. Raise your arms." I pass the tape behind his back and measure his chest.

"Don't tell me what the number is," he says. "Everyone makes fun of my concave chest at school."

"It's not concave." But it *is* pretty narrow, so I write down the number without inflicting it on him.

"Anyway," he says, leaning back against the wall, "I'm kind of jealous of Alex and Isabella. Me and Raymond—we have to share a bedroom and a bathroom, and that's just awkward. Especially since they keep serving us Mexican food at dinner . . ." He grimaces. "Stupid burrito night. But Alex and Isabella can just see each other when they're looking their best, so it's easy for them to stay romantic."

"Okay, you're done," I say flatly. I've suddenly lost the desire to goof around with him. "Tell someone else in the cast to come in here, will you?"

"Sure. Thanks, Franny. See you at dinner?"

I nod. He leaves with a friendly wave, and I slowly— very slowly—roll up the tape measure so I can stall the moment when I have to leave the dressing room and face Amelia out in the office again. I just need a minute.

You know how sometimes you *know* something, but you pretend you don't? To yourself, I mean? Lawrence just made me realize I've been doing that. For the last few days, Alex and Isabella have managed to sit next to each other at every meal and wander off alone together after dinner, except when she sneaks out for a smoke with Harry and/or Vanessa.

That's when Alex comes to find me. At least once or twice a day he and I have these amazing talks, reminiscing about people we knew in eighth grade and telling each other about our families. Like I know that he wants to be an architect but that his father wants him to go into law, and that his mother has all these little dogs she's more comfortable talking to than she is to people, even her own kids. And he knows that my parents try to act like they're still friends and that I pretend I think they're still friends, but that it's obvious they can't stand to be in the same room together anymore.

Stuff like that. I mean, we really, really *talk*.

But only when Isabella's not around.

I get it. She's beautiful. And sophisticated. And cool. I'm none of those things. But Alex really opens up to me, and that seems like something that could outlast a momentary crush. We've all been together only a few days. Isabella makes a stunning first impression, but there's the whole tortoise and the hare thing, right? And who's more of a tortoise than me?

But after what Lawrence said, I force myself to watch Alex and Isabella at dinner that night—really watch them together. And I see how she puts her hand on his arm when she wants to make a point and how she pretends to be tired so she can lay her head on his shoulder and how he kind of lays his own head on top of hers. And how she snags french fries off his plate like she has a right to them.

So whatever's going on between them, it's progressed

a lot more than whatever's going on between him and *me*. We're not eating each other's food or snuggling up together. We started off talking and we're still just . . . talking.

It's a blow. I feel this connection to Alex, and I want it to turn into something. And it *could*, because we both live in Phoenix and could actually have a future together.

Isabella laughs at something he says and gently brushes her fingertips along his wrist. He nudges her shoulder with his and smiles down at her.

I look away.

Across the table, Julia is making googly-eyes at Harry Cartwright like she always does, but I don't get the same starting-to-get-serious vibe from the two of them that I'm getting from Isabella and Alex. Which is probably a disappointment to Julia, but I think she's better off not getting in too deep with Harry. The guy flirts with every girl in sight. And with some of the boys, too. He pretty much preens and glows at the slightest sign of admiration. He's like a dog rubbing up against anyone who'll pet him.

When we all walk outside after dinner that night, Isabella and Harry excuse themselves and stroll into the shadows together.

Alex instantly comes over to me.

"They're going to come back smelling like cigarette

smoke," he says, with a sort of pained half smile.

"They always do." But I think, *You don't like that she smokes—doesn't that say something about her? Or about you? Or about your potential as a couple?*

He says, "My mom smoked when she was in college. She stopped pretty soon after that. She said it wasn't hard to quit." There's a pause. Then he says, "No one's perfect."

"There is that."

He studies me with affectionate interest. "What's *your* fatal flaw, Franny?"

"Oh, you know . . ." I shrug. "I'm too perfect for this world. It's rough."

"I wouldn't worry about it," he says. "The gods always punish hubris sooner or later. You'll get yours in the end."

"That's supposed to be reassuring?"

"Well, yeah—to those of us who *aren't* perfect." Then he glances away again, toward the darkness at the side of the building, and says, "Smoking's not a big deal, right? Tons of people do it for a few years and then stop."

"If you don't mind the smell . . ."

"I hate the smell," he admits with a laugh.

"Me too."

We're silent for another moment and overhear a snippet of someone else's conversation: ". . . *most amazing fireworks* . . ."

"Fourth of July next week," Alex says. "You excited about seeing fireworks, Franny?"

"Who doesn't like fireworks?"

"That's not an answer. That's an evasion."

I step closer to him. "Okay, honestly? They scared me when I was little. I never wanted to tell anyone, so I'd go with my family and just keep my eyes closed tight the whole time. But I could still hear them."

"Poor little Franny." There's sympathy in those kind Alex-blue eyes.

I say, "You're the only person who knows this, by the way. I've always been kind of embarrassed about it."

"I won't tell anyone." He leans toward me and adds in a whisper, "And I also won't tell anyone that you're still a little scared of them."

"How did you know?" I whisper back.

"You're easy to read." He grins down at me.

Am I? The thought that I might be transparent makes me instantly duck my head so he can't see my eyes anymore, and while he tells me how worried his mother gets about her dogs on the Fourth of July—they hate the sound of fireworks, even when it's in the distance—I pretend to be fascinated by the gravel at my feet.

Yesterday I'd have been fine with letting him know how much I like him, but if Lawrence is right and Alex and Isabella are already a couple and it's obvious to everyone there, I have to be more careful.

Less readable.

Julia comes over and immediately launches into a complaint about Marie, who's driving her crazy now that they're in the same cast.

"Do you know how she got them to switch her from the cast she was originally put in?" Julia asks us. "I just found out. She said one of the guys in the first cast had said something 'inappropriate' to her and she didn't want to name names and get him in trouble but she didn't feel safe being in that environment. Can you believe her? She made the whole thing up so she could be in the play she wanted, and because of it all the guys in that cast had to go to a special meeting where they were told that if there were any more complaints, there would be serious repercussions. And they didn't do *anything*."

"Why'd she want to switch so badly, anyway?" I ask, and Julia gives me a look. A *duh* look. And I say, "Oh, yeah, never mind." Because we both know that Marie is all over Harry Cartwright, flirting with him every chance she gets.

And I also know that Julia is doing the exact same thing. I'm not sure why she thinks she has more of a right to flirt with him than Marie does, except I guess that she was in his cast *first*, and legitimately.

As far as I can tell, Harry doesn't prefer either Marie or Julia or any of the other girls who fawn over him. He just flirts with whoever's nearest at any given moment.

And then probably goes off to study himself in the mirror—spending time with the one person he *truly* loves.

"Thank God she's not going to the beach on Sunday," Julia says. The students get Sundays off, and the directors have arranged transportation and a picnic for anyone who wants to go to the beach on the Sunday that's coming up.

"Did you sign up for the bus yet?" Alex asks her.

"Not yet, but I'm going to."

"Why isn't Marie going?" I ask.

"Her boyfriend's taking her somewhere." Julia smirks. "I made sure Harry knew that. Are you coming, Franny? It'll be fun."

I hesitate. Now that the directors have all settled on what they want for costumes, Amelia and I have a ton of work to do. She's expecting me back in the Sweatshop right now to get in a couple of hours before heading home to her apartment and has made it clear to me that she expects us to work all through the weekend.

Alex says, "You've got to come with us, Franny. It won't be as much fun without you."

And I nod, thinking, *Hell, yeah, I'm going—just try to stop me.* And then, less happily: *Why, oh why, didn't I buy a new bathing suit before coming here?*

Somehow I talk Amelia into letting me go. She

complains and grumbles and says, "With everyone gone, we could get so much work done," and I say, "But it's Sunday and everyone else is going," and we go on like that for a while, her making objections and my saying "It's *Sunday*," and finally she says, "Fine, go, but know you're going to have to make up for the lost day of work—no more lingering at meals half the day." Of course I say yes. I'd promise anything at this point to go to the beach with Alex.

scene six

Sunday morning I put on the only bathing suit I brought with me, throw a pair of shorts over it, and run over to the campus with a beach bag. Lawrence is climbing onto the bus just when I get there, so we grab a seat together. I try not to let it bother me that Alex is sitting with Isabella a few rows in front of us and that they were holding hands when I walked by them. I mean, I'm going to the beach with my friends. It's all good, right?

Right. Except . . .

Guess who gets a piece of glass in her foot within minutes of arriving at the beach?

Not Isabella, who has belted a long white linen tunic over a brown-and-blue bikini and looks like she stepped out of an editorial spread in *Vogue*.

Not Julia, who's very leggy and lean in Daisy Dukes and a bikini top.

Not Vanessa, who has artfully paired boyish board

shorts with a red bandeau.

Not any of the guys—all of whom, by virtue of their gender, didn't have to think twice about what to wear to the beach or whether they'd look good in it, just slapped on longish swimming trunks and T-shirts and called themselves dressed.

No, the honor of stepping on a sharp piece of glass is reserved for the brown-eyed girl with the ponytail who's wearing a pair of denim shorts over a practical one-piece Speedo (bought by her mother for actual swimming, not for posing on the beach) and who thought it would be a good idea to slip off her flip-flops and really sink her feet into the rough sand near the road as the group walked toward the water.

A few steps later, foot meets shard of glass.

Girl yelps in pain.

Soon everyone is clustered around me, staring down at the ball of my right foot, which I'm cradling in my hand as I lean on Julia so I can inspect it.

"I once had a splinter of glass in my foot so small no one could see it," Isabella says. "Not until my nanny got out a magnifying glass. But it hurt so much I thought I would pass out. Hold on, Franny—don't poke at it like that. You don't want it to break off under the skin."

"Let me see it," Alex says. "Maybe I can pull it out cleanly."

"If I can just find a place to sit down, I can do it." I

look for a nearby bench or rock.

Alex ignores me. "Julia, support her. Isabella, grab her leg and help me get it a little higher." Before I know it, my foot is being hauled way up high. I'm still protesting that I can take care of this myself, but no one's listening to me.

"Anyone have a pair of tweezers?" Vanessa asks, moving in to get a closer look.

"Why would anyone bring a pair of tweezers to the beach?" Julia says.

"You never know."

"My mom keeps a first-aid kit in her car," Lawrence says, peering over Vanessa's shoulder.

"That would be useful information if your mother's car were *here*," says Julia.

"You guys are blocking my light. Move back, will you?" Alex is cradling my shin firmly in the palm of his left hand, angling it around to try to get the best view of my foot. His hand is warm.

I'd be lying if I said I've never imagined feeling Alex's hand on my leg.

Sadly, that daydream didn't include a throng of people staring at us.

"Hold it steady," Alex says to Isabella, like my leg has nothing to do with me, everything to do with her.

"Yes, doctor," she says, and they share a quick smile. He lightly touches his index finger to the skin near where the glass entered my foot, and I yelp again.

"Sorry," Alex says. "Okay. One quick pull. You ready, Franny?" He bends over my foot, but then—

"What's going on?" A new voice. We all look up.

It's Marie. She's got a big beach bag on one arm and her pudgy boyfriend, James, on the other.

"Franny stepped on a piece of glass," Alex explains.

James makes a little clucking noise of sympathy.

Julia says, "What are you guys doing here?"

"I decided a day at the beach sounded like fun, so James drove us here to meet up with you guys." Marie turns to Harry. "I don't see *you* helping out with this operation."

"I'm providing moral support," he says airily. "It's a very challenging job."

"You trying to be moral? I'm sure it is," she counters archly.

"Will you please just take it out?" Julia snaps at Alex. "Or am I supposed to stand here all day holding her up?"

"Okay. For real this time." He bends over me, and I feel his fingers on my foot and there's a stinging moment of pain, and then . . . less pain. "Got it!" he says, and holds up a small sliver of green glass for everyone to see.

He and Isabella release my leg, and I balance carefully on my toe. "And to think I've always loved sea glass," I say. "I even have a collection. But it turned against me."

Alex says, "You guys go find a spot on the beach and put your towels down. Harry and I can carry Franny."

Lawrence and Vanessa head down toward the beach.

"You don't need to carry me!" I say. God, it keeps getting more and more embarrassing. "Seriously, I can just hop. It's a tiny little wound. I'm fine."

They ignore me.

"How should we do this?" Harry asks Alex. "Shoulders and knees? Crossed arms under her?"

"Do you need another set of hands?" asks James.

Alex shakes his head. "For tiny little Franny? Nah."

"I could probably just pick her up by myself," Harry says.

"Oh, listen to the big strong man," Julia says. "We're all really impressed over here."

"Fine. I'll show you." Before I can even say anything, he's pushing her and Isabella out of the way and scooping me up in his arms. His biceps bulge. I know because I'm looking right at them. I wonder if he works out a lot.

What am I saying? This is Harry—of *course* he works out a lot.

"Put me down!" I say. "I can walk."

"Stop wriggling," Harry says. "Or we'll both fall on our faces."

Alex frowns. "Let me help. It's hard to walk in the sand, and if you fall, you could hurt her."

"I'm fine," Harry says. "If everybody would just get out of my way . . ." He takes an unsteady step toward the ocean. "It would help if you'd put your arms around my neck." His voice sounds a little strained.

"Sorry." I sling one arm around his neck and the other in front and clasp my fingers loosely together.

"Tighter," he says.

So I tighten my arms around his shoulders. It feels uncomfortably like I'm hugging him. "I really could walk. . . ."

"I know. I'm proving a point here."

"Why?"

He tilts his head back so he can look at me. We're both wearing sunglasses, so I can't see how green his eyes are, and I feel a funny twinge of regret at the lost opportunity to see them up close. Julia's always talking about how beautiful his eyes are, but I've made it a point not to spend too much time staring at him. He's vain enough as it is. "You know, there are girls who wouldn't act like this was some kind of punishment," he says.

"I'm sorry. It's really nice of you. I'm just embarrassed."

His arms tighten under my shoulders and knees. "Well, don't be." He staggers and lurches to the side with a swear, but steadies himself before we both go down. "Hole in the sand. Some stupid kid just left it like that. Sorry."

"Nice save."

"Thank you. Just think of me as your personal savior. And here we are. . . ."

Is it weird that I'm sort of sorry we got here so fast? That I was starting to enjoy my ride in Harry's arms? Yeah, it's weird. Forget it.

"Now I just have to figure out how to put you down. Hold on, I've got it. . . ." He drops to his knees so I'm pretty much sitting on his lap. I quickly scoot off him and onto the towels. "I'm fairly hopeful you're going to survive this injury, Franny."

"Unless gangrene sets in."

"Gangrene always sets in," he says darkly.

"What are you talking about?" asks Julia as they all gather around us again. "No one gets gangrene anymore."

"They do in old books. If Franny were a Hemingway heroine or something, gangrene would set in and she'd lose her leg. Or her life."

"But I'd be very attractive on my deathbed," I add.

Alex touches my shoulder. "How's the foot feeling?"

"Fine. Really."

"Don't try to walk on the sand. You don't want to grind something in there while it's still an open wound." He looks around. "Anyone want to go in the water?"

"Not me," Julia says. "It's freezing."

"You never like to go in the ocean," Alex says.

"Because it's always freezing. Give me a heated pool any day."

"You're so spoiled."

"You're just as spoiled, so don't pretend you're not."

"Hey, look, volleyball," Vanessa says, pointing to a net that's set up a little ways down the beach. A bunch of other Mansfield students are already there, stripping off shirts and kicking off their sandals. "I'm going to go play. Anyone else?"

"Me," says Lawrence. He glances back. "You sure you're okay, Franny?"

"I'm so beyond okay that I'm going to scream if anyone else asks me that."

"Okay. Bye." He trots after Vanessa, slipping his T-shirt up and over his head as his feet slide in the sand. His thin shoulders are so white they're practically translucent in the sun.

"Harry?" Julia says.

He's already made himself comfortable on the towel next to me, his legs stretched out, his face turned up to the sun. "Mmmm?" he murmurs absently.

"Want to go for a walk?"

"In a minute. I need to regain my strength. I just saved a girl's life, you know. Takes a lot out of you."

Julia drops her beach bag onto one of the towels. "In that case, I'm going to run to the bathroom. I'll be right back."

"*I'm* up for a walk," Alex says, looking at Isabella, who hesitates and says, "But poor Franny's stuck here."

"I'm fine," I say.

"I'll hang out here with her," Harry says.

"So will we," says James. He's been carefully arranging a very thick and plush beach blanket on the sand for the last few minutes, and now he settles down on it, pulling a few wrinkles smooth as he makes himself comfortable. He's wearing baggy swim shorts and an unbuttoned oxford shirt, which reveals a thatch of sandy-colored chest hair and a couple of rolls of waist fat. "Man, that sun's hot today."

"Yes, the sun has a way of being like that," Marie says.

Alex and Isabella tell us they'll be back soon and wander off down the beach.

I watch them go. He's inclining his head toward her, listening intently to whatever it is she's saying. The roar of the ocean makes their conversation instantly private.

"It's hot," James says after a moment.

"So you've already pointed out," Marie replies. She's still standing, her hands on her hips. She kicks a tiny bit of sand at Harry's legs. He doesn't seem to notice. She does it again, only with more sand, and he lifts his head and says, "Don't," and then goes back to sunbathing and ignoring her. She fidgets a bit, adjusting the waist of the leafy-green sarong she's wearing around her tiny waist, then looks up and says, "You should drink something, James. You're sweating like a pig."

"That's because it's hot."

"Yeah . . . You know what? I just remembered that we passed a coffee shop about two blocks back. I think you should go get us all some nice cold drinks."

"But we just got settled here."

"I'm *dying* of thirst."

He rises reluctantly to his feet. "I wish you'd told me that before."

"I know, I'm sorry." She strokes his arm with sudden affection. "You're so sweet. Get me an iced tea, okay? With lots of ice? And two Splendas? You guys want anything?" This last question is to me and Harry. He orders an iced coffee. I pass.

"I don't suppose you want to come with me?" James says to Marie.

"I have to keep Franny company." She slides down onto her knees next to me. "Since she's stuck here and everyone else wants to take a walk. It would be mean for us all to just leave her."

"Okay, then, I'm off. I have my phone if you think of anything else you want."

"Thanks!" Marie says, all smiles and waves. "You're totally my hero! Come back quickly!"

He struggles through the sand toward the parking lot, stopping a couple of times to take off one of his Sperry boat shoes and shake the sand out of it.

"Got rid of *him*," Harry says lightly.

Marie shrugs with a little smile.

A few seconds later she shifts around on the blanket and says, "This is boring. Let's go explore a little, Harry." She rises to her feet.

"But I'm comfy."

"Don't be so lazy." She reaches down for his hand, and he shrugs and lets her haul him to his feet. Like it's more work to resist, which maybe it is. Harry definitely takes the easiest path.

Although he did carry me across the hot sand. Got to give him credit for that.

"We'll be right back," Marie says to me.

"No worries," I say. I honestly don't care.

They head along the beach. As they disappear around the curve, I see Marie's hand start trailing up Harry's ridiculously muscled arm.

I'm alone. I get a book out of my beach bag and try to focus on reading it. Try not to think about Alex and Isabella and how they've completely vanished. And what they're talking about. Or whether they're even talking at all.

A shadow falls over me: Julia is back.

"Where did everybody go? Where's Harry?"

"He and Marie went to explore."

"Are you kidding me? He *just* said he didn't want to go for a walk!"

"They'll be back any second."

She drops down heavily next to me. "She *has* a boyfriend."

"It's just a walk, Julia. They'll be back soon."

"No, they won't," she says miserably. "They're nowhere in sight."

"It's nice just sitting here and reading."

"Nice for you, maybe."

I give up and go back to reading my book while Julia digs her fingers into the sand over and over again.

A little while later . . . "I'm back," gasps a winded James, who hands me a full cardboard drink tray before collapsing down onto his knees on the towels. "Where did Marie go?"

"On a walk with Harry." Julia fixes James with a stare, like she wants him to realize how wrong this is.

James sits on his butt and adjusts his sunglasses on his nose. "It's a little strange to ask someone to get you a drink and then not be there when he gets back."

"*Very* strange." Julia rises to her feet. "I'll go find them and tell them the drinks are here. You stay with Franny." She runs off across the sand, toward the bend in the beach.

That leaves me alone with James. "So," I say, because I feel like I have to make conversation, "what are you up to this summer?"

"I'm working at a law firm."

"Nice. Do you like it?"

"Very much. I'm planning to take a full-time job there when I graduate." He unwraps a straw and threads it into one of the drinks.

"That's great," I say. "What's it called?"

"Rushport Reeves."

"Oh, so is this a gift from them?" I point to the beach blanket, which has *Rushport* embroidered on one corner of it.

"No. My last name's Rushport." I must look confused, because he adds, "My grandfather's a founding partner of Rushport Reeves."

No wonder he has a job waiting for him.

James drinks his coffee and smiles at me pleasantly around the straw. I thumb the pages of my book.

"How's your foot doing?" he asks as he puts his cup back down.

"Fine, really. I'm tempted to get up and walk around."

"Best to play it safe," he says. "Glass, you know."

I nod, not entirely sure what I'm agreeing with.

Another silence. I fidget and watch the volleyball players, who are laughing and jumping and diving in the sand. I would have happily played volleyball. I'm good at volleyball.

We fail at getting a real conversation going, so eventually I go back to reading my book, while James stretches out on the towels and closes his eyes with an "I put on SPF fifty this morning, but I know I'm doomed."

* * *

Last in, first out: Julia returns. I thought she was in a bad mood when she left. It was nothing compared to the one she's in now.

"I couldn't find them," she announces angrily as she drops down next to me, missing the towels and sending a swirl of sand up in the air and into my eyes. "They must be hiding somewhere. This sucks."

I'm finding it hard to be sympathetic: I bet I'm just as wounded by Alex and Isabella's disappearance as she is by Harry and Marie's, but at least I'm trying to make the time pass pleasantly for those of us left behind. Every time she mutters something about how long Harry and Marie have been gone, James looks more disturbed, and I'm starting to feel bad for him. Is Julia really that clueless?

Lawrence and Vanessa come back soon after that, sweaty and exhilarated, followed a little while later by Isabella and Alex.

"Sorry we were gone so long!" Isabella sings out. They sit down close together and she lets her hand rest lightly on his knee, almost like she doesn't know it's there. "There was this strange little rock area up ahead, and I said, 'Let's just walk to there,' but then it was much farther than I realized. And then when we got there, it wasn't even all that interesting." She glances slyly at Alex. "But the walk was nice."

"As we learn from *The Odyssey*, it is not the journey

but the destination that matters," Alex intones with mock pomposity. He leans back so he can pull something out of his pocket and says in his normal voice, "Hey, Franny, I found these for you." He holds out his hand to me, revealing five softly colored, irregularly shaped pebbles. "You said you like sea glass, right?"

I didn't even think he'd heard me.

I put out my hand and he pours the pieces onto my palm. "They're beautiful," I say. "Don't you want them?"

"I was looking for you. Since you couldn't."

"Thank you." I close my hand around my treasure.

Isabella says—a little sharply—"Don't hog all the credit, Alex. *I* found that big clear piece."

"No," Alex says. "I found the clear one—you found the purple one."

"I'm pretty sure I found both."

"Now who's trying to hog the credit?" He brushes his lips against her temple.

"Just trying to keep you honest," she says, her voice softening.

I tighten my fist around the sea glass until it hurts.

Marie and Harry don't return until we're all eating the hot dogs, chips, and drinks that the counselors have supplied.

Marie is in a very good mood. She tosses around

her mane of honey-colored hair as she laughs loudly at Harry's jokes and orders James to wait on her. She seems to think she's impressing everyone with the fact that she has two guys orbiting her, but I don't think either of them seems nearly as delighted with her as she is with herself.

Julia· is unusually quiet, just sits with me and Lawrence, picking at a bag of chips and ignoring her hot dog.

After we've been eating for a little while, Isabella stands up and stretches. With that white linen tunic and her long dark hair pinned up and those sleek sunglasses, she looks sexy and sophisticated. "Anyone want another soda?" she asks, and Alex leaps to his feet to go with her to the barrel of drinks near the volleyball net. Their hands seek out each other along the way, and they stay entwined even when they return to report that the counselors are putting out dessert. Harry and Lawrence head over to the picnic table to grab some for us all.

Harry comes back and tosses a plastic-wrapped brownie in front of me. I toss back a "thanks," and then he drops down next to Julia and holds out another one. "For you."

"No, thank you," she says frostily.

He shakes his head ruefully. "I could have sworn someone told me that girls like chocolate."

"I like *chocolate*," she says.

"So it's me you have a problem with?"

"It was just a joke. Excuse me." She gets up and pointedly walks over to where Alex and Isabella are talking and sits down with them.

Harry looks at me. "I think I'm in trouble."

"Seems like it."

He leans back on his elbows. "Don't suppose you'd be willing to tell me what crime I committed?"

I shake my head. "I'm just an innocent bystander. By*sitter*." Then I relent. "But you probably should have waited for her to take that walk along the beach. I'm only telling you this much because you gave me a brownie."

"I knew I was on to something with that chocolate/girl thing." He turns onto his side so he's facing me, his head propped up on one elbow. "Hey, how's your foot feeling?"

"Totally fine."

"Too bad. I kind of liked carrying you around."

"I'm sure you'll have plenty more opportunities— I'm the world's biggest klutz."

"Well, I'm not going to *hope* that you get hurt, but if you do, remember that you're *my* damsel in distress, and no one else is allowed to carry you."

"I don't remember signing that contract," I say.

"All the more reason to promise me now."

"What if you're not around when I get hurt?"

"Send word. I'll come running."

"How big an injury does it have to be? Because sometimes I do this thing when I stand up too quickly and my ankle kind of twists a little—"

"Sounds serious," he says gravely. "You don't want to put any weight on that. I'd better carry you the next time that happens."

"What if I skin my knee?"

"I'll carry you."

"Charley horse?"

"I'll carry you."

"Chipped toenail?"

"Not worth taking a risk. I'll carry you."

I grin at him and then realize that Julia is watching both of us from over near her brother. And she looks seriously annoyed. Which is ridiculous: I can't help it if Harry flirts with whoever he's near and that happens to be me right now. But I have to admit—he's funnier and smarter than I've given him credit for, and I'm kind of enjoying the conversation. I guess guys like Harry can be good company so long as you don't forget that they're, you know . . . guys like Harry.

act II

scene one

The next day, parts are announced. At dinner that night I can basically guess who got the good roles and who didn't by everyone's expression.

Julia is morose. "It's not bad enough that she switched to our cast?" she whispers to me as we fill our cups together at the dispenser. "They gave her Viola! The biggest female lead!"

"Is she a bad actress?"

She waves her hand irritably, sending drops of Diet Coke flying around us. "She's fine, I guess. It doesn't matter—this is totally sympathy casting; they still think some guy was inappropriate with her. Which is so ridiculous. . . . And you know who's playing the duke?" I shake my head. "*Harry*," she says, like it should have been obvious. "That means the two of them fall in love, which is just what she was obviously hoping for when she switched into this cast. She got everything she wanted by cheating. It's so unfair!"

"Who did you get?"

"Maria." She pronounces it "Ma-rye-ah." "She's a maid. It's not the worst role in the world, but it's not the best. I'm also the duke's musician. I think that gives me one more line."

Marie is sitting with Harry when we get back to our table, going on about the play and their scenes together. "We should sneak off to rehearse whenever we can," she tells him as we sit down. "He said he wants us off book by the end of next week. That's not so hard for people with smaller roles"—her eyes, ever so briefly, graze over Julia—"but I'm terrified!"

"It'll be fine," he says, and greets both me and Julia, who takes a sip of her Diet Coke and says offhandedly, "So where did you and your boyfriend go after the beach, Marie?"

Marie looks vaguely annoyed by the question. "Just some restaurant." She turns back to Harry. "The hardest thing to me is going to be pretending to be a boy—I mean, I could *play* a boy no problem. It's much trickier playing a *girl* who's *pretending* to be a boy. You know what I mean?"

"Don't overthink this one," he says. "Lower your voice, show some swag, grab your crotch, and wear something that hides your boobs. She will, right?" he says, turning to me. "Wear something that hides her boobs? What's her costume going to be like?"

"I'm not allowed to say—Amelia's worried people will start asking for changes if they find out too early on."

"But you'll tell *us*, right?" Harry says, with a beguiling smile. He *does* have an extremely beguiling smile; I'll give him that. Something to do with those under-eye dimples. "We're your friends."

"I'm open to bribery," I say cheerfully.

"I already gave you a brownie," he points out. "How much more can one man do?"

"Two brownies?" I suggest.

Alex and Isabella come over to the table. "I'm Isabella!" she cries out as she gets closer.

"Yeah, we've met you," Harry says.

"Shut up! You know what I mean."

"You got the role!" He holds out his arms and she bends down so they can hug. "I'm so proud of you. I knew you could do it."

She steps back, beaming. "Best of all, Alex is the duke."

"Everyone's a duke," I say.

"Is that what you got?" Isabella asks Harry, who nods. "Fantastic! I'm so proud of *you*." Another hug. What a huggy duo they are. She slides into his lap and rests her head on his shoulder. "Can I share your food?" she asks. "I'm too tired to go get my own."

"What's mine is yours," Harry says, and she rips off a piece of his roll and pops it in her mouth, then rips off another piece and pops it in *his* mouth.

"So you're one of the leads?" Julia asks her brother, who nods. "I'm just the stupid maidservant," she says glumly. "It's not fair. I mean, I'm happy for you, Al, but I care about acting so much more than you do."

"I know, and you're also much better at it than I am."

"I'm not saying that—"

"It's true." Alex is totally channeling William to me right now: my brother would have tried to make me feel better too. "It's just that boy/girl thing—every guy will get a good role because Shakespeare had lots of great male roles and there aren't as many guys as girls here."

"Yeah, Sir Andrew's going to be played by a girl in our production," Marie says. "They're changing the character to Lady Andrea because they don't want a girl playing a boy since Viola is already a girl playing a boy and they don't want to confuse the audience."

"Which means trannies are completely out of the question," Harry says.

Marie taps his shoulder. "Are you going to go see fireworks on the Fourth with everyone? I'm trying to decide if I want to go or not. There's a party I've been invited to—"

"With James?" Julia asks.

Marie gives a curt nod. "But I don't know if I want to go. I hate to miss out on fireworks."

"Girls always see fireworks when they're with me" is Harry's predictable response.

"Oh, I'm sure," she says with heavy sarcasm. "But are you going?"

"Haven't thought about it." He glances at me. "You going, Franny?"

"I guess," I say. If everyone else is going, I'll go. I'm not going to miss out on a fun night away from campus just because I have a stupid childhood phobia.

I look up and see that Alex is watching me. He gives me a little nod and a reassuring smile. I guess he remembers that fireworks make me nervous.

On the night of the Fourth, after the bus lets us off on a tree-lined bluff above the ocean, the graduate students hand out candy and popcorn. They brought Frisbees and footballs, too, and we all throw them around, laughing and enjoying the growing cool as the twilight deepens around us.

It's fun, but there's a knot of anxiety inside me that tightens when someone yells, "They're about to start!"

Everyone gathers at the edge of the cliff, facing the ocean. I quickly slip to the back of the crowd, getting as far away as I can from the actual fireworks.

There's a small *boom* and a sizzling noise as a rocket

snakes up to the sky. It explodes, and blue and white sparks fly down.

People ooh and aah. My heart thuds, and I can feel sweat prickling under my arms and at my temples. I know I'm perfectly safe and should be enjoying this, but my body refuses to believe that. Where's William when I need him? He was the only thing that kept me from fainting when I was little. He'd stand next to me and I'd close my eyes and press my face into his arm.

Two loud *boom*s in a row and suddenly I'm finding it hard to breathe. I move closer to the tree and press my whole body against the rough bark. Maybe I can just kind of shield myself behind it—

I suddenly feel a strong arm behind my back and a warm, steady hand on my shoulder.

I open my eyes. Alex is standing next to me. He doesn't say anything, just keeps his arm tight around me. I'm protected by him on one side and the tree on the other.

Five rockets are set off in quick succession and *boom, boom, boom, boom, boom* above us. I stare up at the shower of lights as each burst breaks through the one before it. I lean against the trunk and think, *It's beautiful*. Because it really is.

Alex's arm is reassuringly solid across my back. I want to relax against it, but I don't, because he's probably just being nice, and I don't want him to think it means anything more than that to me.

I thank him when it's all over. He says, "Don't mention it," gives my shoulders one last squeeze, then walks back to Isabella, who's standing with Harry near the front of the group.

He takes her hand and says something, gesturing back toward me and the tree, and she nods, like she understands what's going on. But the next time we walk by each other, her eyes linger on my face like she's trying to figure something out.

A couple of nights later, I find my friends curled up together in a corner of the common room, talking wistfully about chocolate chip cookies.

"The ones here suck," Julia says. The sofa is full, so she curls up her legs and drapes them across Vanessa's lap, making room on the floor for me to sit below them. "They're always stale. I want bakery ones, all warm from the oven."

"At home I bake cookies all the time," Vanessa says, gently scritching the top of my head in greeting, like I'm a pet. "They're good, too."

"If we had a kitchen, you could bake us some," Julia says.

"Yeah," Harry pipes up from the other end of the sofa. Alex is between him and Julia, and Isabella is once again curled up on Harry's lap with her head on his shoulder. They're such an adorable couple, Harry and Isabella—why can't they just actually be a couple? That would improve *my* life. "We need a kitchen," Harry says. "Then all you girls could go in there and bake stuff for us guys. Preferably in skimpy bikinis and barefoot. But with lots of lipstick on."

Marie is perched on the sofa arm next to him. She pushes at his arm with flirtatious indignation. "You are so sexist."

"I have a kitchen," I say. "I mean, my aunt does."

"Would she let us use it?" Julia asks.

"I think so . . . but I also think we'd have more fun if she's not there." I'm definitely more certain of the second point than the first one. "She doesn't go out a lot, but she said something about a book club this weekend. Let me ask her about it."

Amelia *does* have book club on Sunday evening. "We only read books that expand our horizons," she informs me. "They have to be translated from another language and take place in a foreign country—it's important to learn about other cultures. And they can't just be *fun* books—this isn't about reading for pleasure; it's about becoming better informed. Do you want to come along with me?" I politely decline and ask her if I could invite a few friends over while she's gone.

"A few?" she repeats suspiciously.

"Four or five . . ."

"Just girls?"

I shake my head and say quickly, "But they're all good kids, I promise. Everyone's exhausted. We just want to relax and watch TV." I don't mention the cookie baking—she's such a neat freak she might say no just to keep her kitchen clean.

"No alcohol," she says. "Or anything worse."

"Of course not."

I guess I sound sincere because she reluctantly agrees to let me entertain in her absence.

Sunday's perfect, since the Mansfield students always have it off.

"It was meant to be," Lawrence says, when I tell everyone at our next meal that we're good to go.

"That's a ridiculous thing to say," Vanessa tells him. "Life is all chaos and happenstance and occasional good or bad luck."

"I don't know," Isabella says. "Some things feel inevitable to *me*."

"Like death and taxes," Harry adds.

"What do *you* know about either?" Julia asks him.

"Only that my grandfather's equally terrified of both," he says with a laugh.

After dinner on Sunday, I lead our group to Amelia's apartment, slightly nervous because most of them come from huge, expensive estates—I know they won't make fun of the way we live or anything like that, but I still feel a little embarrassed about it. Which is a feeling I'm used to. Story of my life, really.

At least I know the place is clean: Amelia is meticulous about her housekeeping and expects me to be the same. If she finds so much as a single dirty fork in the sink, she'll grill me on it: Why didn't I wipe it off and put it in the dishwasher? Did I expect her to do it for me? Or our invisible maidservant? Or maybe a little elf? Life isn't all fun and games and letting other people clean up after us, missy. We're responsible for our own messes and if I think otherwise—

It's easier to just clean up after myself than go through *that*.

As we walk toward our entryway, Julia nudges Harry and points to the raised hot tub in the tiny courtyard. Harry nods and says, "I am so in."

Up on our floor, I unlock the door and swing it open. "Here you go. It's not much, but I don't call it home."

They glance around the living room, which is also the dining room and the TV room.

"It's nice," Julia says politely.

Lawrence says, "I have an old maiden aunt too, and her place smells just like this. What *is* that smell, anyway?"

"Age and desperation?" I suggest.

"Bitterness and despair?" Vanessa says.

"Baked fish?" says Harry.

"She does like tilapia," I admit.

Marie sidles up to Harry. "Oh, hey," she says brightly. "Want to go with me to the hot tub?"

"Sure, but I don't have a bathing suit."

"You're wearing boxers, right?"

He turns to the rest of us. "I swear I don't know how she knows that. She must be psychic."

She giggles. "You can wear those. And I can borrow a suit from Franny."

I say, "Okay, but I only have one."

Harry looks over at that. "Do you want to go in the tub, Franny? Because I always say the girl who owns the suit gets first dibs on it."

"You say that all the time, do you?" Isabella says to him, amused.

"Yes, I do. I can't count the number of times it's come up in conversation." He turns back to me. "So do you want to do the hot tub with me, Franny? It's safe: I haven't urinated in a public bathing facility in at least"—he thinks—"four . . . seven . . . carry the two . . . at least two and a half months. I mean, weeks."

"As appealing as that sounds, I'm going to pass. I want to make cookies." I had actually been thinking that Julia might want to borrow the suit too, but she doesn't lay claim to it, just follows me to my room, where I dig out my Speedo while she complains about how the hot tub was her idea—she spotted it first—and it's not fair, nothing's fair, Marie gets everything first, and her—Julia's—life is terrible, horrible, miserable.

"You want this?" I ask, offering her the suit.

"It's too late now," she says, so I go back into the living room, where I give the suit to Marie.

"Don't you have a bikini?" she asks, and when I shake my head, she snatches it out of my hand like she's doing me a favor and disappears into my room to change.

Harry comes out of the bathroom with a towel tied around his waist, and I give him the keys to get into the pool area and then back into the building. I also manage to sneak a quick peek at his chest, since it's standing right there in front of me, and it's really a pretty excellent chest—broad, muscular, smooth. . . . The guy could be a male model. *Should* be one. Then he could strike poses in front of admiring people all day long—his dream job, no doubt.

He lets the keys dangle from his fingers. "After the cookies are done, if you change your mind about joining me in the hot tub—"

"You'll be the first to know," I say.

Once he and Marie leave, Vanessa and Lawrence and I start mixing the cookie dough. Julia sulks on the sofa in the living room, and Alex and Isabella . . .

Where *are* Alex and Isabella?

"They said something about taking a walk," Vanessa says when I comment on their disappearance. "It's probably one of those hot and heavy 'walks.' The kind that don't require any actual walking, if you know what I mean."

"Gee, no," Lawrence says. "You're just too subtle, that's your problem."

Harry and Marie return first—complaining that the tub was more tepid than hot—and are already dressed and eating cookies by the time Isabella and Alex show up.

"It's such a beautiful night!" Isabella says, her eyes shining. Her cheeks and chin are pink, the way they get when you've been kissing a guy who hasn't shaved since that morning.

"And the cookies are done!" Alex gloats. "We timed this perfectly."

"I hope you don't mind that we skipped out on the baking," Isabella says to the rest of us. "Too many cooks and all that."

"You okay?" Alex asks Julia, who's focusing a little too intently on transferring the last batch of cookies to a plate.

"Fine."

Harry looks up at that and comes over to her. "You don't sound okay," he says. "You want to tell Uncle Harry about it?"

She shoots him a venomous look. "Thanks but no thanks."

He leans toward her and whispers something in her ear. She doesn't respond. He whispers some more. She smiles reluctantly. He whispers again, and this time she laughs out loud.

They giggle a lot more together while we clean up. Marie glances at them from time to time, her face growing tighter and angrier with every additional minute that she's left out of their private joke.

We wrap up the cookies to go, and then I usher everyone downstairs—I want them safely out before Amelia returns so I have time to clean up the kitchen.

In front of the building complex, Marie grabs Harry by the arm. "Let's run some lines together as we walk," she says, and he lets her pull him ahead of the others.

After everyone else has moved off, Julia lingers behind to say to me miserably, "One second he's all over me, the next he's all over her."

"She won't leave him alone."

"I know, but then he goes along with it."

"That's the kind of guy he is."

"Whatever. I'm so done with this." She runs to catch up with the others. I'm not sure if she means the conversation or the Harry-Marie thing, but either way I'm glad she's moving on.

It's not until I turn around and reach into my pocket

that I realize I don't have my key. I gave it to Harry but he never gave it back. And I don't have my cell phone with me.

I lean against the door, annoyed at myself. All I can do is wait for someone else to come along who lives in our building. Amelia should be back soon, but I hope one of our neighbors shows up first, because if she sees that I locked myself out, she'll give me a lecture I really don't want to get.

But then Harry is suddenly racing toward me from across the street.

"I'm an idiot," he calls out as soon as he's close enough. He tosses me the keys as he comes to a stop in front of me. "I have no memory of even putting these in my pocket."

I snatch the keys eagerly. "No problem—you came back just in time."

"Okay, then," he says with a nod. "Good night."

He's turning when I say, "Harry?"

He instantly swivels back. "Yeah?"

"Can I ask you a question?"

"Of course. Anything."

"I was just wondering if you knew that you kind of hurt Julia's feelings tonight."

His face falls—this clearly wasn't the topic he was hoping for. "Did I?"

"You really didn't know?"

He glances off to the side uncomfortably. "I guess I kind of knew," he says after a moment. "But it seemed sort of stupid. If she wanted to go to the hot tub, she should have just said so."

"Face it: there's some kind of weird triangle thing going on with her and you and Marie."

"Weird triangle thing?" he repeats, his lips twitching.

"You know what I mean."

"If there is, it's not my fault." He holds his hands out. "I'm just being friendly."

"But if people's feelings are getting hurt . . ."

"So am I supposed to do something about it now? Go find Julia and apologize or something? I'm not sure what I'd be apologizing for, though."

"I don't think you need to apologize, exactly."

"What then?"

"I don't know." I make a helpless gesture. "I guess all I'm saying is try to be aware of how what you do affects people."

"I get that," he says. "And I'll try." He steps a little closer to me. "And what about you, Franny? Are *you* aware of how what you do affects people?"

I force a laugh, suddenly a little uncomfortable. "Not an issue for me, Harry."

"I don't know about that. Us talking right now?" He lowers his voice to a throaty whisper. "I think maybe it's affecting me."

I can't tell if he's joking or not. So all I say is, "Thanks for not just telling me to screw off."

"Wouldn't dream of it."

"I know you're just enjoying all the admiration, but Julia's more fragile than you'd think. Don't forget that, okay?"

"Yeah, I'll keep it in mind." There's a pause. He slides his eyes toward me. "So you think people admire me, do you?"

"You know they do."

He grins with sudden delight, then holds his hand out and I take it, thinking he wants to shake or something, but instead he bends down and kisses me lightly on the cheek. "You know, if you're going to take me aside when I'm behaving badly, I may start behaving worse. Just to get some attention from you." His eyes briefly catch the light and glow gray-green for a moment. "Possibly even some admiration."

"Harry . . ." I take a deep breath and raise my face to look him in the eyes. "Don't flirt with me, okay? Not if you want us to be friends."

He drops my hand and scuffs at the cement stoop. "I was being sincere," he says.

"Whatever. Doesn't matter. Just talk to me normally, okay?"

"I *was*." A pause. He kicks at the step some more, then glances at me. "Do you *want* us to be friends?"

"Of course."

"Okay, then, I'll tell you what: I'll promise to try not to flirt if you'll promise . . ."

"What?"

He cocks his head at me. "Not to assume that everything I say to you is insincere."

"Even if it is?"

He shakes his head. "Ah, Franny. That's not even trying."

"Sorry. I'll do better."

"Liar," he says, almost fondly, and leaves.

scene two

ere are some of the things people say to me on Monday, while I'm measuring them for costumes:

"I'm taller than you'd think from my measurements."

"Subtract a few inches—I like things to fit really tight."

"I can only wear cotton or I break out in hives."

"My waist is *not* twenty-nine inches, thank you very much! I wear a size two—zero at the Gap."

"Don't let her put me in something ugly."

"Hey, watch those hands! LOL."

"I know you're not supposed to tell us what our costumes are going to look like, but you can tell *me*. I won't tell anyone else."

"You know what would be cool? If I'm the only one in the cast who's wearing red."

"Kneel before Zod!"

* * *

"What does 'Kneel before Zod' mean?" I ask Lawrence at dinner.

"*Superman* reference. From the eighties movie with Christopher Reeve. Zod's a supervillain from Krypton. Why?"

I point across the room at a tall, thin, redheaded boy who is walking with his tray to a table. "Sam Carson said that to me when I was measuring his inseam."

"He's such a nerd."

"Hey, *you* knew the reference."

"I never said I wasn't a nerd."

"Gay or not gay?" I ask, gesturing again at Sam. It's a game we all play here.

"Gay as the night is long," Lawrence says. "He and Brian Emmanuel hooked up a couple of days ago."

"People are pairing off like crazy," I say, watching Isabella and Alex jostle each other in line.

It's possible I sound a little bitter.

"Tell me about it," Lawrence says morosely. His relationship with roommate Raymond has taken a downturn—not only did they decide that there was no romantic future there but now they can't even stand each other. Apparently Raymond is a pig who won't empty the trash can, not even when it's his turn and not even when he's just clipped his toenails into it, in front of all his roommates. "Toenail clipping is the enemy of love," Lawrence said when he told me that story.

"Let's stay single together," I tell him now. "We have each other—who needs romance?"

"Not I," Lawrence says. A beat. "Well, maybe I a little bit."

"I a little bit too," I admit.

"Mind if I sit here?" Harry takes the empty chair next to me before I even respond. He's been doing that all week: sitting next to me if he can. It's fine with me; he makes me laugh. And whenever he says something at all coy or flirtatious, I shoot him a look, and usually the next thing he says is normal again.

Julia's not thrilled about our growing friendship. "I thought you didn't trust him!" she says to me a little while later when we're both waiting in line for ice cream.

"I don't. But that doesn't mean I don't *like* him."

"Well, I think it's strange that you're always telling me how shallow and unreliable he is, and now he's like your best friend."

I shrug and don't say what I think, which is that it's probably a relief for Harry to talk to someone who *isn't* in love with him. Maybe he likes a break from the hard work of living up to his reputation.

"It's not like I care," Julia says. "Personally, I mean. I'm over him."

"You are?" It's news to me.

"There's this other guy in our cast . . ." And she launches into a description of Manny Yates, who's playing a couple of different roles in *Twelfth Night*. He's cute, he's straight, he's interested in her, and he's more shy than flirtatious. "I'm done with guys who are in love with themselves," she says. "I want someone who actually pays attention to me."

"Really? I want someone who doesn't even know I'm alive."

The joke is wasted: Julia, as usual, barely registers my words. "Just don't do anything stupid," she says with all the superiority of someone who stopped doing stupid things a couple of days ago. At the *most*.

Back at the table, Marie is in my chair.

"Um," I say, "I was sort of sitting there."

"Sorry," Marie says, with an indifferent shrug. "Harry and I were going to try to run some lines right now. Do you mind switching?"

"It's fine." I take my ice cream and water glass over to her former seat on the opposite side of the table, feeling vaguely annoyed: Harry could have made an effort to save my seat for me. But he's Harry. Whichever way the wind blows . . .

The wind blows him and Isabella and Vanessa off for a stroll together after dinner while the rest of us gather in front of the dining hall.

I'm soaking in the warm night air and my last few minutes of freedom before returning to the apartment—on Thursdays Amelia likes to watch *The Real*

Housewives of Blahdy-blah-da while she and I do whatever hand-sewing work she's brought home with her—when Alex comes over to me. "Hey, Franny."

"Cigarette break?" I nod after Harry, Vanessa, and Isabella's retreating backs.

He sighs. "She told me she wants to stop. The problem is, Harry's always getting her to join him—"

"You're blaming *him* for her smoking?"

"Well, he is her smoking buddy."

"He's not exactly holding a gun to her head," I snap.

Alex draws his head back in surprise at my tone. His light blue eyes flit up to my face, then quickly dart away again. "Sorry. I guess I should be more careful what I say. Isabella told me that you and Harry—" He stops.

"Isabella told you that me and Harry *what*?"

"You know," he says, which by the way is the most maddening thing a person can say when you've made it clear already that you *don't* know.

I can guess, though. "Did Isabella say we were, like, into each other or something?"

"Are you?"

"No. Not that it's any of Isabella's business."

"I'm not prying, Franny," he says. "But you rushed to defend him and—"

"I wasn't rushing to defend him! I just don't think you can blame anyone for the fact that Isabella smokes except Isabella."

"Still . . . I mean . . . Isabella says he likes you. That he keeps talking to her about you."

"God, it's like a game of telephone around here!" I flick my palms up. "People say stuff and other people repeat it and no one has any idea what they're talking about!"

"Why are you so mad about this?"

Because Isabella got you to believe I like someone I couldn't care less about. And because I can't tell you who I really like. "Because," I say out loud, "there's nothing going on with me and Harry Cartwright, but people are talking about us like there is. I hate that." That was true enough in its own way.

"Everyone talks about everyone here."

"Yeah, I definitely know way more about you and Isabella than I want to."

His eyebrows draw together. "What's that supposed to mean?"

"Nothing." I'm an idiot. Why'd I say that? "My point is, I don't start throwing it in your face."

"What exactly did I throw in your face? All I did was apologize—"

"It was an inappropriate apology!" There's a pause while we stare at each other. I'm not sure which of us laughs first, because we both crack up at the same time. "Okay," I say. "That sounded really stupid."

"I'll try to apologize more appropriately in the future."

"See that you do."

He smiles, and all the tension goes away. "I'm kind of glad, though. . . ."

"About what?"

"That Isabella's wrong. About you and Harry. I know it's none of my business, but I'd be bummed if you started going out with him."

I freeze in place. I force myself to sound casual. "Why's that?"

"I just think he can be kind of a jerk. At least when it comes to girls." He lowers his voice. "You deserve better, Franny."

"Yeah?" I say.

"Of course," he says even more quietly. "You're amazing."

I stare at him, stunned.

What am I supposed to say to that? *Thank you?*

Or: *Do you mean it?*

How about: *If you think I'm so amazing, why are you with Isabella?*

I want him to say more. But while I'm still wondering what I can say to make him know how badly I want him to say more, he goes, "Oh, hold on a sec," and darts over to the dorm entrance, where one of the custodians is trying to get out with a huge bag of garbage. Alex holds the door for him and then helps support the bag as they take it around the building to the back.

By the time he's done with that, the three smokers

have returned from their walk, and I'm thinking that I'm reading too much into a compliment from someone who just likes to be nice to everyone he meets.

Now that I've measured the waist, hips, bust, and inseam of everyone there is to measure—and that's a lot of everyone, since there are almost fifty kids in the program—Amelia has put me to work altering existing costumes from the basement archives. Mostly it's making things smaller. These are high-school kids, and the Mansfield actors are college-aged and dealing with the fallout from the freshman fifteen. Which is lucky for me: it's always easier to take in than let out, especially since some of these costumes have already been used and altered a few times and there's just no extra fabric left to play around with, which means I have to add in panels when I need to widen the waists or bodices.

It's all precise, difficult work that makes my neck ache from bending over the fabric, ripping and sewing, so on Tuesday morning I happily jump at Amelia's request that I bring some yellow knit swatches to the theater where the *Twelfth Night* cast is rehearsing. She needs the director to pick out the one he wants her to use for Malvolio's stockings.

I make my way down the hallway and through the exit door near the base of the stage, where the entire cast is assembled. Charles sees me come in but puts up a *wait a sec* finger, and I'm more than happy to take a front seat and watch them go on with the scene. I'm in no rush to get back, and I've been dying to see how the shows all look.

The actors are still using scripts, and the blocking seems pretty rudimentary, but the more I hear them say their lines, the more I'm impressed. Not surprised, though: I looked at the Mansfield application online, and I know you have to provide a performance video and that there's a lot of competition—forty-eight kids get in from more than four hundred applications—so the ones who make it are some of the best high-school actors in the country.

My school did *Twelfth Night* a few years ago, and I remember enough about it to know that the scene they're doing comes at the end of the play, with all the confused-identity stuff getting sorted out and the right couples uniting at last.

The scene is progressing nicely, when there's too long a pause. Everyone looks around uncertainly.

"It's Antonio's line," Charles says, checking his script. "That's you, Wilson, isn't it?"

Wilson, a cherubic-looking kid with glasses, says, "Sorry—I'm getting confused here. I'm already in this scene as the clown."

Charles drops the F-bomb, then quickly adds, "You didn't hear that, guys."

Harry flutters his hand in front of his chest and says, "Heavens, I believe the young man uttered a curse word. Our innocent young ears will be ruined!"

"Shut up, Harry." Charles shakes his head. "I forgot that Antonio and Feste are in a scene together."

"I could have a hat for each role," Wilson says. "And keep switching back and forth . . ."

"That's ridiculous," Marie says.

"I guess I could just cut Antonio out of this scene, but we'd lose some good stuff." Charles swings his head around, like he's hoping he'll see something useful.

And what he sees is *me*, sitting quietly in the front row, clutching my little stocking samples.

He takes a step toward the edge of the stage and peers down at me. "You're Amelia's kid, right?"

"God, no," I say. "Her *niece*."

"Right, sorry, that's what I meant. Listen, could you do me a favor? I need an extra body to stand up here and read the lines for this one character—I just want to see whether I need him or not in the scene. You mind?"

"Not at all." I'm thrilled: an excuse to stay away longer from the workroom *and* a chance to act, however briefly. I race over to the steps up to the stage and take them two at a time. Julia waves at me. I wave back. Harry salutes me. I salute him back. Marie flaps her fingers unenthusiastically at me. I flap back with an equal lack of enthusiasm.

Charles hands me his script and tells me where to stand. "Do you know the play?" he asks. "Do you know who Antonio is?"

"He's the guy who rescued Sebastian from drowning, right? And there's something about some money he lent him, only he actually gave it to his identical twin sister who looks just like him because she's dressed like a guy. Right?"

Charles laughs. "That's exactly right. You know your Shakespeare."

"Just a lucky guess," I say.

"Yeah, right. Okay, gang, let's go back to Sebastian's entrance." He taps my script. "Right here—uh, forgot your name." I supply it for him, and he nods. "Okay, right here. Oh, wait—do you need those?"

I look down and realize I'm still clutching the fabric pieces. "They're for Malvolio's stockings—you have to pick one."

"Will do." He takes them from me and sticks them in his pocket. "Okay—and don't worry about how well you read or anything like that, Franny. This is just to let me see whether or not Antonio adds something to this scene."

"Got it," I say.

The scene starts, and pretty soon we get to Antonio's lines—he basically has to stare at Marie (Viola) and the guy who plays Sebastian (Lawrence's roommate

Raymond, who doesn't look much like Marie, but I know their costumes will be identical and they'll wear matching temporary hair dye, so that will help them look alike) and react with amazement at how similar the twins look, and realize that he confused them before.

Antonio has only a couple of lines, but I milk them for all they're worth, circling the two actors in astonishment when it's my turn to speak and letting my voice squeak with excitement.

Charles laughs out loud, which makes me happy. Harry catches my eye and gives me a quick grin and a thumbs-up, and Julia nods approvingly. Marie doesn't even look in my direction.

We finish the scene fairly quickly—Charles has shortened it a lot. The script is filled with blacked-out lines. He starts to discuss some blocking changes with the cast, so I'm heading toward the stairs when I hear him calling my name. I turn around.

"Do you need to rush back, or can you do me another favor?" he asks. "Because I'd really like to see you do the first half of this scene as Antonio, if you've got the time."

I don't care that Amelia will probably be all worked up about how long I was gone when I finally get back to the Sweatshop—I'm enjoying this too much to worry about it.

I've worked hard to forget how much I love being on

a stage, first when my parents told me to focus on other things, and then this summer, being the only kid not in a show here. But just these few minutes of acting remind me how much fun it is.

I'm mostly playing off Harry—the duke—in this part of the scene, and that's part of why it's going so well. For one thing, I know him and I feel comfortable with him. For another . . .

Our drama teacher in middle school used to talk about how actors can be generous or selfish onstage. A generous actor doesn't always call attention to himself, but sets up the other actors to shine too. A selfish one is constantly making you look at him. "You may remember a selfish actor after you see a play, but you won't remember the play," he'd say.

Anyway, the point is, Harry is generous as an actor, willingly playing the straight man to my bewildered, angry Antonio. It's surprising, given his need for attention *off* the stage, but I guess maybe that gets it out of his system. Even with some of the lines cut for time, I get to deliver a pretty long speech, and he doesn't do anything distracting during it, just listens intently. When I finish, he bursts out with an enthusiastic "fantastic, Franny!" and Marie, who's supposed to deliver the next line, hisses at him to "stay in character."

We go through the rest of the scene, and then Charles tells everyone to take a five-minute break and get ready to do Act 1, Scene 5. Then he beckons to me and leads me into the wings.

"I really enjoyed watching you do that," he says.

"Really?"

"Yeah, you're good. Did you apply to the program here? You're the right age, aren't you?"

"Yeah, but I needed to work this summer, and Amelia said she could use an assistant, so I ended up here for a completely different reason."

"Got it." He tilts his head and studies me thoughtfully. "So this is a little unorthodox . . . but I'm thinking, why not? Would you be interested in jumping in and doing a little acting since you're here anyway? Be our Antonio?"

"I would love that," I say, and I mean it. My heart does a little happy turnover at the thought. "So much. But I know my aunt's worried about how much work we have—"

"I'll talk to her about it," he says. "The good thing about Antonio is that he's only in a few scenes. We can work around your schedule and try to take up as little of your time as possible."

"I still don't know if she'll be okay with it."

"Just tell me honestly whether or not this is something you want to do. If it is, I'll work it out with Amelia."

"What about the guy who had the role before?"

"I don't think he'll mind," Charles says. "I had to cut

a lot of his lines as the clown because he had too much to do, but I can expand that role if it's all he's doing."

"Then yes," I say. "Yes. A thousand times yes."

He holds out his hand and we shake on it.

I race back to the workroom. Amelia looks up and says, "What on earth took you so long? I tried texting you, but then I realized you left your phone here."

"I had to wait for them to finish a couple of scenes. Charles was busy."

"You could have just left the fabric samples. They're not worth losing an hour of work over. So which one did he choose?"

"Um," I say, because it now occurs to me that the samples are still in Charles's pocket. "One sec." I go running back out of the room.

Amelia calls after me, "I don't know what you're up to, Franny, but you'd better come back quickly this time!"

Back in the theater, Charles is standing in front of the stage having a conversation with all the cast members, who are sitting in the front few rows facing him. I enter in time to hear Marie say, "But don't you think it's too confusing to have a girl playing a guy, when I'm already doing that as part of the show?"

"We'll make the character *Antonia*, then," Charles says. "Easy solution." He waves his hand at me. "Hey, Franny."

"I just think it's weird," Marie says, and then adds, "Oh, she's here," like she hadn't noticed.

"Sorry to bother you," I say to Charles. "I forgot to get your Malvolio stockings choice."

"Oh, right." He pulls the samples back out of his pocket, asks the boy who's playing Malvolio—Roger—what he thinks, and together they pick out a bright sunshine yellow. I take the fabric and head toward the exit.

Harry reaches up to touch my arm as I walk by his seat. "Welcome to the cast, Franny," he whispers.

Charles comes to the sewing room a little while later, right before lunch. He tells me to go eat, so he can talk to Amelia alone. "We'll figure this out," he tells me. "No worries."

"Figure what out?" Amelia says, so suspiciously that I'm very happy just to slip away and let Charles handle it.

Julia and Harry clap and cheer when I join them at the table with my tray of food.

"You were so good!" Julia says.

"Yeah, you were great," Marie says unenthusiastically. "But I just don't see how Charles can legally cast you. The rest of us had to audition and pay to be here and everything. I mean, we're getting a lot of instruction, right? That's the whole point of this. We're paying to learn. I mean, I want you to join us,

Franny, of course—I think you'd be a great addition to the cast and all that. I just don't think you should get your hopes up that this is definitely going to happen, because it's really possible someone might complain about how it's not fair."

"Let's hope no one does that," Harry says, shooting her a dark look.

"Wilson was really unhappy he lost the role," she says, with a toss of her head. "You can't really blame him—"

"Are you kidding me?" Julia says. "He told me like two minutes ago that he's getting way more stuff to do as Feste, which is what he wanted. And it wasn't like *you* were in our cast originally, either, so I don't understand why this is so hard for you to accept."

"I'm fine with it!" Marie snaps. "I must have misunderstood what Wilson was saying." She turns to me. "I totally want this to work out for you, Franny. Will your aunt be okay with it, though? I mean, you keep saying there's so much work for you both to do. . . ."

I just shrug and say, "We'll see," but I'm wondering what Charles and Amelia are saying to each other and getting more nervous with every second. I can't stop watching the door. I'm trying to stay cool about it, but the truth is, if she says I can't do it, I'm going to be crushed. I want to be part of a show—I've been on the outside looking in for long enough.

Charles finally enters the dining hall a little while later, gets his food, and sits down at a table with a couple of the other directors, which makes me even more nervous. Not that he said he'd come looking for me . . . but wouldn't he, if he had good news?

When I'm done eating, I bus my tray and then try to look nonchalant as I walk by his table. He calls out to me.

"We're all set," he says.

"Really?" I come closer and scan his face to make sure he's not joking. "Really?"

He nods, a little wearily. "I'm not going to say the negotiations were easy . . . but we worked it out. I promised I wouldn't take up too much of your time, so we may have to do some intense rehearsal cramming, but it's a go, if you're up for it."

"So up for it," I say, and we high-five.

"I promised I'd write out a rehearsal schedule for you and submit it to Amelia for her approval."

"I'm sorry," I say.

"Hey, you're the one doing me a favor here. No worries."

"Thanks," I say, and head toward the door. I give a little skip—I get to perform! I get to be in a play with my friends!

I hear my name and look around. Isabella catches up with me. "Do you have a second?" she asks. She smells like cigarette smoke and perfume. She's wearing short fawn-colored boots with white denim shorts and a striped top. Her hair is put up in that sloppy-chic knot she usually wears, and she has on her elegantly sloping sunglasses. Just once I'd like to see her in a baggy top with sweat stains at the armholes and unflattering pants that make her look hippy. I'd like her better if she weren't always so perfect.

I *think* I'd like her better anyway. I'll never know for sure—I doubt she'll ever not be perfect.

I tell her I have to get back to work, but she's welcome to walk me over to the theater.

"Perfect, I'm headed there myself." She falls into step next to me as we walk along the path. "So are you going on this trip Sunday to Portland?"

"What is it?"

"There's going to be a bus into town," she says. "With a few different drop-offs so we can go to whatever neighborhood sounds like the most fun to us. Alex and I already signed up. We don't want to do anything major, just wander around, do some shopping, eat at a nice restaurant. . . . Some people are going to see a movie in one of the big malls, which sounds like a waste of an exploring opportunity to me, but whatever. Anyway, Harry's interested in going with us, but he said he doesn't want to feel like a third wheel all day, so I think you should come too." She touches my arm lightly. "He's always asking me about you, you know. You're his favorite topic these days, like whether I think you're as nice as you seem and whether I've noticed what pretty eyes you have—stuff like that."

I shake my head wordlessly. I don't know what's going on here, but it fits with what Alex was telling me—that Isabella thinks Harry and I could become an item. But it's not going to happen.

She reads my silence as coyness. "You don't believe me, do you?" She gives my arm a jovial squeeze. "I should have known. There are girls who think every guy in the world has a crush on them, and then there are girls who can't believe *any* guy would have a crush on them and miss all the signals."

I'm pretty sure I'm neither of those types. "Look, Isabella, I know Harry's a good friend of yours, and he's a lot of fun. But he's also . . ." I stop, uncertain how to put it.

"The kind of guy who flirts with anything that moves?" she supplies.

I nod, surprised by her honesty.

"I know, I know." She rolls her large, expressive eyes. "Believe me, I know. There's like this long trail of wreckage behind him at our high school. Girls always think he likes them more than he does, and it gets him in trouble all the time. Just look at Julia and Marie." She dismisses them with a flick of her long fingers.

"Anyway, the point is, you're right—he's a total flirt. But that's just what he's like on the surface. Deep down, he's a good guy."

"I'm sure he is," I say politely, even though I'm not.

"Anyway, I didn't mean to turn this into a big deal: there's no pressure on you if you come with us. I'm not setting you guys up or anything—I just think we'd all have fun as a group."

"I'd like to go, but I'm kind of scared even to ask Amelia. I'm already cutting into my work time with this rehearsing thing—"

"I'll talk to her for you," she says confidently. "I can always get people to do what I want."

"That must be nice," I say.

"I may be exaggerating slightly." We're almost at the theater. She stops abruptly and turns to me. "Can I ask you something?" I nod, and she says slowly, "This may sound weird, but I've noticed that you and Alex . . ." She hesitates, then starts again. "I mean, I know you've known Alex and Julia since middle school. Maybe that's why sometimes I get the sense that you and he . . ." Another pause. "You're obviously good friends, which is great. But I was wondering—is there anything I should know about you guys? Because I'm starting to really like him." She gives a short laugh. "Big surprise, right? I haven't exactly been hiding it. And I don't think Alex is the kind of guy who would . . ." She stops. "It's just that you two seem really close, and if there's something I should know—"

"No worries," I say. "We're just friends."

"You sure? I see you two talking sometimes."

This sucks—why am I stuck in the position of having to reassure *her*? She's the one he's chosen. But whatever. I say, "Honestly? I think he's totally one hundred percent into you."

She nods slowly, absorbing that, studying me intently like she's trying to hear something I'm not saying. "I hope you're right," she says simply, before walking me the rest of the way to the Sweatshop, where she turns on the charm for Amelia.

It takes less than five minutes for her to get her way. She compliments Amelia on the costumes, tells her how lucky Mansfield is to have found her, launches into what good friends she and I have become, then says, "Now, you have to let Franny come with us on Sunday, because it's the only day all summer that we get to explore Portland and it won't be fun without her."

To my astonishment, Amelia just nods and says, "Of course she should go."

"All set," Isabella says to me with a satisfied smile as she leaves for rehearsal. "I'll tell Harry and Alex you're coming."

Once she's gone, Amelia's attitude flips 180 degrees. She grumbles about how much work she has, how she needs me 24/7, how it was bad enough knowing she'd be losing so many of my work hours to play rehearsals, and do I even appreciate what a sacrifice she's making just so I can have some fun and—

I say, "Fine. I won't go." As soon as the words are out, I feel disappointed—the idea of not going makes me realize how much I actually do want to go.

Amelia waves her hand. "I already gave my word that you can go, and *I* don't break my word." The way she emphasizes *I* is almost an accusation: like I've somehow betrayed her by making this plan to go out for a few hours one day. I decide I'm done offering to stay. She grumbles some more under her breath as I take up my stitching, and it's so annoying that I actually ask her to turn on her folk music.

What's truly scary is that I think I'm starting to like Joan Baez and Joni Mitchell. Pretty soon I'll be drinking herbal tea and wearing homemade skirts and spending my free time adding tassels to sofa cushions.

Just shoot me now.

scene three

haven't had a lot of opportunities to dress up, so on Sunday I decide I might as well put on the one nice summer dress I brought with me. It's dark green and tight across the bodice, with a narrow waist and full skirt—very 1950s. I found it at a thrift store. I don't think it's actually vintage—I think it was designed to be retro—but it's still pretty nice. I want to pair it with my sexy spike heels—the only good shoes I've brought— but I'm worried we'll have to walk a lot, so I stick to comfortable sandals. I use a curling iron to create waves in my light brown hair and put on some makeup. I check myself out in the mirror. Not bad. I've spent a lot of time this summer staying cool and comfortable in shorts and ponytails, so it's a nice change to go for pretty instead of practical.

I meet up with Isabella near the dorm. She seems very pleased that I've made an effort to look nice.

"Harry's going to melt when he sees you," she says.

"He won't care," I say. "We're just friends."

She smiles a little smile and shrugs.

As we fall into step, heading back toward campus, I wonder why she seems to want something to happen between Harry and me. She's his best friend, so I've got to assume she's on his side and that he's into the idea. And if that's true—if Harry told her he likes me—how do I feel about that?

I'm not sure. Like I told Julia, I don't trust the guy, but I've come to like him more than I thought I would when I first met him.

And he's very good-looking.

And maybe you can have fun with someone you don't trust, so long as you remember you don't trust him. My mistake with my previous boyfriends was caring more than they did. Couldn't it be fun to have some kind of summer fling where neither of us takes it seriously at all?

An interesting thought . . .

Alex and Harry are waiting in front of the dining hall, close to the bus that everyone's already starting to board.

"Any chance you two pretty ladies might be interested in spending time with some manly men?" Harry asks as they greet us.

"We were hoping to do better," Isabella says with

a toss of her head. "But there's no shame in settling, I suppose."

Alex touches her arm. "You look nice."

"Nice?" she repeats. "Try harder, Alex."

He flushes adorably. "Really nice," he says.

"Next time, try this," Harry says. He reaches for my hand. "Franny, I didn't know what beauty was until I saw you walking toward us a minute ago."

"I like his better," I say, pulling away. "At least he sounded like he meant it."

"I meant it," Harry says, almost irritably. But a guy like Harry Cartwright doesn't stay unhappy for long. A moment later he's hauling me onto the bus with an enthusiastic "I call window seat!" So I guess we're sitting together. Alex and Isabella take the bench across from us.

Julia is sitting with Manny Yates a couple of rows behind us. She waves at me when I glance back and gives a little head bob in Manny's direction: *Look who I'm with!* I give her a thumbs-up before settling down in my seat.

Once we're buckled in, Harry slides as close to me as our seat belts will permit. He glances at my face. Then he laughs and gives my leg a friendly pat. "Relax, Franny," he says. "It won't be that bad."

Our group gets dropped off in some random little neighborhood that supposedly has lots of good shopping and restaurants. We're the only ones getting off there.

It's cute, with a small-town feel even though I'm pretty sure it's technically still part of Portland. There are a few crisscrossing main streets lined with small boutiques and cafés. It's a nice place to wander around and explore on a warm and cloudy summer day.

Alex and Isabella soon move ahead of me and Harry, holding hands.

Harry and I walk behind them. *Not* holding hands.

"So," he says after a moment. "How's life?"

"Really?" I say. "'How's life'? Harry, we see each other every day. You have to come up with a better conversation starter than that."

"I know, I know. You're right. Can I have another shot at it?"

"Sure. We got nothing but time."

"You don't have to sound so glum about it." A pause, while he thinks. Then: "Okay. I've got one. Do you think Pluto should still be considered an actual planet in its own right?"

"Much better. And yes, I do. I had to memorize the planets when I was in third grade, and it was one of them, and I don't like having to relearn things."

He gently knocks his elbow against mine. "If you want Pluto to be a planet, it's a planet, as far as I'm concerned."

Isabella looks over her shoulder at us, grins, and whispers something to Alex, who looks back and doesn't grin, just observes us for a moment, then faces front again.

"Whose idea was this outing?" I ask.

"Isabella's," Harry says. "But she was doing it for me."

"You have a special fondness for corny little neighborhoods with lots of tiny shops?"

"No, for corny little girls in green dresses."

I look down at my green summer dress. "My goodness," I say. "I do believe you mean li'l ol' me!" Then, in a more normal voice: "You said you wouldn't flirt with me, Harry."

"I just called you corny and said you were wearing a green dress. That's, like, the least flirtatious thing anyone's ever said."

"I'm willing to believe it's the least flirtatious thing *you've* ever said."

"Why are you so hard on me when I'm so nice to you?"

"Why are you so nice to me when I'm so hard on you?"

He claps me on the shoulder. "Nicely played, Pearson! You win that round. But the game isn't over yet. Hey, look . . ." He pulls me over to look at a store window. "If you had to buy just one of these cupcakes, which one would you get?"

I point to one that's thick with chocolate frosting. "That one. You?"

He shakes his head, like he's amazed. "The. Exact. Same. One. It's like we're the same *person*, Franny." He glances down the street. "We'd better hurry up—those guys are getting away from us."

We've walked a few more blocks when Isabella and Alex stop suddenly, wave at us, and point to the store they're in front of. They go on in, and when we reach the spot, I see it's a used-book store.

"Shall we?" Harry says, and I nod eagerly. We push through the door and into the store, which looks small at first, because it's so narrow and crammed with books and old wooden tables (which are also crammed with books), but as we wander down the main aisle, I see doors leading off the sides and back of it and realize it's a lot bigger than it looked.

Isabella is flipping through books on a shelf that says DRAMA/THEATER—big surprise there—and calls to Harry as she pulls one out. He comes over and she shows him the cover, with a smile at some private joke. They share a lot of those.

I wander on to the back room, where the walls are lined with fiction. I used to love reading novels before high school ruined the fun of it for me, forcing me to read one assigned piece of literature after another. I just want to read for pleasure again, because something looks interesting and not because it's going to be on an AP exam. And now that it's summer, I could actually do that—although the SAT prep book my mother made me pack keeps peeking out from under my laptop. But I've gotten very good at ignoring it.

After a while, I feel someone come up beside me. It's Alex. "Find anything good?"

I show him the stack in my arms. "Lots. But I don't know if I should get them—I don't really want to lug them around all afternoon."

"I'll carry them for you. I don't mind. I like doing things for you, Franny."

I feel my cheeks turning hot. Is that just a friendly thing to say? Or is he saying I'm special to him? He's holding out his hands, like he's ready to carry the books right away, and waiting for me to respond. I shove the books back onto the shelf together. "It's okay. I don't really need any of these."

"You sure?"

"Yeah. Plus I should be saving money." I turn around. "I'm ready to go if everyone else is."

We find Isabella leaning against a case marked COOKBOOKS, leafing through something.

"Wow," Alex says. "A cookbook? That's so unexpectedly domestic of you."

She shakes her head with a laugh and shows us what she's reading: it's a coffee table book of haute-couture fashion. "Sorry to disappoint you."

"I'm not disappointed," he says. "I'm relieved. The

world has been restored to order."

She makes a face at him, and he laughs and kisses her lightly on the lips. Right. They're a couple. And a very affectionate and adorable one at that.

"Where's Harry?" I ask. Might as well get *my* buddy back.

Isabella inserts her book back between two others. "He got bored and left to see what else was on this block. He said they didn't have a good enough graphic-novel section here and he'd meet us in front in a minute."

"You two go ahead," Alex says. "I want to ask the guy up front if he has any antique books about the care and feeding of dogs. My mother collects them."

"Really?" Isabella says. "My mother collects diamond bracelets."

"My mother collects headache medications," I say.

Isabella and I slip down the narrow aisle and out onto the sidewalk, where the clouds are getting darker by the second.

"Do you think it will rain?" I ask.

"I hope so. I love a good summer rain. We don't get many in L.A. None, really." She's wearing a dark blue maxidress with narrow straps that crisscross her slender back. At least three different guys stopped to stare at her in the bookstore as we walked through. I couldn't tell if she didn't notice them or was just pretending not to notice them. Or maybe she's just so used to male admiration it barely even registers anymore.

We look up and down the street, but no Harry yet.

"Aren't you glad you came today?" Isabella asks as we wait for him.

"I was until we were both abandoned. Do you think Alex slipped out the back and he and Harry ran off together?"

"I'd believe it of Alex," she says, "but Harry's not going to run away today—not on the day you've actually agreed to go out with him."

"About that . . . ," I say. "When exactly did I agree to go out with him?"

She gives an airy little shrug. "You know what I mean. He's just really happy we're all here together. And I am too, Franny. I've been wanting this to happen."

"Any special reason you feel that way?" I ask.

She smiles her Mona Lisa smile, the one that always seems to slay Alex. "I like seeing Harry happy, that's all."

On cue, Harry emerges from a store at the other end of the block and gives us a jaunty wave. I watch him as he walks toward us and wonder if I'd be falling madly in love with him if I'd met him for the first time today. Probably. He's cute and funny, and I really do like him. A lot. But all that history with Julia and Marie—all his flirting, and playing them off each other, and not caring if he made one or the other miserable—that still bothers me. Plus he's Isabella's best friend in the world. They've both said so a bunch of times. You can judge people by their friends, right? And I don't trust her at all.

He reaches us just as Alex comes out of the bookstore.

"Here." Harry holds a small white waxed-paper bag out to me. "This is for you, Franny."

I open it. Inside is the cupcake I picked as the best-looking one in the window. "You didn't have to get it for me!"

"I know. I wanted to." He grins at me.

I try to remember all the arguments I was just making about why he's not boyfriend material. Because when Harry grins like that, he seems like *very* good boyfriend material. I've mentioned those little divots under his eyes, right? The ones that are maybe dimples and sit right below those gray-green eyes that catch the light no matter how little there is? Even on a cloudy day when there's practically no light at all?

"What did *you* get?" Isabella asks Alex, who, I now notice, is carrying a plastic bag filled with books.

"Found some stuff for my mom." He leads the way down the street.

I spot a Starbucks on a street corner less than a block away, so I suggest we all get something to drink and split the cupcake.

"No sharing," Harry says. "That cupcake is for you and you alone."

"Gee, thanks," Isabella says. "Did it even occur to you to buy me one too?"

"Nope," he says.

"You've known me for years longer than you've known her." But she's smiling. She doesn't really mind.

"It's my cupcake," I say. "I can share it if I want to. Sharing makes things taste better."

"You know, not everything they tell you in preschool is true," Harry says.

"They were right about that running-with-scissors thing."

"But not that everyone in your class was your friend."

I nod. "Yeah, Alana Fonsberg was definitely *not* my friend. She was a pusher."

"Drugs?"

"Backs. But I still want to share the cupcake. It's huge."

Harry heaves a mock sigh. "There's no making you selfish, is there, Franny? That will be our goal today— to make Franny do or say one selfish thing."

Alex is half a step ahead of the rest of us, but he looks back. "Give up now. It's not going to happen."

"How about we get Franny to do one selfish thing and Isabella to do one *un*selfish thing?" Harry suggests. "I'm not sure which would be harder."

Isabella flicks at his arm. "Why are you being so mean to me?"

"Because I love you," he says.

She scowls. "Does that ever work?"

"On my mother it does."

"I'm not your mother," she says.

"I know that already, because I'm enjoying your company."

We're still sitting at an outdoor table with our coffees, the cupcake I insisted on sharing reduced to crumbs, when Isabella picks up the bag Alex was carrying. "So what did you get your mom?" she asks, putting it on her lap so she can pull out and examine the books. She holds one up. "I thought you said you were getting her dog books. These are all novels."

"They're for Franny, actually," he says, with a slightly sheepish nod in my direction.

"Really?" I lean forward so I can see them better. "These are the books I picked out at the store! But I put them back—"

"They were all still in a pile together. So . . ." He trails off.

"And you were just going to lug them around all day without telling me?"

"I wanted it to be a surprise." He makes awkward jazz hands. "Surprise."

Isabella sticks the books back in the bag and drops it on the ground. "I don't see any of the ones *I* was looking at in there."

"Oh, sorry," Alex says. "I'd have happily bought you anything you wanted. I just knew Franny really wanted these—"

"So why didn't *you* get them?" she asks me sharply.

"I don't know," I say uncomfortably. "I guess I was being lazy. I didn't want to have to carry them. At least let me pay you back," I say to Alex.

He waves his hand. "Nah, it was my idea to buy them."

I protest, but he's adamant.

"It's interesting." Isabella crosses her arms tightly over her chest. "Both of you guys got something for Franny. And no one got me anything. Anyone care to analyze this?"

"Someone's feeling left out," Harry says.

"Come on." Alex stands up and holds his hand out to her. "Let's go get you a present. There are tons of stores here. I'll buy you whatever you want."

"That's not the point." She ignores his outstretched hand. "You both wanted to surprise Franny. Neither of you thought about surprising *me*."

"Here." Harry grabs a book out of the bag and holds it out. "For you, 'Bella. Surprise!"

She glares at him. "I'm touched."

"Seriously," Alex says. "I'll figure out something that will surprise and delight you. Maybe even shock and awe you, but I'm not making any promises."

She slowly rises to her feet, giving him a long sideways look, dark eyelashes swooping down over narrowed eyes. "You'd better. Or I'll start thinking you like Franny better than me."

"Franny?" Alex pulls her against his side with a shake of his head. "Franny's the sister I never had. And by that I mean a *lovable* sister, unlike the one I actually have." He winks at me.

Impressive: he just destroyed any pleasure I'd gotten from his gift.

But I can tell from his cheerful expression that he has no idea how deeply his casual comment cut me. I glance at Isabella and see the glint in her eye. She gets it, even if he doesn't. She's pleased. And I wonder whether part of the reason she's throwing me in Harry's path is to get me out of Alex's.

Not that I'm particularly *minding* being in Harry's path.

In fact, given Alex's last comment . . .

"You and I can split off and do something on our own," I say to Harry.

He snatches eagerly at the idea. "Take Isabella shopping," he tells Alex. "I suggest you distract her with something sparkly, then text us when you're ready to meet up for dinner."

"Sounds good," Alex says, and reaches down for the bag of books.

Harry says, "I'll carry that." In kind of a proprietary way. Like even though Alex bought the books, Harry is the one who should carry them. Because they're mine. Which you'd think would mean *I* should carry them . . . but apparently not if you factor in stupid sexist male posturing.

Alex and Isabella head down the sidewalk, bodies close together, and he's whispering something in her ear, and her head is tilted in a way that suggests she's listening and she *will* forgive him . . . but he's going to have to work for it.

"Poor Isabella." Harry's also watching them go.

"Really?" I say, turning back to him, my eyebrows raised. "Poor Isabella?" That's so not how I'm thinking of the situation.

"Absolutely. She's a mass of insecurity. That's why she can be hypersensitive sometimes. I shouldn't have teased her."

"Come on," I say. "She's rich, gorgeous, smart—"

"And wildly insecure. Especially when it comes to guys and relationships. Trust me: I'm the one she calls at two in the morning when she's convinced she's unlovable."

"Wow," I say. "She sure doesn't come across as insecure."

"Yeah, well, you can't judge anyone by appearance."

"Not even you?"

"Depends. What do I look like to you?" He strikes a he-man pose, elbows raised, hands in fists.

"Like someone who's spent a lot of time flexing in front of mirrors."

"Hmm . . . uncannily accurate . . ." He relaxes. "Okay—I guess with me what you see *is* what you get. But I'm the rare exception." He looks around. "So what do you want to do now that we've dumped those losers?"

"I don't know. Something indoors—it's about to rain."

"No, it's not."

I eye the clouds, which are thicker and darker than they were ten minutes ago. "I really think it is."

"I finally have you to myself," he says. "I won't let it rain."

"I so admire a man who can control the elements. Come on." I stand up, and we both reach for the bag at the same time. "I can carry my own books."

"I know. I *want* to carry them."

I roll my eyes.

"I mean it. It makes me feel all manly." He gathers the bag handles in his fist and curls and lowers his arm a few times. "Look at that? See that? See my guns? Aren't you impressed?"

"Stop or I'll faint."

"Yeah, I have that effect on all the women." As we

move away from the Starbucks, heading in the opposite direction from Isabella and Alex, he switches hands and insists I now check out *that* arm's bicep muscle. "I'm not a one-arm wonder, Franny. Both sides are equally magnificent. This is what you call fearful symmetry."

"Why do you ever wear a shirt?" I say.

"For the mystery of it, Franny. For the mystery."

scene four

We have fun, we really do. Harry keeps me laughing for the rest of the afternoon, leading me into stores, where he makes up a different story for each salesperson, telling one we're twins who were separated at birth and have reunited for the first time that day, and another that we've escaped from a summer program where they've kept us locked up in a shoe factory stitching sneaker parts together (which I later point out to him isn't all that different from the truth—at least for me), and asking a third if she knows a minister who can perform a quickie wedding.

The salespeople ask concerned questions, which Harry somehow manages to answer with a straight face, embroidering the original story with more brilliantly funny details, but I can't say a word, too afraid I'll crack up and give it all away if I do.

"Do you always do this kind of thing?" I ask him

when we finally extricate ourselves from the last woman's concerned pleas to "think long and hard before you kids do something you might regret."

"Yeah, but you inspire me to new heights of imagination."

"New depths of dishonesty is more like it." I wince as a cool drop of water hits my cheek. "Can I inspire you to notice that it's raining?"

"Do you want me to stop the rain?" he says. "I'd do it for you, Franny. Or die trying."

"Yeah, that's not over the top. How about you just figure out a place where we can stay dry? Preferably without making me pretend to be your sister bride or anything like that."

"I never said you were *both* my sister and my bride. That's just wrong." He shakes his head in disgust. "Really, Franny. I had no idea what a depraved mind you have. Also? I'm saving that for when we meet someone important, like a senator or something."

"You're still talking, and I'm getting wetter by the second."

He looks around. "Let's see. . . . This way." He leads me across the street and pulls me into a small grocery store, the kind you'd stop at to grab a carton of milk or a pack of gum but not to do your *real* food shopping. It's very dim, the darkness of the rain clouds outside deepening the natural gloom of the cramped store. The owner is slumped at a stool near the entrance, watching a small TV next to the cash register. He squints suspiciously at us, then goes back to his show.

We duck to the back corner of the store, where the metal shelves are filled with dusty cans of beans and ancient boxes of pasta. It feels like no one's been back there for decades. We slip around one of the high racks so we're hidden from the owner's view.

"Don't say I never take you anywhere nice." Harry sets the bag of books on the floor. "We can stay here until the rain lets up or that guy comes after us with an ax—whichever comes first."

"Maybe we should call Isabella and Alex and make a plan to meet them soon."

"Sure," he says, but then he stops and stares at me.

"What's wrong?"

"You have drops of rain in your hair. They look like diamonds."

I laugh. "Oh, please. That's like a pickup line you'd use in a bar."

"It would have to be raining inside the bar."

"Fine. A pickup line you'd use *outside* a bar."

He says quietly, "It's not a line, Franny."

And then he leans forward and kisses me softly and quickly on the mouth. Before I can even decide how I feel about it, he steps back. He holds his hands up. "No, sorry, that's all you get. Don't embarrass yourself by begging for more."

"Harry—"

He drops his hands. "Don't be mad at me, Franny. That was just an impulse. I won't push anything. I get it."

"Okay," I say. "Thanks."

"But know that I like you 'for realers,' as my little cousin would say. Okay? And I'm not going anywhere, not unless you send me away. Or that guy axes me."

I think for a moment, staring down at the unswept cement floor. Then I look up and say, "I'm not going to send you away. Not yet anyway."

His face breaks out in a happy grin. "How is it that you say more with a few careful words than most girls say in an hour of chattering away?"

My laugh is shaky but genuine. "*You're* going to criticize other people for talking too much?"

He steps back and surveys me. "You like to tear me down, don't you, Pearson?"

"Yeah," I say. "I kind of do."

"You'll have to keep building me back up again, then, won't you?"

"I guess so." I realized I'm reaching out for him. It's almost like my body is doing it more than my mind. I don't trust him. But he's so good-looking and so near and that kiss made me curious. Eager, even. I touch his upper arm. "So what's the best way to build you up?

Should I say something about how strong you are?"

"That would work." His voice sounds slightly hoarse.

"Oh, Harry, you're so big and strong," I say, not sure if I'm making fun of him or me.

"Yeah?" His arm snakes around my waist.

"Was that enough? Do I get to tear you back down now?" I have to tilt my head back to look at him now that we're so close.

"Not quite yet."

This time, when he kisses me, I kiss him back, and we both take our time. It's a slow, long, lingering, exploring kiss. The kind that leads to more kisses. The kind that makes me hope it keeps raining for a while so we have an excuse to stay right where we are, all alone in that dingy little area, surrounded by dusty shelves and ancient cans of food.

"If that guy's going to kill me, I hope he does it soon," Harry whispers at one point. "I might as well die happy."

Over the top, as usual. But right now I don't mind his exaggeration. I even kind of like it.

An hour or so later, we're all seated at dinner together.

Harry and I are the ones who hitch our chairs closer together. Isabella and Alex keep a slight distance between theirs, and when Harry asks what gift Alex found to surprise her with, Isabella raises her elegantly arched eyebrows and says icily, "I told him not to bother. He was acting like it was a chore."

"That's not fair," Alex says. "I wanted to get you that bracelet. You just kept saying that there was no point since it wouldn't actually be a surprise. You wouldn't *let* me get you anything."

"You didn't try very hard." She waves her hand dismissively. "We saw some nice stores, though. And I got to walk in the rain, which I love. How about you guys? Did you have fun? What did you do?"

"Pretty much what you'd expect," Harry says. "I spent most of the afternoon fighting off Franny's advances."

"In his dreams," I say with a snort.

"Pinch me, then, because I've been dreaming all day." He holds his arm out to Alex, who shoves it away, more violently than seems necessary.

Isabella stands up. "I'm going to the ladies' room." She touches Alex's shoulder. "Do you want to hold my cigarettes while I'm gone? Or would you rather just sniff at me suspiciously when I come back?" She turns to Harry and me. "I can't even go to the bathroom without being sniffed up and down afterward. It's like dating a DEA dog."

"Whatever," Alex says.

"I'll join you." Harry jumps up. "We can powder each other's noses."

"Sadly, that's not a euphemism," she says with an exaggerated sigh. They wrap their arms around each other's waists as they walk across the floor together.

Alex and I are silent for a moment. Our eyes meet.

I say, "I don't think I ever thanked you for getting me those books. It was really nice of you. I'm sorry if I got you in trouble."

"You didn't," he says. "I can buy books for a friend if I want to." He takes a sip of water. We've ordered our food but have so far gotten only our drinks. Isabella and Harry got glasses of wine—they both have fake IDs, but the waiter didn't even ask to see them. Still, Alex and I just got water. "You and Harry seem to be having a good time," he says flatly, putting the glass back down with a little thump.

I shrug. "It's been a nice day."

"Glad to hear it." He doesn't look glad. He looks . . . not like his usual cheerful self.

"Is everything okay?" I ask.

"Why wouldn't it be?" he snaps.

I shoot him a look. "Really, Alex?"

He holds his hands up in sudden apology. "Sorry. I honestly don't know why I'm in such a bad mood. It's just . . ." There's a pause; then he leans forward abruptly. "Hey, Franny? Be careful, okay? With Harry, I mean. I've spent a lot of time with both him and Isabella, and you have to . . ." He stops himself. "Not that they're the same. It's just . . . I mean, they're from L.A., you know? People are just different there. And for someone like you . . . You shouldn't rush into trusting people. So don't. Rush."

"Maybe you should be careful too," I say sharply. Why does he assume I'm some naive little kid who needs his advice? Who's more careful than me? I'm so careful I haven't even kissed a guy yet this summer.

Oh, wait, yes, I have. An hour ago. I kissed a guy a lot.

Cool.

"Isabella's not like Harry," Alex says.

"You just said she was. And, by the way, they're best friends, so if you don't like him, you should be wondering about her taste."

"I never said I didn't like him. I just don't think you can trust him completely."

I don't actually disagree with him, but I'm too annoyed to let him know that. "Harry's been nothing but nice to me."

There's a pause. Then Alex says, "All I know is he doesn't deserve you."

"What do you mean?" I suddenly wish we had more time alone, but I can already see Harry making his way toward us from across the room.

"Just . . ." He gestures helplessly with his hands. "Just know that I'm here, Franny. And that I care about you. A lot."

I'm still turning those words around in my head, trying to figure out what they mean, when Harry arrives at the table, drops down into his chair at my side, and puts his arm along my shoulders.

I shift toward him, briefly closing my eyes to regain my balance, which feels a little unsteady since Alex's last comment.

"You smell like smoke," I tell Harry.

"And you smell like girl," Harry replies. "I may have snuck out for a sec. Were you worried about where I was?"

"Nope."

"Did you not see me go off with another woman?"

"I did. And I hope you two had fun together."

He makes a face. "Damn it, Pearson, why are you so hard to make jealous?"

"Oh, sorry," I say. "Was that supposed to bother me?"

"Forget it," he says with mock hurt. "Just forget it." Then he murmurs in my ear, "Someday I'll make you wild with jealousy. You'll see."

"Yeah?" I say, and raise my water glass to my lips. My eyes meet Alex's over the rim, and he's watching me drink and I watch him watching me, and it's like Harry isn't there next to me; it's like there's no one else in the whole restaurant except for me and Alex, Alex and me, for that one split second before everything goes back to normal.

* * *

When the bus returns to pick us up, Isabella grabs my arm and tells the guys that the girls want to sit together. News to me, but I let her guide me to a window seat. She plops down beside me. The seat across the aisle from us is already taken, so Alex and Harry move on and sit somewhere behind us.

Once the bus is moving, Isabella says, "You probably think I was being a jerk at dinner."

I shake my head silently.

"I know I acted like a baby about the books." She leans her head back and gazes absently ahead. "I don't know why I was doing that. I *like* that Alex is the kind of guy who'd get those books because he knew a friend wanted them. I guess I just felt a little left out. I'm used to being the one who gets the presents." She glances at me with a little laugh. "Selfish to the core, right? Just like Harry said. He knows me well."

"Nah," I say. "Who doesn't like presents?"

"Anyway, I just wanted you to know that it had nothing to do with you, and that Alex and I are fine, even if we have these moments. We just . . ." She wiggles her fingers uncertainly. "I don't know. It's almost like it's too intense sometimes." She sits up, then leans toward me confidingly, lowering her voice. "Like we like each other *too* much. You know what I mean?" Her big dark eyes bore into me. She sounds like she's asking me a question, but I think she's telling me something.

I get it. He's hers. *But she doesn't know that he said Harry doesn't deserve me and that he cares about me.* "I get it" is the only part I say out loud. The rest I just hold on to, to think about later, when I'm alone.

"When we were together, Harry totally reamed me out about making you feel bad," she says, shifting back and smoothing the navy fabric of her dress over her knee. "He was all, 'Get as pissy as you want with Alex but leave my Franny alone.' Seriously. That boy is so all about you right now—I'm sure he'd rather be fighting dragons to prove his love, but he's stuck with fighting *me*. The Gorgon."

I smile politely.

"So?" she says. "You and Harry? Yes?"

"What am I saying yes to exactly?"

"*You* know. I don't think I've ever seen you laugh as much as you did with him today."

"I probably never have," I admit. "I had a lot of fun."

"You know what's even better?" she says. "I've never seen Harry think about anyone other than himself, but all day today I could see he was trying to figure out what *you* wanted. You're good for him." Her cell phone buzzes, and she pulls it out of her purse. "Sweet," she says, studying it with a smile. "It's Alex. He wants to know if I'll trade places with Harry. Says he misses me. What do you think?"

"Yeah, you should go." I'm happy to make the trade.

She wasn't really waiting for my approval anyway: she's already sent back a text. She puts her phone away and pats my knee. "I'm glad we got to talk." She unbuckles her seat belt and gets to her feet, then makes her way to the back of the bus, swaying with its movement, passing Harry as he makes his way forward.

The fat, old bus driver glares into the rearview mirror and barks out, "Will you kids stop moving around? Stay in your seats or I'll stop the bus and come back there and bust your asses."

"What a charmer," Harry says as he drops into the seat next to me with a cheerful (and therefore deliberately infuriating) wave toward the angry driver. "With his people skills, I'm shocked he doesn't have a more high-profile job. Like as a fish descaler." He buckles in, then turns and looks at me. "Hi," he says.

"Hi."

"This is better. A lot better. Alex is a terrible kisser. All tongue and no finesse. I couldn't wait to get away from him and come sit with you."

"I'm glad you thought of it. Oh, hold on . . . you *didn't*. It was *Alex* who wanted to be with Isabella. You didn't care at all."

He shakes his head. "You're an idiot, Pearson. And you don't check your texts. Look at your phone."

I pull it out of my purse. There are four new texts

from Harry, all suggesting I change seats with Alex, except for the last one which is *You're not even reading these, are you?*

"What's that?" he says, leaning closer. "I didn't quite hear that. Did you just say, 'I'm sorry for doubting you, Harry? I'll never doubt you again'?" His eyes are dancing. This close, I can see the separate flecks of gray within the green.

"Let me whisper it in your ear," I say.

He obligingly leans over even more. I gently brush my lips over his ear without saying a word. He shivers.

"That's not fair," he growls, drawing back. "You can't do something like that *here*, on a bus, surrounded by people."

"No one saw."

"Yeah, but they'll see this." He twists toward me, takes me by the shoulders, and kisses me full on the lips. The girls across the aisle make loud hooting noises. "See what I mean?" he says with a mock sigh. "Now there'll be gossip."

And I think, *I don't care if I trust him or not. I like him.*

scene five

stay up late that night, video-chatting with William—whenever he has time to talk to me, I jump at the chance, even if I'm half-asleep. I text him once or twice every day, and he usually texts me back, but most of the time it's *Sorry, no time to talk. <3 you, Frannygirl.*

The thing is, when your brother is twenty and has a serious girlfriend and is living in New York, it doesn't matter that once it felt like it was the two of you against the world or that you used to crawl into his bed when your parents were fighting or that you sat next to him on the sofa when they told you they were getting divorced and the only thing that kept you from falling apart completely was knowing he was there at your side.

I know he loves me and he's there for me if I need him, but he's got his own life these days and doesn't need *me*. So I'm grateful for any time he can give me.

He asks me if there are any boys in my life, so I tell

him about Harry, keeping my voice low so I won't wake up Amelia if she's asleep—and she won't be able to eavesdrop if she's not.

"How does he compare with Tyler?" William asks.

I think about that. "Less serious," I say. "And probably not as smart. But funnier. And cuter."

"Yeah? You becoming shallow, Franny? Only caring about a guy's looks?"

"It's summer. I'm supposed to just have fun, right?"

"I guess. But it's not fun to spend time with someone who turns out to be a jerk."

"I don't think Harry's a jerk." I hesitate for a moment, then say, "To be honest, there's another guy here who I like more. He's definitely not a jerk. He's really sweet. And sometimes I think he likes me. But he's already going out with someone."

William tilts his head toward me. Or toward his laptop camera, at any rate. He's handsome, my brother, but at this angle you can see that his hair is already thinning on top. He's going to be bald before he's thirty, just like our grandfather. "If he's going out with someone else, why do you think he likes *you*?"

"Just the way he talks to me sometimes. And he does really nice things for me. Like he bought me these books today, just because I said I wanted them."

"And how did the girlfriend feel about *that*?"

"She was a little pissed off," I admit.

"Hmm."

"That's a pretty disapproving-sounding *hmm*."

"Just take care of yourself, okay, Franny? Don't fall in love with anyone who might hurt you. Which both these guys sound like they could do."

"I'm not falling in love with either of them. I'm not an idiot."

"Smart people can be stupid about this stuff."

"Wow," I say. "Can I quote you on that?"

"Shut up. I'm making a good point." But he drops it.

A few minutes later we say good-bye, and I close my laptop and wonder whether I was telling the truth, whether I'm really not in love with either Harry or Alex. I think it's true. But only because they're both around. It's like when two people in a comedy sketch try to go through a doorway at the same time and get stuck. If I didn't have Alex around—if I didn't feel like he was the kinder, more trustworthy guy—I'd probably have a crush on Harry. And if Harry weren't around, actually paying attention to me, I'd probably still be mooning over Alex, waiting for him to see the light and leave Isabella for me.

Guess I'll have to wait for one of them to get unstuck.

Or give up on the whole idea of romance and just watch reality shows with Amelia every night. I'm sure I could learn to find *Antiques Roadshow* fascinating.

* * *

I sleep late the next morning and don't have time to go to the dining hall for breakfast, so instead I just grab a protein bar from Amelia's supply. They're all "formulated for a woman's needs," which makes me roll my eyes every time I take one—I wonder what would happen to a man who accidentally ate one. Not that that's likely to happen in Amelia's apartment.

I walk to campus with my aunt, and on the way she quizzes me about my outing the day before. She was watching TV when I got back last night, too absorbed to do more than nod when I said hi on the way to my room, but now she's curious. I tell her we found a great bookstore, and she nods approvingly.

"I have to say, I like to hear about kids your age who are more interested in books than anything else. It's very refreshing."

"We stayed there for most of the afternoon." I figure I'll exaggerate a little, score some points. "We went into a couple of other stores, had dinner . . . nothing too exciting."

Somehow I don't get around to mentioning the part where I hid in the back of a store with the hottest guy at camp and we kissed for an hour.

There's a folded piece of paper taped to her workroom door, with both our names on it. Amelia plucks it off and opens it, and I stand on tiptoe so I can read over her shoulder. It's the schedule Charles has worked out. He's clearly done his best not to take up too much of my work time: For the next couple of weeks, he's only got me down for about six two-hour rehearsals, all of them late in the afternoon, close to dinnertime. The week after that—the last week before the final performances—he's marked out some longer sessions, and of course the days of the actual performances are completely blocked out.

Amelia's frowning. "I don't mind losing you during show week—we'll basically be done by then. But that last week of rehearsal is when I need you the most. That's my busiest time."

"Maybe I can take some hand sewing with me to rehearsals," I suggest. "And work on it when I'm not actually onstage."

She considers that. "It's not ideal," she says begrudgingly. "But I suppose we could try that when the time comes."

"It'll work out," I say.

I guess I sound a little too blasé or something, because she narrows her eyes and waves the piece of paper in my face. "I hope you appreciate my generosity here. This was not part of the bargain when I hired you to be my assistant. In fact, I told your mother there would be no special considerations for you and that you'd have to work as hard as any stranger. And yet here I am, bending over backward for you, making my life harder, just like I said I wouldn't do."

"I *am* grateful," I say. "Truly. And I'll work extra hard the rest of the time."

"Yes, you will."

"Nothing will distract me." I swear I mean it when I say it. But just a couple of hours later, when my phone vibrates, I pounce on it eagerly.

Amelia says, "You're like Pavlov's dog. That thing buzzes and you salivate."

"Woof," I reply absently, reading the text. It's from Harry, who's breaking the rules by using his phone during the day. I wonder how he managed to do it without getting caught. I'm guessing the men's room.

Find a way to sneak out at 10:30. I'll meet you at the bench in front of the dining hall.

No *please*. Just a command. He assumes I'll go.

At ten twenty-five I say to Amelia, "I'm falling asleep here. I'm going to go grab a cup of coffee at the dining hall. Want anything?"

"I can make you a cup of tea," she says, nodding toward her electric kettle. "Peppermint can be very invigorating."

"Sorry—it's got to be coffee."

"Fine." She waves her hand and goes back to the work she's doing, embroidering the fairies' dresses for *A Midsummer Night's Dream*. I slip out the door and run across the courtyard toward the dining hall.

I don't even make it that far: Harry comes racing toward me from the theater building. He catches me up in his arms, swings me around, kisses me so passionately that my heart starts racing, then suddenly sets me back on the ground and steps back.

"Oh, sorry," he says. "I thought you were someone else. My mistake." He sticks his hands in his pockets and starts to walk away, whistling.

"I get that a lot," I call after him. "People are always confusing me with someone else. But usually I get better kisses out of it."

He stops and turns around. "Those are fighting words," he says seriously.

"You accept the challenge?"

"Hell, yeah." He reaches out, grabs my arm, and pulls me around the side of the building. Then we get busy kissing for a while.

"Don't you have to get back to rehearsal or class or whatever it is you do here during the day?" I say eventually.

He mutters something vaguely obscene that might suggest a rehearsal could have sex with itself and tries to go back to what we were doing.

I push him away. "Think how bad it would be if you got kicked out of here. I'd have to find someone else to make out with. It might take me *hours*."

He lets go of me and steps back. "Don't say stuff like

that, Franny. I'm too worried it's true."

"I'm just teasing."

"I know." He takes my hand. "It's just that I get the sense I really do like you more than you like me, and it's not something I'm used to feeling."

"I like you plenty," I say. "I just want to take things slowly."

"I know. I get that." He slips his fingers between mine and gathers me toward his chest. "I'll work hard to be worthy of you."

"Oh, please," I say. "'Worthy'? Who talks like that?"

He's silent a moment. Then he says, "How about, *You don't have to worry, Harry. I'm crazy about you*?"

I squeeze his hand. "You don't have to worry, Harry. I like being with you."

"I'm not getting anything helpful out of you today, am I?"

"I'm not about to stand here massaging your ego, if that's what you were hoping for."

"Humph." He absorbs that for a moment. Then he shifts and says hopefully, "Speaking of massages . . ."

I shove him. "Time for you to go."

"Don't forget me," he says, and shoots me one last lingering, wistful look while he clutches his hand to his heart. The guy is always acting, always playing around. He's never serious. He just plays at being serious now and then for a minute. For the fun of it.

* * *

When I join the cast at rehearsal late that afternoon (this time they're in one of the practice rooms above the dining hall), Marie glares at me. Eyes like daggers.

Julia pulls me aside to tell me, laughing, that Marie complained to *her* that morning that there was something creepy about how I had targeted Harry, made him carry me at the beach, then hijacked that excursion the other day—

"Where *was* she yesterday, anyway?" I interrupt. "I figured she'd find a way to zone in on Harry, but I never even saw her."

"Oh, my God, it was the funniest thing ever!" Julia says. "Her boyfriend had said that he'd take her to some fancy restaurant on Sunday, and she was bragging all about it for days, and then she found out about our day trip. I heard her on the phone to him, trying to cancel, but I guess he had worked hard for the reservations and said they had to go, and she was all like, 'Fine, but don't expect me to enjoy it!'"

"She's a delight," I say.

"She better start being nicer to him," Julia says, "or she's going to lose him, too."

"Too?"

"You know what I mean. So how *are* things with Harry?"

"I'm not sure."

She doesn't ask me what I mean, because she doesn't really care. She asked only so she could launch into how great things are going with her and Manny. I'm happy for her, and I listen and I say the right things and squeal when it's appropriate to squeal. But pretty soon Charles needs me for a scene: true to his word, he's making good use of every minute I can spare from sewing.

I jump to attention the second he calls on me and come flying in at my cue. I'm so happy to be acting, I have to work hard to stay in character and not keep grinning the whole time I'm onstage.

act III

scene one

A few days later, at the end of our rehearsal, Marie sidles up to Harry and tells him she'd really like to run lines with him after dinner. He agrees that they could use the extra practice; then he turns to me and says I should come too.

"Are you implying that I need to work on my lines?" I ask with a slightly pained laugh. The truth is, I did forget a bunch of lines during this last rehearsal. Charles has been patient with me because I started two weeks after everyone else, and I know I shouldn't expect to be perfect yet, but I hate the look of panic that crosses his face whenever I mess up.

"If I say yes, will you join us?" Harry asks.

"I can't. I have to go back to the Sweatshop." I wish I didn't. I don't love the idea of the two of them going off alone together: Marie still flirts with Harry every chance she gets, and even though he and I have been an established couple for close to a week now, I feel like she's breathing down my neck.

"Come find us in the common room as soon as you get out," he says.

"We should go somewhere more quiet than that. Just text us when you're done," Marie tells me. "We'll probably still be working." She's wearing a lot of makeup today, with smoky eyes and deep red lips. Since her character is supposed to look like a boy, it was a little unsettling to see her like that during the rehearsal, but she looks pretty hot. She may be annoying and self-centered and dishonest, but she's also incredibly cute and knows how to work what she's got. All the straight guys watch her whenever she's walking across a room. She has the whole übergirl hip-swaying, hair-tossing thing down. It's affected, but it's also apparently effective.

After we all have dinner, I tell Harry I'm heading back to the sewing workroom. He tells me to "blow off the old lady," but when I say I can't, he shrugs and says, "Fine, but come back when you can." Easygoing as always. I kind of want him to protest more. Maybe it's silly, but it just feels like he doesn't really care, like, yeah, maybe he'd *rather* be with me, but if he can't, he's perfectly happy to be with Marie, who's already tugging on his arm as I say good-bye.

It puts me in a bad mood. I'm mad at myself for caring. Wasn't *not* caring supposed to be my MO when it came to a relationship with Harry?

Amelia and I wrap up the night's work around eight thirty. She says, "Where do you think you're going?" when I head toward the door.

"To hang out with my friends. It's still early."

"It would be nice if you'd spend an evening with me now and then," she says. "You're always dashing off. I thought this summer would be our chance to get closer."

"We just spent the entire day together."

"But that was work," she says. "That's not the same. You think I don't know how to have fun, but I do. Like tonight I was thinking we could make popcorn and watch an old movie in our pajamas. Doesn't that sound nice?"

"Yeah, really nice," I lie. "But I promised some of my friends I'd come by."

"You could text them and say you can't make it."

"I'll only be an hour or two. I promise."

"Fine," she says. Her lips tighten, and she closes a drawer with a violent shove. "Do whatever you want. You always do." She adds in a low, vicious hiss, "You're just like that father of yours."

"Excuse me?" I stop and turn around. "What did you say?"

"Nothing." She waves her fingers toward the door. "I thought you were in a hurry."

"Were you dissing my dad?"

She puts her hand across her chest. "I would *never* say anything negative about him. Not in front of one of his kids. He may have been a bad husband, but he's still your father, and I will always be respectful of that."

"He wasn't a bad husband!"

"I certainly won't argue the point with you. I'm not that kind of person."

I take a deep breath and get control of my temper. "Whatever. I'm off. Don't wait up for me." I open the door.

"You said you wouldn't stay out late."

Yeah, that was before we had this little talk, I think, but the only thing I say out loud is "good-bye."

Now my mood is even worse. First of all, I hate Amelia for casting my father as the bad guy in my parents' marriage. I was there and she wasn't, and maybe he and my mom didn't always get along, but it wasn't like he was some kind of villain and she was some kind of saint. They both acted like jerks to each other a lot of the time. Never to us, though. Neither of them was ever mean to me or William. I remember wishing they could be as nice to each other as they were to us, but for some reason they just didn't seem to be able to do that.

And it's crazy for Amelia to complain that I'm not spending enough time with her. All I *do* is spend time with her.

Most important, the whole time I was standing there

having that miserable conversation, Harry and Marie were rehearsing alone together.

I get to the dorm and check out the common room. It's quiet tonight. I look around for friends, but they must all be off doing something else. No Harry or Marie in sight.

Guess the big rehearsal is still going on.

I'm reaching into my pocket to get out my phone so I can text Harry, when Alex enters from the other hallway. He spots me and comes over.

"Franny!" he says. "I'm glad you're here. I wanted to play a round of darts and there was no one to play with."

"Where's Isabella?"

"With her roommates. Apparently they needed to have a serious talk about bathroom hygiene. What about Harry? Where's he?"

"Rehearsing with Marie."

He kind of raises his eyebrows but doesn't say anything.

I shove my cell phone back in my pocket. "Let's play darts." I don't really want to send Harry a text anyway—I don't want to *tell* him to stop rehearsing with Marie and come be with me. I want him to stop because he's had enough. Which clearly he hasn't, since he's not around.

Alex leads the way back across the common room. A bunch of people are sprawled on the sofas—and on top of one another—watching *SpongeBob SquarePants*. A girl comes in right after us and squeals, "I love this show so friggin' much!" and squeezes herself in between two seated guys. One of them grabs her hand and holds it tightly, but there's nothing romantic about it—it's just a moment of shared glee. They cheer and wave their joined hands when SpongeBob bursts into song.

We have to wait for a minute until Raymond and Wilson finish their game of darts, and then Alex high-fives the winner (Raymond) and we take over.

"Go ahead and throw first," he tells me. "I want to see if you're any good."

"Any good?" I say. "I'm like practically a professional." I throw the darts and manage to miss the target with every one of them. The darts mostly hit the wall and bounce off, landing on the floor. "Maybe I should clarify that." I scoop the darts up off the floor and turn around to face him again. "I've never actually played before."

"Okay," he says. "The first rule is don't kill anyone."

"Oh, don't start making up rules *now*. That's not fair."

"Fine," he says. "Kill people. Just know that you don't get any points for it. Here," he adds, and gently bends my elbow a little and moves my wrist. "Try holding your arm like this and flicking your wrist more when you throw."

I try not to think too much about how close Alex is to me. His touch is light and respectful, but it's still kind of . . . intimate. I'm suddenly glad Harry and Isabella are somewhere else. Even if it means Harry is with Marie.

"Okay," Alex says, stepping back. "Give it a try."

"Like this?" I try to do what he said. After a few more throws, I'm still not landing the darts anywhere near the bull's-eye, but at least they're sinking into the target and not bouncing off the walls. "Ready to play a real game?" I ask.

"Am *I* ready?"

"Prepare to be humiliated."

We play a round, and he beats me by a lot. "I went easy on you," I say.

He tilts his head and gives me a fondly skeptical look. His eyes are so blue. Blue is the best color for eyes. "I'll spot you seventy points this time," he says.

"You sure you want to make it that easy for me?"

"I'm sure."

I lose again. "See?" I said. "You made it too easy for me—to lose."

"No offense, Franny, but you kind of suck at darts."

"Yeah, but I have incredible team spirit." I raise my hands in the air and wave invisible pom-poms. "Go, me!" I drop my hands. "All you have is skill."

"That's all?"

"Well, you do also have a certain indefinable something . . . that's hidden and indefinable . . ."

"You said 'indefinable' twice," Alex points out.

"It's *really* indefinable. Possibly even nonexistent."

He laughs. So do I. It's one of those moments where you laugh because you're happy more than because you're amused. There's a pause. "Want to watch *SpongeBob*?" he asks.

"Yeah, I guess." I'm glad he doesn't want our time together to end either.

"Or we could . . ." His voice trails off. "I don't know," he says. "What could we do?"

I gesture toward the big windows. "It's a really beautiful night."

"Let's go outside," he says, so quickly it's almost like he was waiting for me to propose that.

No one looks at us twice as we leave the dorm. We always hang out together, Alex and I. Just not usually alone like this. But no one else is thinking about that. Only me. And maybe him.

I'm tense. In a good way. A trembling, *could something happen tonight?* kind of way.

I briefly wonder if I should be more worried about Harry and Isabella. Technically, we're going out with them. Technically, there are rules about this kind of thing. Technically, there are ideals of fidelity and honor.

But it's summer and we're only here for a few more weeks and plenty of people have gone out and broken up already.

Anyway, as much as I don't want to hurt anyone, I don't think either Harry or Isabella is likely to be hurt for too long. If something happens between me and Alex, the two of them will cuddle up together with a couple of cigarettes and then go make some other people fall in love with them.

I've liked Alex longer than Isabella has, anyway.

I glance at him, wondering if his thoughts are running along the same lines as mine, if he's trying to square everything away so he doesn't need to feel guilty, no matter what happens. But he's looking down at the ground, and I can't see his eyes or his expression—the sun has set completely and it's dark. There are fireflies lighting up the branches of the trees. A bunch of kids are playing Frisbee in the courtyard with a glow-in-the-dark disc, and it streaks across the sky like an alien spaceship.

We move away from the players and spectators, toward the greater darkness between the buildings. Neither of us is leading, as far as I can tell. We just both choose to walk that way.

"How's your summer going?" Alex asks after a moment of walking in not-uncomfortable-but-oddly-weighty silence.

"Okay, I guess. Today wasn't great. I got reamed out by my aunt for being a bad niece. Which I guess I am."

"I doubt that."

He's so nice. Have I mentioned that? How *nice* Alex is? From the moment he gave me that stupid rose in eighth grade, I've been aware that this is a nice guy. "It's true I'd rather be hanging out with my friends than with her."

"Well, of course you would. Who wouldn't?" We've reached a small circle of trees behind the building. We stop and Alex leans against one of the trunks. "What's it been like working with her?"

"She's not a barrel of laughs. But it's fine. I'm glad I'm here—especially now that I get to be in a play. I almost feel guilty, getting to have the fun part when I never even had to apply or try out or anything."

"From what I heard, you totally earned it, as much as anyone here." We're completely in shadow now, far from the splashes of light that the streetlamps throw off. But there's enough moonlight for me to catch the quick glance he throws at me. "And Harry?"

I pluck at the bark on the trunk closest to me. "What about Harry?"

"Is he improving your summer?"

"I don't know. He's Harry, you know? He's a goof." I sound more dismissive than I feel. But right now I want Alex to think Harry's no big deal to me. And clearly I'm no big deal to Harry—he's still with Marie and hasn't even bothered to check in with me. Maybe they're just really into rehearsing. But maybe not.

"I can't get used to it," Alex says. "You and Harry."

"Me and Harry what?"

"You know. Isabella says you're totally a couple now."

"Well, if Isabella says it, it must be true."

"Is it?"

We've both been lowering our voices during the whole last exchange. We're practically whispering now.

"Of course not," I say. "I'm not an idiot. We're just having fun, that's all."

"Good," Alex says. "Harry's not the kind of guy you want to see a girl you like getting too involved with." I don't know what to say to that. And what does the *like* mean in that sentence?

Like is such an ambiguous word. So open to interpretation.

He says, "I don't want to see you get hurt, Franny."

"I'm tough."

He shakes his head with a gentle smile. "That's not how I see you."

"How do you see me?"

"I don't know," he says, which is disappointing. But then he reaches out and catches my hand in his. "Franny," he says, and I wait, my throat tightening with my caught breath. But suddenly there are voices near us and he lets go of my hand. "It's getting late," he says. "We should probably go back inside."

I don't want to. I want to stay in the dark with Alex, who I've had a crush on since middle school. It's dark and it's warm and I know that something could happen and everything could change.

Something *is* happening: I can feel it.

I draw closer to him. "Alex? Do you remember giving me a flower?"

"A flower?"

I tell him the story.

"Wow," he says. "I totally forgot I did that. But now it's coming back to me. You were so cute with your costume and makeup and all, but no one was there for you. And everyone was making this huge fuss over Julia—as usual. And I thought, *Someone should give that girl a flower.* So I did. And then I was so embarrassed I ran away."

"It was really nice of you."

"It wasn't that nice. It was Julia's bouquet."

"But it was your idea."

"And you've remembered it all this time."

We look at each other.

"I'm glad I gave you a flower," he says.

"You gave me a lot of books, too."

"I guess I like giving you things."

"Why's that?" I take a step toward him. He reaches out to me. His hand finds mine and pulls me toward him. In the dark, we hug. Like friends? No, not like friends, I think, and I raise my face to his. His lips brush against the corner of my mouth. He whispers my name, and I freeze, afraid that if I move, I'll break the spell. I feel his lips close to mine again, their warmth only an inch away. Then they're brushing lightly but deliberately against mine—

And then I hear the sound of a girl laughing nearby.

Alex startles and drops my hand. He turns away from me.

"We should go back," he says, and starts to walk.

I follow him silently, but I don't want to just leave things like this. My heart is pounding. My skin is prickling all over, like it's woken up from some kind of deep sleep. But I'm not sure exactly what happened—I mean, I know what *happened*; I just don't know what it *means*. Or what's supposed to happen next.

"Wait," I say as we're about to round the corner.

He halts and glances back at me. It's lighter here, but that actually makes it harder to see his eyes. They're in deep shadow, while the light picks out the planes of his forehead and the bones of his cheeks.

"It was fun," I say a little desperately. "Playing darts tonight. Being with you."

"I know," he says. "It was amazing. Franny, I—"

And then suddenly Isabella appears around the corner of the building.

She studies us both coolly. "I thought I heard your voices." Smoke escapes from her mouth with each word.

"There you are!" Alex says with excessive enthusiasm. Well, it sounds excessive to me, anyway. "Thought you were still with your roommates!"

"We finished. So Harry and I . . ." She gestures with the cigarette held between her long fingers just as Harry appears next to her, also holding a cigarette, only he holds it pinched between his index finger and thumb. It occurs to me that I've never actually seen him or Isabella smoke before: they're always so careful about getting far away before lighting up.

Or maybe it's because their cigarette breaks are my chance to have Alex to myself, so I've never even thought about following them.

Harry puts his cigarette to his lips and sucks briefly at it as he looks at me and Alex standing there in the dark together.

"Hi," I say unsteadily. "How was your rehearsal?"

"Fine," Harry says. "You were supposed to text me when you were done with work."

"Sorry. I came over and didn't see you and figured you and Marie were still rehearsing, and then I ran into Alex and we just started talking." It's the truth. So why does it feel like a lie?

"Kind of a dark place to talk, don't you think?" Harry says.

Isabella says, "Definitely." She flicks a bit of ash off her cigarette, puts it back between her perfect lips, and sucks at it so the tip glows for a second. It's pretty the way it lights up, and I stare at it. It's easier than meeting anyone's eyes.

"We were playing darts," Alex says. "It was really hot in there, so we came outside for a minute."

"Uh-huh." Isabella drops her cigarette on the ground and neatly swirls the sole of her ballet flat on it.

Alex touches her lightly on the elbow. "Want to go get something to drink?"

"What did you have in mind?"

"Soda in the dining hall?"

"I'd rather walk into town and get a real drink."

"Okay." He looks at his watch. "We only have about an hour until curfew."

"Better get going, then. You guys want to come?" She looks at Harry, not at me.

"Franny?" He waits for my response, head politely cocked.

It feels oddly like we're all onstage, stiffly reciting lines we've barely memorized. Nothing sounds natural.

I shake my head. "I promised my aunt I wouldn't be late. I should head back." I'm so uncomfortable right now . . . I want to be away from them all. No, wait, not

Alex. I don't want to be away from Alex. I want him to pull me back into the shadows. Or—even better—to stand right here in the light and tell Isabella that he wants to walk me home.

But he doesn't say anything.

He doesn't even meet my eyes.

It's Harry who says, "I should walk you back. It's late."

"You don't have to." I don't want him to. I need time alone to think. To figure out what just happened.

"I'll take Franny home and then meet up with you guys," Harry tells Isabella. "Text me when you know where you're going."

"Okay." She suddenly throws her arms around him. "I love you," she whispers.

"I love you too," he says soberly, and hugs her back.

They release each other, and then Isabella and Alex move away.

Harry and I stand there for a moment watching them go. Then he says abruptly, "What were you and Alex doing out here?"

"He told you—getting some fresh air."

"Right."

"I don't know why you're acting like this," I say, snappish because I feel guilty and confused and it's easier to feel angry than either of those things. "Like *I've* done something wrong—you were the one who went off with Marie for half the night. And you're always flirting with her, but I never make you feel bad."

"I asked you to come with us tonight. And told you to let me know when you were done with work. Which you didn't do."

I shrug irritably. "The point is, we both spent time with members of the opposite gender tonight. Who cares? This isn't the eighteenth century."

"There's nothing else going on, right? With you and Alex? Because Isabella . . ." He stops.

"What?"

"She thinks Alex has a thing for you."

"That's ridiculous," I say. "He's been in love with her since we got here." But my voice sounds too high, because I'm excited: if Isabella is worried that Alex likes me, that's just more evidence that he really does.

"True," Harry says. He takes a quick, audible breath. "Franny, this is weird for me. I don't do the whole jealous thing. To be honest, I've never had to. So just tell me everything's cool and I'll believe you."

"Everything's cool," I say.

He takes my hand. "Now look me in the eyes and say that. And it wouldn't hurt if you said something reassuring about how Alex looks a little like a frog with those bulgy eyes of his."

I take a deep breath, squeeze his fingers, raise my gaze to his, and say again, "Everything's cool—"

He bobs his head. "Okay then."

"—but we never said we were going to be exclusive, you know." I'm not sure why I feel the need to add this. I guess I just want to make something clear to both of us.

He drops my hand. "That wasn't all that reassuring."

"I'm just saying. Not that it matters, necessarily. But since you're the one asking all these questions, I think it's important to be honest and . . . and clear about these things. Right? So no one gets hurt." I'm babbling and I know it. I force myself to stop. Which only makes me more aware of the silence that falls as soon as I do.

"Are you mad?" I ask after a moment goes by.

He shakes his head, slowly, like he's distracted. Like he's thinking.

Some kids walk by us and open the dorm door. Light streams out. They go in and it gets dark again. Then Harry says slowly, "There are some things I guess I thought went without saying. But maybe I'm wrong about that."

"We have fun together," I say. "That's all that matters, right?"

"That's all that matters," he repeats, almost absently. "So if you suddenly felt like 'having fun' with someone else, then that would be all that mattered. Right?"

"I guess." Part of me wants to keep everything all right between us. And the other part wants to make everything completely shattered between us and then go tell Alex that it's shattered. And that part is desperately hoping that he's busy shattering everything with Isabella right now.

"And the same would go for me?" Harry asks. "Just to be clear? We're both free to 'have fun' with anyone at any time?"

"Oh, come on, Harry," I say. "You know you already do whatever you feel like. Especially when it comes to girls. None of it really matters to you, does it? Not in any serious way."

He takes a step back. His eyes glitter in the glow from a courtyard streetlight, which looks like an old-fashioned oil lamp but only because it's a fake. "Do you really think that?"

I say quickly, "It's not a criticism—not at all. It's just who you are. Which is fine. I'm not trying to change you."

"I'm so glad," he says. His tone is mild, almost amiable, but he hunches his shoulders forward like he needs to protect himself against an imminent attack.

"I like that you're easy to be with, Harry. It's a *good* thing. You're the most fun guy I know."

"Just so long as you don't make the mistake of thinking I could ever be serious?" he says.

"We've both wanted to keep things casual."

"Give me a break, Franny." His voice is suddenly sharp with anger, something I haven't heard from him before. I'm so surprised I just stare at him. I didn't think Harry *got* angry. "You decided what kind of person I was without even giving me a chance. In what way haven't I been a good boyfriend? In what way have I treated you badly?"

"I never said you did. And I wouldn't—you've been incredibly sweet." I touch his arm.

He flings my hand off. "Don't call me sweet! Jesus. That's what you call your old aunt who smells funny. I don't want to be your old maid aunt, Pearson. You already have one of those and you hate her."

"I didn't mean it that way."

He shakes his head. "Everything you're saying to me tonight—you're *damning* me with your words. I'm fun. I'm sweet. I'm a flirt. God, kill me *now*. Why are you doing this? Does it have something to do with Alex?"

I ignore that last question. "You can't deny that since you've gotten here, you've flirted with every girl in sight."

"Flirted, yes. Actually liked? One girl. Actually kissed? One girl."

"Come on," I say. "You spent an hour in the hot tub with Marie. You going to tell me you didn't kiss her?"

"*She* kissed *me*."

"Oh, please."

"It's a real distinction!"

"You guys disappeared on the beach—"

"Right. We went for a walk together. She flirted with me like crazy and kept grabbing at me, but I wasn't interested. I've never been interested in her. If I had been, we'd have hooked up." He pounds his fist against his thigh. "God, Franny, *I'm* not the one playing two girls against each other. *I'm* not the one who waits for his girlfriend to walk away so he can go grab hold of someone else."

"Alex doesn't do that! He—"

"I've *seen* him do it, over and over again! It drove me nuts for Isabella's sake, but I thought that at least he didn't have a chance with you—that you were too smart for that kind of shit."

"Alex and I are old friends," I say. "We like to talk to each other, that's all." Which has been true, right? Up until tonight. "But the stuff between you and Julia and Marie—that was ridiculous, and it went on for days. You sucked up all their adoration and let them slug it out."

He raises his hands, like he's strangling the air. "That was their fault, not mine. I never claimed to be involved with either of them. They were interchangeable to me."

"Who isn't?"

He just stares at me, and I writhe uncomfortably under his silent gaze.

"Anyway," I say, "I don't actually care. The thing with Julia and Marie . . . it doesn't matter. I was just making a point."

There's a pause. Then he says, "You really don't 'actually care,' do you?"

"I just said I don't."

"I mean about me. About . . ." He points at me, then at himself.

"Of course I care about you," I say. "You're one of my best friends here, Harry."

"Right," he says coldly. "And let's not forget that I'm sweet and fun."

"You say that like it's a bad thing." I sneak a sideways peek at him. Maybe he'll laugh. He likes to laugh.

But he doesn't laugh. He just stands there, waiting for me to do or say something else. But I don't know what to say or do. Now it's like I'm caught in that narrow doorway with him and Alex. *None* of us can pass through.

When the silence has gone on for an entire minute . . .

"Screw this," he says, and walks away.

I call after him—I don't want him to go away mad—but he just flicks his fingers in my direction and keeps walking. It looks like a friendly wave from a distance, but it's not.

A noisy group of girls is also heading toward the dorm door. As they get closer to the light, I realize Marie is one of them. Harry spots her at the same time. He glances back at me. Then he strides forward with sudden energy, grabs her by the arm, and pulls her away from the other girls and against his hip. She laughs and clutches at him as he spins her around so they can head away from the dorm together.

Harry doesn't look back at me, but Marie does. With a smile and a toss of her head. Which she then leans against his shoulder as they disappear into the dark.

I feel a spasm of anger and something else, too: something like pain. Did he really just run off with her? Like *that*—two seconds after telling me I was special?

I guess he's as unreliable and changeable as I thought. I should feel glad that I escaped before I got so tangled up with him that he had the power to hurt me. It's pretty clear right now that any girl who really likes Harry Cartwright is going to end up getting hurt.

I should feel good about this. To hell with him.

I stand there for a while, trying to appreciate how good this should make me feel, but I'm still not convinced when I finally turn around and head slowly back toward Amelia's apartment.

What else am I going to do? I have nowhere else to go right now.

scene two

I don't know who's more surprised that I'm home at such a reasonable hour, Amelia or me. I immediately tell her I'm tired and just want to crash in my room with a book. She's riveted by the show she's watching—people are screaming at each other—so she lets me go without an argument.

I fall down on my bed and curl up so my feet are sticking out over the side, since it feels like too much work to take off my shoes. I pull my cell phone out of my pocket and spin it around on the blanket.

I feel unsettled. On edge.

There's this weird little bubble of happiness inside of me—Alex kissed me!—and then this bad feeling that has to do with Harry walking away furious and clutching Marie to his side.

Why'd he have to grab her like that? I know I shouldn't expect anything else from him—but still . . . it was rude and deliberately hurtful.

But Alex, I remind myself. *Alex.*

Some time passes. I sit up and pick a book off the stack on my desk and try to settle myself down with some reading, but then I realize it's one of the books Alex gave me on our day trip, and that gets me started all over again: thinking about whether Alex bought the books because he liked me, remembering how much fun Harry and I had that day, wondering whether Harry was just trying to teach me a lesson when he disappeared with Marie right now or if something happened when they were alone rehearsing that had him already planning to do that.

My phone buzzes, and I snatch it up instantly.

Come to the window.

It's from Alex.

I scramble to my feet and look out.

Alex is standing in the courtyard, gazing up at Amelia's room. The fact that he's confused about whose window is whose makes me melt toward him.

Not that I needed any extra heart-melting in his direction.

I open my window—only a crack because Amelia's put in some kind of thief-deterring hardware that keeps it from opening any wider—and call out a muted but very happy "Wait there!" through the inch of open space. He turns and sees me, so I wave before ducking down and running into the living room. I'm in luck: Amelia has disappeared into her bedroom, so I'm free to creep through unchallenged. I close the apartment door behind me very quietly.

He's right below the front step as I come out. His eyes search my face eagerly.

"I wanted to make sure you were okay," he says. He's wearing the same blue T-shirt and jeans he was wearing when I last saw him an hour or so ago. Of course he is. Why would he have changed? Nothing's changed.

Unless everything's changed?

"I'm fine," I say. We're both speaking in whispers. People are asleep in the buildings all around us. I hope Amelia is asleep.

"Harry and Marie . . ." He stops, sticks his hands in his pockets. "He was with her when he met up with us, and they were all over each other. . . . I didn't know if you knew about it. I thought you should."

"Yeah," I say. "But it's fine. I don't care."

"So you guys broke up?"

I wave my hand dismissively. "We weren't going out enough to call it breaking up. I mean, I knew all along that he and I didn't really belong together."

"So you're not upset?"

"God, no."

"Good. I hated the thought of you being here alone, feeling sad . . ." He glances at his watch. "Shoot—it's almost curfew."

"You'd better go."

"Yeah." He looks up at me, a sideways glance full of hope and uncertainty. It's a killer look. "Franny, if you need anything . . . a friend, a shoulder to cry on, a bodyguard, a physical trainer, an oral surgeon . . . I'm here for you."

"All of those things sound nice," I say with a little laugh.

"Anything," he repeats. He studies my face. "Man, you're pretty," he says. And then he comes up onto the step and presses his mouth against mine.

It's a real kiss—I can feel his lips hard against mine—and my knees almost buckle with the unexpected thrill. I want it to last a long time, but he breaks away too quickly and steps back down. "This conversation isn't over," he says, his eyes intent on mine.

"Good," I manage to say. I'm shaking all over.

"I'll see you tomorrow."

I nod. He kind of salutes me and then he walks away. From across the street, he glances back and sees I'm still watching him. We hold up our hands briefly in a sort of motionless wave. And then he heads down the sidewalk and I watch him disappear around the corner. But that's okay.

Because this conversation isn't over.

I go back to the apartment, keyed up, excited and anxious and a little desperate for something else to happen.

Another text. A spray of pebbles on my window. A phone call. A plague of locusts.

Nothing.

I put on my pajamas and brush my teeth.

Nothing.

I toss and turn in bed, still waiting.

But I know nothing more is going to happen tonight.

It doesn't matter: I can't sleep. I'm thinking about how I made a choice tonight. I didn't make it on purpose; it just kind of happened, and I'm still a little confused how. But it was the right choice: Alex over Harry. Substance over style. Kindness over selfishness. Steadiness over unreliability.

I choose you, Pikachu.

The nonsense words—from some stupid old animated show William used to watch—pop into my head for no good reason and keep repeating themselves. The more I try to ignore them, the more they bug me. *I choose you, Pikachu.*

I keep flipping over, from one side to the other, trying to find a cool spot on my pillow, wishing I could block the noise in my head, fairly certain I flicked the switch to start something new and glad of it—but slightly unsettled by the way I had to end something to do it.

Alex over Harry. The right choice.

And the weird little sore spot I'm feeling somewhere in the back of my throat or my stomach or my head—I don't know where; it keeps moving—that's probably just because Harry and I fought and I don't like to fight with anyone. He was angry at me—I didn't expect all that anger. Other people's anger sucks.

Also . . . he grabbed Marie so quickly that it was like he was *relieved* to have an excuse to leave me and go to her. He's like the worst of my old boyfriends combined—he doesn't take anything seriously and especially not me. I'm at the bottom of the list of things he cares deeply about, and Harry doesn't even *have* a list.

My ego is hurt, I think. That's the problem. I want to be with Alex, but it was flattering having Harry—who everyone's got a crush on—act like my boyfriend. If I just take my ego out of the equation, then I'll see that the best thing for me is having Harry happily off pursuing Marie.

I spend some time trying to take my ego out of the equation.

But the sore feeling doesn't go away.

I fall asleep at some point after sunrise, and the next thing I know Amelia is shaking me awake. "Throw some clothes on quickly," she says when I crack open my eyes. "I want to leave here in five minutes and you'd better be with me."

I don't have time to shower, so I pull my hair into a ratty ponytail. I know I'll feel grungy and sticky for the entire day, but at least I don't have to face people at breakfast—as eager as I am to see Alex and to continue the conversation, I'm equally dreading seeing Harry. It just feels easier to postpone both for the moment.

I choose you, Pikachu.

Rats, it's still in my head.

When we reach the Sweatshop, I can hear a rehearsal going on in the theater. The casts rotate in and out: every day one gets the stage for the morning, two have shifts in the afternoon, and one rehearses there after dinner. The rest of the time, the casts rehearse in practice rooms on the second floor. The schedule changes daily, but it gives them all an equal opportunity to get used to the space before performing in it.

Amelia and I don't actually go through the auditorium, so I can't tell which cast is in there right now.

But Amelia checks the rehearsal schedule once we're in her office. *"Twelfth Night,"* she says. "Your cast, but Charles didn't ask for you until this afternoon, which is good, because you can help with the fitting I want to do now—the costumes are almost done. Charles can send the kids back here when they're not needed onstage."

I hide the groan that rises to my lips. Of all the casts . . .

It hadn't even occurred to me until now that I've got to go rehearse with them later today. That I'll have to see Harry and Marie *together*. I can still see him taking her arm last night and her laughing and clutching at him . . .

But it's good, I remind myself. By running off with Marie, Harry made it okay for me to obsess about Alex. I was on the verge of feeling guilty, and he freed me from that. There's still Isabella to consider, I guess, but if Alex likes me better than her, then he'll just have to make that clear to her. Maybe he already has.

That thought momentarily cheers me up.

Still, rehearsal is going to be awkward. At least it's not until later, and most of my scenes aren't with Harry or Marie, and sometimes Charles pulls me out to rehearse with—

"Franny," Amelia says sharply, interrupting my train of thought. "How many times do I have to ask you to go?"

"Go where?" I ask, genuinely confused. She talks at me so much when we're alone that sometimes I don't bother listening.

"To the theater to tell Charles to send the kids back here to try on their costumes. Hurry up."

I enter the auditorium through one of the side doors. Charles is standing just below the stage, tilting his head back so he can talk up to the kids who are on it. The ones who aren't performing right now are down in the audience.

Harry and Marie are sitting side by side. She sees me

before he does and whispers audibly, "What's she doing here? Charles said she wasn't coming until later."

Harry turns, and our eyes meet. He nods at me coldly, then turns back to Marie with an indifferent shrug. She snuggles in as close to him as their separate seats will allow, and he curves his arm around her.

How cozy.

I have to walk by them to get to Charles, and when I do, Harry doesn't release Marie, just stays like that and says calmly, "Hey, Franny."

"Hey," I say stiffly. "I'm just here to talk to Charles."

"He's over there." Harry nods in his direction, even though I'm already headed that way.

"Right." I scuttle past them, bile burning suddenly in my throat.

Julia is onstage, listening to Charles's direction. She notices me waiting there and gives a little wave, and Charles looks my way. "Franny?" he says, and glances at his watch. "I wasn't expecting you this morning."

I explain to him why Amelia sent me, and he nods. "Okay, we can do that." He glances around and spots Harry and Marie. "You two—go back with Franny. Try on your costumes quickly and come right back."

Oh, great. He had to pick *them*.

"I know you, Harry," he adds. "You'll take any opportunity to loiter. So get your butt back here as soon as possible."

"Sir, yes, sir," Harry says with a comically exaggerated salute. He stands up, and pulls Marie to her feet. "Lead on, Franny."

I head back out the door. They follow behind me, arms entwined. She's whispering, loud enough for me to *know* she's whispering in his ear but not loud enough for me to hear what she's saying. Not that I want to.

I stop outside the Sweatshop entrance and gesture inside. Marie releases Harry and sweeps by me.

Harry hesitates halfway through the doorway, but as soon as I look at him, he evades my glance and moves on.

Amelia's rising to her feet. "Remind me who you are," she says.

"I'm Marie—"

"Not your names," Amelia says irritably. "Your *roles.*" She only ever calls the actors by their stage names. It simplifies things for her.

Normally, this exchange would have amused me, but now, stumbling in behind the two of them, I feel too miserable to laugh at anything.

I hate myself for caring that Marie keeps shooting little glances at Harry and he keeps smiling at her the way he was smiling at me a day ago.

Alex, I think. *It'll be okay if things work out with Alex.*

And then I think, *I hate girls who can only be happy if they have a boyfriend.*

So then I think, *I hate myself.*

And that sounds about right at this particular moment.

Amelia is rustling through a rack on wheels that has a sign saying *Twelfth Night* taped to one end. "Here," she says, pulling out a costume and handing it to Marie. "This is for you. And this one"—she rifles through some more hangers and finds it—"is for the duke. We only have one changing room—"

"I'm up for sharing if you are," Marie says, giggling to Harry, who raises his eyebrows and says, "Sounds like fun to me."

Amelia continues, her voice tighter: "—but one of you can change in the bathroom. Hurry now. None of us wants this to take forever."

They disappear into the two separate rooms.

I sit down, grateful for the break.

Amelia is shaking her head. "Honestly. Sometimes..." It's clearly a complaint, but not a very specific one.

Harry is out first. He's now wearing a tuxedo that's designed to look like it's from the 1920s, which is when Charles is setting the production.

Harry looks incredible in it, like the hero in an old black-and-white movie, his shoulders exaggerated and broad, his legs slim and long. The only thing that's missing is a cigarette between his fingers—but, knowing him, he'll probably have one there before too long, in character or out of it.

He hasn't buttoned the top of the tuxedo shirt, and the bow tie is undone and dangling. His neck is bare. I've kissed him on the hollow right at the base there.

I look away. No point reminiscing—it's not going to happen again.

Amelia studies him and gives a satisfied nod. "Not bad. We'll find shoes with a bit of height, so we don't have to hem. Open the jacket for me." He does, and she circles around, then grabs the pants at the waistband. "We'll need to take these in. The vest is huge, too, but there we can get away with just adjusting the tabs. Franny, hand me the—"

She's interrupted by Marie, who calls out from the changing room, "I can't figure out the buttons on this thing."

Amelia spins around. "For God's sake, don't pull at anything!" she shouts toward the door. She grabs her wrist pincushion off her desk. "I'll help her in there. Pin the duke's waist, Franny. Looks like he needs to lose about an inch." She knocks briskly on the changing-room door and enters without waiting for a response, shutting the door behind her.

Talk about awkward. Neither of us says anything for a moment.

Then: "Alone at last," Harry says, which is a typical Harry thing to say, but there's a flatness to his tone that's never been there before—at least not with me.

"You'll need to take off the jacket and vest," I say.

He silently complies, while I find a box of pins. I come over to him. He's holding the jacket and vest in his arms. I take them and put them over the back of a chair and then turn back to him. His shirt is hanging out. "We have to tuck this in first," I say, and together we stuff the shirttails into the waistband.

"If you're going to put your hand down my pants, you could at least pretend to enjoy it," he says. Again, Harry's words, but in an unfamiliar voice.

I don't respond, just circle around behind him and gather some of the fabric at the waist to see how much I need to take in. I'm honestly not trying to give him the silent treatment or anything like that—it's just hard for me to talk right now. My eyes are stinging and my throat is swelling.

I know that feeling: I'm close to tears. What I don't know is *why*. Everything's fine. Harry has proven he's the inconstant flirt I always thought he was. That should be comforting. All's right with the world.

Except I hate Marie. Have I mentioned that? She's a repulsive pig.

"You look good in the tux," I manage to croak out, because the silence is going on too long. The worse I feel, the more I don't want him to know how bad I feel. My voice sounds really weird, so I swallow hard and force myself to speak more clearly. "You're lucky. The *Winter's Tale* cast has to wear these ugly ski pants and down jackets. They'll boil onstage."

"Franny . . ." He twists around, like he's trying to look at me.

"Don't do that, or I'll stick a pin in you." I give a shaky little laugh. "It might even be by accident."

"Franny," he says again, and then the door to the changing room bangs open.

"—can't even breathe in there!" Marie bursts out, followed closely by Amelia. "How do I look, Harry?" She's wearing a man's suit: it's a little boxy, but she looks cute in it.

"Fabulous." Since when does Harry use words like *fabulous*?

She accepts the compliment with a broad smile. "Oh, my God, you're gorgeous!" she says. "You should wear that every day!" She comes closer to him and strokes her hand down the front of his tuxedo shirt. I can see Amelia's face darken behind her. Probably because Marie didn't wash her hands first.

"You should see it with the jacket on," Harry says.

"I like you half-dressed." She rubs her cheek against his arm and makes a purring sound.

I want to say to him, *Really? You like this? This is the kind of thing you like? Really?* But of course I don't. Anyway, he *looks* like he likes it. He has a half smile on his face, and his bedroom eyes look even bedroomier than usual.

"She'll have to bind her chest when she's wearing this," Amelia says brusquely. "Turn around. Let me see the jacket buttoned."

"It's too big on me," Marie says, looking down at herself, pulling the jacket tight behind her to show off her little waist. "That always happens to me with costumes. I'm very narrow."

"It's made for a man," Amelia says, jerking the fabric out of Marie's grip and smoothing the jacket back into place. "Of course it's too big—it's not supposed to fit perfectly. Your director wants it to look like you bought it off a rack in a hurry to disguise yourself as a man."

"So much for looking good onstage," Marie says with a dramatic sigh.

"Are you kidding me?" Harry says. "You look fantastic, babe."

"Babe"? Who is this guy?

I stick another pin in his waistband, and I guess his shirt still isn't tucked in correctly because my fingers brush briefly against his warm back. I feel him stiffen under my touch, like he wants to move away. I quickly ram in the last pin and stand up straight.

"I'm done," I tell Amelia.

She glances over. She's still fiddling with Marie's jacket.

"Okay, Duke," she says to Harry. "Get changed and go back to rehearsal. Watch out for the pins as you take the pants off."

"You bet I will," he says, and disappears into the bathroom.

"Let me know if you need any help in there," Marie calls after him gaily.

Amelia says, "Franny, are you responsible for the way that jacket is just tossed over the back of the chair?"

"I guess so." I hastily pick it up and smooth it out.

She shakes her head, tsking. "I expect you to take better care of the costumes than that. You'll have to press it now."

"Oh, poor Franny," Marie says with barely repressed mirth. "As if it's not hot enough in here already. Now you have to iron! I feel so bad for you."

I want to kill her.

Harry comes out of the bathroom, once again in jeans and a T-shirt and holding the rest of his costume. "Who do I give this to?"

"Franny will take it," Amelia says, adding to me, "and please be more careful than you were the last time."

Harry hands the costume to me. I accept it silently.

"Oh, Harry, I almost forgot to tell you," Marie says. "Someone's organizing a trip to a bar—" She stops, and glances at Amelia, then giggles again and says, "I mean, to a *restaurant* tonight for anyone who's not rehearsing. I said we'd go. You don't mind, do you, babe?"

We? They're a *we?* That happened awfully fast.

I suddenly find myself very involved with folding the pants. I have to smooth every inch out just right. Staring fixedly down at them the entire time.

"Sounds good to me," Harry says. "You know how much I love going to 'bars, uh, restaurants.'"

"Oh, sorry, Franny!" She spins around, her hand to her mouth, like she *just* remembered I'm there. "I didn't mean to leave you out. I'm sure you can go too, if you want to."

"I probably have to work tonight," I say.

"Too bad." She paints a sympathetic look onto her face.

Amelia tells her to go change into the dress she'll be wearing in her first scene. Marie touches Harry on the hand. "See you soon," she says, and tickles his wrist before going back into the changing room.

"You need me for anything else?" Harry asks Amelia. "I can try on other people's costumes too, you know. I'm able to alter my height and weight at will. It's my superpower."

"We're done with you for now," my aunt says, not amused. "Send one of the other actors in."

"Okay," he says, and then, "Bye," sort of in my direction but not exactly in my direction.

I raise my hand silently.

While Marie is changing, Amelia excuses herself to go to the bathroom and is still in there when Marie comes back out, now wearing a dark red flapper dress that's been distressed to look like she swam in it. "Here," she says, handing me her suit. "Make sure you hang it up carefully, will you, Franny? It's really important to me that my costume not get all crushed and wrinkled, since I'm the one who has to wear it onstage." She rotates in front of the mirror on the changing-room door, admiring the fringe on the dress. "Wish Harry had seen me in *this*. It's so much more flattering than that stupid suit." She looks over her shoulder. "Oh, sorry, Franny. Is it awkward for me to talk about him in front of you? You two sort of had something going on for a little while, didn't you?"

"Did we?" I say, and thread the pants onto the hanger.

scene three

'm nervous as I walk into lunch that day. I don't know where I should sit. Not with Harry, obviously—and that's been my place for days.

Julia finds me while I'm still getting my food. "What the hell happened last night?" she asks. "I go off alone with Manny for like two hours, and come back to find you and Harry split up and Marie sitting on his lap?"

"We weren't ever really together," I say, but I'm thinking, *Marie was on his lap last night?* Then: *Why am I surprised?*

Julia raises her eyebrows. "Could have fooled me. But you were the one who kept warning *me* about what a flirt he was, and we all know how available Marie's made herself to him, and even though she's the biggest rat I've ever met, a lot of the guys think she's cute." She smiles suddenly. "Although, BTW, and just between us, Manny told me he doesn't think she's nearly as pretty as *she* thinks she is, but he's, you know, one of the good guys. And I think sometimes he says things like that to me because he thinks they're what I want to hear. I hope he doesn't think I'm high maintenance." She pauses. "Are you upset or anything?"

I shake my head, and that's enough for her. She goes on. "Marie's been bragging all about how she and Harry totally hooked up last night, but it's such a lie: we all went into town and then when we got back, he went off with Isabella and they disappeared for ages, and Marie was in our room before it was even curfew."

"Really?" I find this very interesting. "So you think she was lying about hooking up with him?"

"Marie's not exactly known for her integrity. Oops, there's Manny—he's waiting for me—got to go." She races off and throws her arms around Manny Yates, who smiles fondly down at her even though she made him spill some of his soda.

By the time I'm done getting my food, Vanessa and Lawrence are at a table together, which means I have people to sit with.

"Look who's here," Lawrence says as I put my tray down next to him. "The girl who's always too busy for us."

"That's so not true." I sit down and take a sip of my soda. "It's just that with rehearsals for *Twelfth Night* and all the costume work piling up—"

"Oh, I'm sure it has *nothing* to do with your being joined at the hip to Harry Cartwright," Lawrence says. "I've finally conceded, by the way: he's not gay."

"Um, Lawrence?" Vanessa says. She points to Harry and Marie, who are walking into the dining hall together, her arm tight around his waist, his arm draped loosely over her shoulder.

"Excuse me?" Lawrence says. "What are *they* doing together?" He turns to me. "What's going on, Franny?"

"We broke up." It's amazing how calmly I can say it.

Vanessa says, "Marie told me last night, but I wasn't sure . . . I mean, I never believe anything she says." She puts her hand on my arm. "Franny . . ."

I cut her off. "If either one of you expresses sympathy for me, I'll scream and throw food. I'm so okay with this I can't even begin to tell you."

"Really?" she says.

"Want me to swear on my aunt's dead body? I'd have to kill her first, but I'll do it if it proves my point."

"You'd like an excuse to do that, wouldn't you?" Lawrence says. I'm glad I can still make other people laugh. I'm faking it myself at the moment—seeing Harry smile down at Marie makes my skin crawl.

Alex, I tell myself sternly. *Remember about Alex. He's the one who matters. Not Harry.*

Where is Alex, anyway? I need some reassurance that I wasn't imagining what happened last night, because it's starting to feel very unreal in the light of day.

Vanessa picks up an apple and rotates it, searching for imperfections. "All I'm going to say on the subject is that any guy who would prefer Marie to you is an idiot." She takes an emphatic bite of her apple.

"I agree," Lawrence says. He stands up. "Anyone else want a glass of milk?"

We shake our heads, and after he leaves, Vanessa leans over to me. "Seriously, Franny, about Harry . . ."

"I'm fine."

"And it's over?"

I nod.

"Good. I didn't want to say anything, because it's none of my business, but I thought the whole thing was a mistake. Guys like Harry don't really care about anyone but themselves."

I nod, relieved to hear someone I trust confirm my decision. Especially since it wasn't entirely my decision. "Hey, where are Alex and Isabella?" I ask casually. "Why aren't they here?" I'm wondering if there's any gossip going around about them, about how they've broken up or something like that. Or maybe he's breaking up with her right *now* and that's why they're not in the dining hall.

Except they are: Vanessa points past my shoulder and says, "They're right over there." I turn and see Alex and Isabella sitting with Julia and Manny at a table in the corner. Their backs are to the room, so I guess I just didn't see them.

Now I feel like I've been punched in the stomach. He's been here the whole time I've been here. With her. Just sitting there. Not even looking for me.

Like nothing happened last night.

Am I losing my mind? Didn't Alex kiss me? Didn't he say the conversation wasn't over?

Vanessa's sharp eyes are studying me curiously. "Something going on you're not telling me?" she asks.

I shake my head, and fortunately Lawrence comes back to our table right then with his milk and a plate of cookies and she's distracted.

I sneak another peek at Alex and Isabella. Their chairs are close and their knees are touching.

Maybe I'm just an idiot. Maybe I just didn't understand how the rest of our "conversation" was going to go. Maybe he was planning all along to say, *And, by the way, even though I kissed you, I'm not leaving the really gorgeous girl I'm already seeing. And, hey, how about those Mets?*

That's making conversation too, right?

When I clear my tray, I have to walk by their table. His eyes flicker up—and then suddenly he's very busy eating a cookie.

The afternoon feels endless. We do costume fittings with the *Winter's Tale* cast, and then I spend a couple of hours ripping out hems and seams.

And then it's time to go to rehearsal.

I'm lucky. Charles wants me and Raymond—who plays Sebastian—to work on a short scene that just the two of us are in. I quickly suggest we go off by ourselves and work in the hallway so the others can keep rehearsing in the practice room, and Charles says that's fine and he'll go back and forth.

Marie is whispering to Harry when Raymond and I walk out.

She's always whispering to him when I'm around. You'd think he'd get tired of her sputtering in his ear like that.

With just two of us in the scene, I don't have any downtime, which is good. I have to remember my lines, respond to his, focus on where to stand, figure out how to create the character—I don't have time to obsess about why Alex was ignoring me at lunch or about the curling feeling I get in my stomach every time I see Harry with Marie.

I'm lying.

I still think about all that.

After we've worked on the scene alone for a while, Charles joins us and has us run it through for him. He gives us a few notes, then tells us to follow him back into the practice room so he can give some general notes to the whole cast.

I sit next to Julia. When Charles dismisses us, she

and Manny say they're going to dinner. "You coming?" she asks me.

"I should check in with my aunt first." That's just an excuse—I'm planning to skip dinner tonight. I don't need to see Isabella with Alex, Marie with Harry. I don't need to feel ignored and passed over up close. I can enjoy those feelings just fine from a distance.

Amelia is still sewing away when I show up. "What time is it?" she asks, looking a little dazed.

I tell her, and she asks me if I want to go to dinner. When I say I don't, she puts me to work ripping out some seams. We work in silence for about an hour—well, silence except for her folk music—and then she sends me down to the costume archives to see if I can find a red scarf. She's sure there's one in there somewhere. I find one that's dark red—but plaid—and one that's a solid red—but orangey—and bring them back up the stairs and outside, where I'm suddenly pounced on by Vanessa and Lawrence.

"We've been waiting for you," Vanessa says. "Amelia told us you were down there. We're kidnapping you and taking you out on the town."

"Now that you're a free woman again, we want you back in our lives," Lawrence says.

"I was never out of them!" I protest.

"We accept your apology," Vanessa says. They walk me back into the Sweatshop, where the two of them explain to Amelia—with straight faces—that it's a

Very Important and Special Night for all the Mansfield actors, and that we're not allowed to tell her anything about this very important and special night, now or ever, but that she should know that it might go very late because it's so very important and special.

She *buys* it. That's the weird thing about Amelia: she's nervous and negative and theoretically suspicious . . . but she's also oddly gullible. She nods and reluctantly says that it sounds too important and special for me to miss, and thanks the two of them for including me.

She doesn't have to tell us twice. We're out of there before she finishes her sentence.

"Where should we go?" Vanessa asks as we race away.

"Can we run back to the apartment for like ten minutes so I can shower?" I ask. "Please? I promise to be fast. I just feel like such a grunge ball right now. I don't want to go out like this."

"You *look* like a grunge ball," Lawrence says. "Whatever that is. No offense."

"Is there anything to eat at your aunt's?" Vanessa says. "I was waiting to eat and now I'm starving."

I try to think of what I can offer her that's at least slightly appealing. "There's Greek yogurt and hummus and protein bars and rice cakes—"

"I love hummus!" Vanessa says.

Hey, maybe my luck is changing.

* * *

I take a shower and come out of the bathroom wrapped in a towel to find Lawrence and Vanessa standing around my bed, studying some clothes they've laid out there. Lawrence says, "We got bored so we picked out an outfit for you."

"You have to wear it," Vanessa says. "Because we were nice and came back to your apartment and waited for you and the hummus sucked. You didn't tell me it was homemade."

"You didn't ask."

"It was like solid chickpea. Someone needs to introduce your aunt to the wonders of tahini." She points to the clothing on the bed. "Hurry up and get dressed. My blood sugar's dropping, and if I don't get dinner soon, I'll turn into a raging lunatic."

"How will we know the difference?" Lawrence says.

"I just have to dry my hair first," I say. "Don't be mad."

"Be fast and I won't be mad."

"Be mad and I won't be fast."

"Both of you shut up and maybe we'll get out of here before midnight," Lawrence says.

They leave the bedroom, and I put on the outfit they picked out: dark skinny jeans with a silky pink tank that has ribbons crisscrossing its bodice. They've even laid out shoes: the strappy spike heels that I wanted to wear with the green dress but didn't because they're so impractical. I put it all on, like an obedient child. I'm happy to have someone else making choices for me. I'm glad Lawrence and Vanessa are here.

I blow my hair dry quickly, leaving it naturally wavy since that's the fastest way to get it dry, but at least it's clean and soft and *not* in a ponytail. While I'm finishing up, the two of them knock on the door, and Lawrence says he wants to try putting makeup on me because he's never done it before and he thinks he'd be a good makeup artist.

"I'm not going to let you train on my face!" I say.

"I've done stage makeup," he says. "Just not girl-going-out makeup. What's the difference?"

"About ten pounds of foundation," Vanessa says. "Let me show you how it's done." She sorts through the makeup in my toiletry kit. Amelia and I have to share one bathroom, so I've never really unpacked my stuff; I just keep it all in the bag so I can bring it back to my room when I'm not using it.

"This is fun," Vanessa says, as she brushes blush on my cheeks. "You're so pale and smooth, it's like painting on a blank canvas." She looks pretty drop-dead herself tonight, her crazy corkscrewing hair swept up in a big pouf that's held in place with one of her wide headbands. The headband shouldn't work with the big black glasses, but it does. It's all about style, I think. And bone structure. I gaze at her as she goes to work on my face, leaning forward to dab and brush, shifting back to study her work. Yeah—if you have the right cheek- and jawbones, like she does, you can do crazy stuff with your hair and glasses and people still know you're pretty.

I don't have her bone structure, but as Vanessa finishes and I turn to the mirror, I have to admit that I've come a long way from grunge ball. She didn't go overboard with the makeup, just kept it soft and flattering, so I look like me, but me on my best and prettiest day.

Miss Smith after she's taken off her glasses.

Who said that?

Oh, right. Harry.

Forget that, then. It's a stupid compliment. And he's long gone.

"What are you doing?" Vanessa asks Lawrence.

He's leaning close to the mirror, carefully outlining his eyes in black pencil. "What do you think?" he asks, turning to us. It's astonishing what a difference it makes. Usually he looks like he's barely fifteen and kind of nerdy, but with the guyliner he suddenly looks dark and goth and sensual.

"I think your poor little Midwestern mother would have a heart attack if she saw you," Vanessa says.

"Good thing she's hundreds of miles away, then," he says. He fluffs out his curls, tells me I look gorgeous, and declares himself ready to go.

Out on the street we link arms and I feel warm and happy. Like Dorothy with the Tin Man and the Scarecrow, I think.

Although . . . maybe Vanessa is Dorothy. Or Lawrence. Maybe *I'm* the Tin Man. He had no heart, right? Sounds pretty appealing to me right now. I'm ready to give mine up. It's done nothing but get me in trouble. And ache.

Amelia lives just a few blocks away from downtown Mansfield, which is about halfway between her apartment and the college campus. We walk briskly in that direction now, Vanessa's heels and mine echoing on the concrete sidewalks, Lawrence's rubber-soled boots silent.

"I thought we'd just go grab some fast food for dinner, but now I'm thinking we're too beautiful for that," Vanessa says. "I mean look at us. Just look at us. We are three very fine-looking individuals."

"So where should we go?" Lawrence asks. "If I don't eat soon, I'm going to start gnawing on my own arm."

"You'll have to share it with us," I say. "We're hungry too."

"Won't work for me," Vanessa says. "I'm a vegetarian."

"You can have my toe jam," Lawrence says.

"You are so gross. How about this place?" She stops and points to a sign that says Mansfield Pub. "There's a menu in the window." We study it for a moment and agree it looks fine. I push open the heavy door and we go in.

The place is big on wood—the tables, the chairs, the stools, and even the floor are all made out of the same kind of fake-weathered oaky stuff. It's pretty dim inside and moderately noisy, and crowded enough to make me hopeful the food will be decent. There's loud rock music playing through the system, but someone is setting up band equipment on a small platform in the back of the room, so it looks like there will be live music soon.

Vanessa spots some people paying and nabs their booth the second they're on their feet. "Takes a New Yorker to score a table before anyone else," she says smugly as we slide in.

A waitress brings us menus. Lawrence and I order hamburgers and fries and Vanessa gets spaghetti marinara. We polish off a basket of bread just in time for the food to come.

Vanessa stops eating the fries off our plates long enough to check her phone when it buzzes.

"You guys mind if Julia and Manny join us?" she asks absently as she punches back a response to the text. It's not really a question, so we don't bother to answer it.

Julia and Manny show up just as the band (guitar, bass, drums) starts tuning their instruments.

But they're not alone. Harry, Alex, Marie, and Isabella are with them.

"Oh, God, Franny, I'm sorry," Vanessa whispers when they all file into the restaurant. "Julia didn't say anything about the others!"

So much for our low-key evening. I feel my entire body tense up.

On the other hand . . . Alex. I haven't talked to him since he showed up on my doorstep last night and kissed me. I'm curious about seeing him face-to-face.

After the way he ignored me at lunch today, I'm wary. But still curious.

They descend on us.

Marie says, "Oh, Franny, *you're* here?" and glances sharply at Harry, but he's not even looking at me. Isabella's greeting is equally unenthusiastic.

It's kind of funny when you think about it: Isabella and Marie are both acting like I'm some kind of threat, and meanwhile *I'm* the one who's there without a date.

Alex says a general and pleasant hello to all of us.

The live music has started, and the pub has completely filled up in the last half hour, which means there aren't any free tables, so everyone squeezes into our booth. I'm grateful I'm already sitting between Vanessa and Lawrence, since it saves me from having to squish up against someone less friendly. The guys nab a couple of extra chairs to pull up to the open side of the table, and Alex and Manny take those. Marie curls up tightly on the booth bench against Harry, who rests his arm on her shoulders and smiles affably at no one in particular.

The waitress comes over. "These booths aren't meant to hold this many people," she mutters. But she doesn't tell us we have to move. Harry, Marie, and Isabella order mixed drinks, and she says, "I can't serve you if you're underage." Harry and Isabella pull out their fake IDs. She scrutinizes them and then hands them back with a begrudging "okay, I guess."

Marie makes a big show of searching her clutch. "I think I left my ID back in my apartment," she says with a little laugh. "I'm so stupid. But I'm with them, so . . ."

"No ID, no drinks," the waitress snaps.

"Maybe I should speak to your manager."

"Be my guest," the waitress says. "Want me to call him over?"

"Oh, just forget it," Marie says. "Give me a Diet Coke." The others also order sodas, and the waitress leaves. "She is so not getting a tip," Marie says to Harry.

"Yeah," Harry agrees. "What a jerk. Actually obeying the law and keeping herself from getting fired."

"Oh, please. She could have served me. No one cares." She shrugs. "Oh well—I'll just share yours."

"Where'd you guys get your IDs, anyway?" Lawrence asks, leaning forward.

"Isabella has connections," Harry says.

"I do," she agrees, with a little smile.

Alex fidgets in his seat. Our eyes have met a couple of times, and each time he smiled at me—and then looked away. Since he's on a chair, he and Isabella aren't snuggled up together, but there's enough PDA going on in the room with Marie practically in Harry's lap.

Julia says, "What do we think of the band?"

"I like them," Manny says.

"So do I," she says with sudden conviction.

"Oh, look, people are starting to dance!" Vanessa says. She sways a little in her seat, in time to the music. "We all need to dance tonight. When else are we going to get the chance?"

"Mansfield Mayhem is next week," Julia says. I have no idea what that is—but I assume it's some kind of party. I miss a lot of information because I'm working when they're all at morning assembly. "But Vanessa's right—we need to dance. Come on, everybody. Especially you, Manny." She slides out of the booth, and Lawrence, who's next to her, eagerly follows.

"Come on, Franny," he says, and I let him pull me out of the booth.

"You coming?" Vanessa asks Harry and Marie as she wriggles her way out after us.

"Want to dance, babe?" Marie asks Harry.

"Once I get my drink."

"I'll wait for you. I want some too."

Now that the booth is less crowded, he takes his arm off her shoulders and shifts away a little. "Look at *you*," he says to me. I'm standing near the booth, waiting for whoever's going to dance. "You never got all glammed up like that for me, Franny."

I shrug. What am I supposed to say to that?

"Hoping to pick someone up tonight?" Marie asks me.

"Oh, yeah," I say. "That's the goal. Preferably a homicidal maniac, if someone would only introduce me to one."

"We dressed Franny tonight," Lawrence tells the others proudly. "Vanessa and I picked out her clothes. Doesn't she look great?"

"Beautiful," Isabella says coolly.

But she's the one who's truly beautiful tonight, in a shimmery nude spaghetti-strap top and a gauzy scarf artfully draped around her neck, her hair pulled back into that elegant, twisted knot.

"You guys coming to dance?" Julia asks them.

"Yeah. Come on, Isabella." Alex stands up abruptly.

"I haven't gotten my drink yet," she says. "But you go ahead." She doesn't mean it. She wants him to say he'll wait for her. I know, because *I'd* say, "Go without me," and I'd want my date to refuse.

Guys are stupid. Alex says, "Okay. Meet you on the dance floor in a couple of minutes, all right?"

"Fine," her lips say, but her eyes narrow. I can see it. Doesn't he? Or does he see it and not care?

We all go together to the tiny dance area, a slice of floor wedged between the band and the bar. We start off all dancing together in one group, but it's instantly clear that Lawrence was telling the truth about how he takes a lot of dance classes, and Vanessa quickly nabs him as a partner. She has mastered a gawky-cool style of moving, arms dangling, feet turned in, shoulders slouching. I wish I could pull that kind of thing off, because it's so much hipper than the way I dance, which is your basic wriggling to the music.

Julia and Manny gradually move closer together, and pretty soon they're touching and pretty soon after that their dancing devolves into more or less making out to the beat.

Which leaves me and Alex facing each other. He's not the best dancer I've ever seen. He overconcentrates, listens to the music too intensely and then tries too hard to move his shoulders and arms in rhythm. And he gets this slight frown of concentration on his forehead. I don't want to think it's cute, but it is—it's very cute.

I'm careful to keep my distance from him, like we're at a middle-school dance where the chaperones say stuff like *We'd better be able to see air between you two!*

Our eyes meet. He smiles at me, and this time he doesn't instantly look away again.

I bite my lip, not sure how I want to respond. On the one hand, there was last night and the kiss he gave me on the front stoop of my aunt's apartment.

On the other hand is everything else since then, which is precisely nothing.

He says something to me that I can't hear, so I lean forward and respond with a brilliantly insightful "huh?"

"You look nice tonight." He has to shout since we're close to the band. "How are you doing?"

"Me?" I shout. "I'm great. I'm fantastic. I'm like so incredibly wonderful."

The music stops suddenly, and the word *wonderful* rings out loudly in the moment of silence before people clap. "I hate when that happens," I say, embarrassed.

"Me too," he says, and smiles at me again.

The new song starts. It's really slow. Too slow to dance to, unless, like Julia and Manny, you're happy just to clutch each other and barely move.

Alex and I stand there awkwardly.

Vanessa touches my arm. "We're sitting this one out. It stinks."

"Yeah, I agree."

Alex and I follow her and Lawrence back to the table, where Marie is on her feet, trying to pull Harry out of the booth.

"Come on!" she's saying. "I love slow-dancing when I have a good partner."

"You want me to find you one?"

"Don't be so lazy. You're so lazy. Isn't he lazy?" She appeals to Isabella, who takes a long swallow of her drink—emptying it—and shrugs, then rises to her feet, saying, "Come on, Harry. Prove you're not lazy. Dance with me."

He gets up, gently pushing Marie aside so he can join Isabella. "All right."

Marie crosses her arms. "You're going to dance with her, not me?"

Harry shrugs. "What can I do? She has this power over me. Always has."

"Isabella . . . ," Alex says, but she ignores him and takes Harry by the arm.

"Life is confusing," she tells him, resting her cheek on his arm.

"Tell Papa all about it," he murmurs, briefly resting his own cheek on the top of her head as they move toward the dance floor.

"Better grab a blanket, because you're spending tonight in the doghouse," Vanessa says to Alex as she and Lawrence scoot back into the booth.

"I'm always in the doghouse," Alex says with a pained laugh.

"Ever think maybe there's a reason?" Vanessa asks.

"What would that be?"

She doesn't answer, just exchanges a look with Lawrence.

"This is so annoying," Marie says, plopping down

angrily onto one of the wooden chairs. "If those two love each other so much, why don't they just go out?"

"They're best friends," Alex says.

"I don't dance with *my* best friends." No one responds to that, and Marie's eyes fall on me. "I'm really surprised to see you here, Franny," she says. "Your aunt was saying she was worried about how much work you still have to do. The costumes *have* to be ready on time, you know. We can't all just go onstage naked because you decided to go out and have some fun—"

"Shut up, Marie," Lawrence says.

"God!" she exclaims. "Why is everyone ganging up on me tonight? I was just joking!" She jumps up from the table. She's wearing a very tight, short, electric-blue dress and high silver heels. She's a little too dressed up for the pub we're in, but she definitely looks hot, and I see several guys at a nearby table swiveling to get a better look at her. She pulls on Alex's arm. "Come on, Alex. Let's go break in on them. They should be dancing with us, not each other."

He hesitates.

Marie snaps, "If you don't want to dance with her, then fine. Stay in the doghouse."

"No, you're right," he says. "Let's do it." He glances toward me uncertainly. I look away and take a sip from my water glass. It's his choice.

Come to think of it, it's always his choice. And I'm

always sitting around waiting for him to make it.

I don't think I like that.

He rises to his feet and follows Marie across the pub, toward where Harry and Isabella are deep in conversation. They're supposed to be dancing, and they *are* swaying to the music, hands clasped behind each other's waists, but really what they're mostly doing is talking.

Isabella turns her head as the other two approach. She studies Alex gravely, thoughtfully. We all watch. Marie says something to Harry. He shrugs and releases Isabella, and Marie smiles smugly and moves into his arms. But over the top of her head he's looking at Isabella, who's not moving toward Alex, even though he's holding out his hand, clearly asking her to dance with him.

"This is interesting," Lawrence says, and Vanessa agrees: "Better than TV."

"If it were *Jersey Shore*, someone would punch someone else very soon," Lawrence adds.

"My money's on the dark-haired girl," Vanessa says.

The dark-haired girl shakes her head, refuses Alex's extended hand, turns on her heel, and walks back to us, her chin high, her shoulders back.

She comes straight over to *me*, to where I'm sitting at the edge of the booth, and she says, "Franny?" and for one giddy second I think she's going to ask me to dance and wonder what I'll say, but of course she doesn't. She says, "Will you come with me to the ladies' room for a second?"

"Okay," I say, too curious to refuse. I stand up.

"Can I come too?" Vanessa asks eagerly, peering at us from behind those thick glasses that don't distort her eyes at all—it occurs to me for the first time that they're probably fakes, just clear glass.

"No," Isabella says. "I want to talk to Franny alone." She nods toward the back of the pub. I'm just starting to follow her as Alex comes back to the table.

"What's going on?" he asks, looking back and forth between us.

"Franny and I need to talk," she says, and leads me away from him.

scene four

Our path takes us by the tiny dance floor, where Marie is now curled up against Harry's chest. She's smiling and talking and rubbing her cheek against his T-shirt. He barely seems to know she's there. He's shifting rhythmically from one foot to the other, but his eyes are on me and Isabella as we go past him.

Isabella opens the restroom door and we go inside. It's a one-room kind of thing. She locks the door, and we have just enough room to stand at a slight distance and regard each other warily. So we do.

"Are you going to beat me up?" I ask.

"Oh, for God's sake," she says, her lips twitching into a reluctant smile. "If I decide to shank you, Franny, you won't see it coming."

"How *was* your time in prison? I've always wanted to ask."

"Seriously . . . ," she says.

"Seriously. Why are we in the bathroom?"

She leans her hip against the sink and regards me. "Harry says I should trust you."

"Excuse me?" She starts to repeat it but I stop her. "No, sorry, I heard you. I'm just surprised. Harry told you to trust me? That's the last thing in the world I'd have expected him to say. He hates me."

"No, he doesn't." She tilts her head back and regards me through half-closed eyes. "He *should*. You've treated him like shit. But Harry's not a hater. Anyway, he says that if I ask you to be honest, you will be. Is that true?"

"What's the point of asking me that? If I'm a liar, I'll just lie about being truthful. And, by the way, I didn't treat Harry like shit."

"*Are* you a liar?"

"Not usually, no."

Our eyes meet, and she gives a little nod, like she believes me. "What happened between you and Alex last night?"

I hesitate. But Harry said she could trust me to be honest, and that makes me want to tell her the truth. "He came by my aunt's apartment."

"And?"

"He didn't stay long."

"But long enough?"

"I'm sorry," I say, and I mean it. "I thought he had broken up with you. Or was just about to."

"I get it," she says. She turns and looks in the mirror and unpins her hair with a single fluid motion. It falls down around her shoulders. "It's not like I'm surprised. After I saw you guys alone together . . ."

"He kissed me last night, but it was the first time, I swear."

"And did he tell you he was breaking up with me?"

"Not in so many words. Would it sound stupid to say he kind of implied it?"

"A little," she says.

This whole conversation feels surreal. I expected accusations and anger, or tears and recriminations. But we're both pretty calm. It's like we're trying to figure something out. Together.

"I've liked him for a long time," I say abruptly. "I think you kind of knew that. But I swear I wasn't trying to steal him away from you or anything like that. He always seemed to like you much better. It's just . . . last night it seemed like maybe he had changed his mind, and I honestly thought he was going to tell you so. I didn't think we were doing anything sneaky. But today he was right back to being with you—"

"Until it was time to dance. Then he went with you."

"Well, it was sort of in a group . . ."

She just gives me a look.

"Look," I say. "I don't know what Alex was thinking then or last night. All I know is that up until last night, he always seemed pretty into you."

Isabella sweeps up her hair in skilled fingers, twists and repins it swiftly. "Pretty into me. A little into you." She shrugs. "'The Boy Who Couldn't Choose,'" she says. "It's not a very original story."

I press my back hard against the wall. "I'm sorry."

"It's okay. Apparently you have nothing to feel sorry about." She turns around and faces me, leaning back against the sink. "That's what Harry says, anyway. He blames Alex for everything."

"He doesn't like Alex very much, does he?"

"He hates him." She minutely adjusts one of the silver bracelets on her arm. "Doubly now."

"What do you mean, doubly now?"

"Harry's very protective of me. And we know how he feels about *you*."

"Yeah," I say. "We know that I was the girl he went out with before he switched to Marie, who'll be the girl he goes out with before he switches to whoever's next."

Her nostrils flare. "You don't know what you're talking about."

"Look, I know he's a good friend of yours—"

"Yeah, he is," she says. "So it's been hard for me to forgive you for being such a jerk to him, but he wants me to."

"That's not fair," I say. "I just said I didn't think things were all that serious between us, and two seconds later he went running off with Marie. Which kind of proves I was right."

"Let me see." She taps her chin, dark eyes searching mine. "Was this before or after we came across you and Alex making out in the dark?"

"We weren't making out. We barely even—"

"Before or after?"

"After," I say reluctantly.

"Uh-huh." She raises and lowers her shoulders.

"What's that supposed to mean?"

"You hurt him. He wanted to hurt you back, so he grabbed whatever weapon he could get his hands on. And Marie always makes herself available." Her lip curls. "Bless her greedy little heart."

I sink down onto my heels so I'm squatting, my back to the wall. I don't want to sit on the floor—it's a bathroom and not even a particularly clean one—but I don't feel like I can stand upright at the moment. I'm so confused. Thoughts are banging around inside my head.

"So," she says, absently fingering a beaten silver earring. "What do we do?"

"About what?"

"Alex, of course. Actually, forget that. I know what *I'm* going to do about him. Enough's enough." She shakes her head. "At some point I'll fall apart about all this, but right now I've got some clarity, thanks to Harry. But what are *you* going to do?"

"Clarity?" I repeat, confused. I feel like she's way ahead of me, and I'm only falling more and more behind.

She bites her lip and says slowly, "I liked Alex because he was so much sweeter to me than any guy has ever been before. He was just so nice, all the time, and not just to me, to everyone—"

"I like that about him too," I say.

Our eyes meet, and Isabella lets out a sudden and surprising bark of rueful laughter. "There's nice," she says, "and then there's *good*. They can be two different things. Being overly nice to more than one girl at a time—"

"—isn't all that good."

"Harry says I deserve better."

"You do."

"I don't know," she says. "I haven't had a lot of luck when it comes to guys."

"Me neither."

"Yeah, you did; you just didn't appreciate it," she says.

Someone knocks on the door. "You okay in there?" an adult woman's voice asks. "There's a line out here."

"Oh, God." I scramble to my feet. "We'd better go."

Isabella shrugs indifferently. "We have every right to be in here."

"Yeah," I say, "but it's the *bathroom*. People have needs, you know."

"Fine." She crosses to the door and flings it open. "All yours," she says to the woman at the front of the line.

I'm stunned by our entire conversation, so I just follow her wordlessly, happy to let her lead the way.

Everyone's back there now except for Julia and Manny, who are over by the bar, talking close together. The band is still playing, but the dance floor is empty.

Alex jumps up when we come close. He looks uneasily back and forth between me and Isabella, and then his gaze settles anxiously on her.

"Hello, everyone," Isabella says, looking around the table. "I have an announcement to make. Since we're all good friends here and since news travels fast anyway, I think you should all know right away that I'm breaking up with Alex."

"What?" he says. "What?"

She turns to him. "I know you like secrets. But I'm different—I like to keep things very clear and honest."

"Hear, hear," Harry says, his voice lazy—but his eyes are keen and protective as they keep a close watch on his best friend.

"Anyway, it's been real and now it's over." She sits down on one of the chairs. "I'm ready for another drink."

Alex says to her, "Can we please talk about this? I don't even know what's going on." He glances uncertainly in my direction. "What were you guys talking about in there?"

The glance isn't lost on Isabella, who says, "Nothing you don't already know. Don't worry, Alex. Look at it this way: I'm setting you free. Spread your wings, little birdie. Fly away." She wiggles her fingers at him.

"What exactly went on in that ladies' room?" Lawrence asks Vanessa.

"Oh, to have been a fly on the wall," she intones dramatically.

He says, "Ew, you want to be a fly in a bathroom?"

Alex touches Isabella on the arm. "Please. Come outside with me. Let's just—"

Harry cuts him off. "She said she doesn't want to talk to you. Leave her alone."

Alex wheels around angrily. "This isn't any of your business, Cartwright."

"I promised Isabella's father I'd look out for her while we were here," Harry says calmly. "So, yeah, it is."

"You did not!" Isabella says to him indignantly.

"I so did. When you were upstairs with your mother. He was all, 'She's my little girl, you know,' and I was all, 'Don't worry, sir, I'll take care of her,' and he was all, 'Good man, here's my cell phone number.'" Harry raises his right hand. "Swear to God."

"Oh. Well, you should have told him I don't need looking after or any of his sexist crap—I can take care of myself."

"I know," Harry says. "But you can't blame us both for caring. And for someone who can take care of herself, you make an awful lot of needy calls at two in the morning."

"Is that a problem for you?" she asks.

He pats her head. "Never."

Alex sinks into the chair next to Isabella. "I don't understand any of this." His blue eyes look sad.

And vaguely frog-like. They bulge maybe a little more than eyes should bulge.

Wait, what made me think that? I've always loved Alex's beautiful blue eyes.

It's Harry's fault. He put that thought into my head.

Harry. I glance over at him. Why is Marie always basically right on top of him? It's disgusting. I have a sudden urge to leap across the table, grab Marie by her honey-colored hair, and drag her face off Harry's chest. And then maybe smash it into the edge of the table. Gently. Gently smash her face into the wood. Over and over again. At least it would wipe that smug little smile off her face.

No one says anything for a while.

Lawrence breaks the silence. "It's getting close to curfew, guys."

"Yes, as much fun as this is," Vanessa says, "we should probably get the check and head out."

I jump up. "I'll get the waitress." I'm grateful to have a reason to get away from the booth. I find the waitress, and she promises to bring the check right away; then I stop by the bar to tell Manny and Julia the rest of us are going to leave as soon as we've paid.

"Is everything okay?" Manny asks me, nodding toward our booth, where people look somber. He's a pleasant-looking guy: not exactly hot, but appealing, with sandy hair, light gray eyes, and an impressively adoring gaze whenever he looks at Julia—which is probably all he needed to make their relationship work. "Did we miss something?"

"Yeah, about that . . ." I tell Julia she might want to talk to her brother, that he's just been publicly dumped.

"Oh, poor Alex," she says. "Why would she do it in front of everyone? That's so mean."

Neither Manny nor I try to answer that question.

We reach the table at the same time as the waitress. Vanessa grabs the check and starts telling people what they owe. "Good thing I rule at math," she says. "Want to know what I got on my math SAT?"

"No," we all say at the same time.

"Seven eighty," she says anyway.

I pull some bills out of my wallet and look up to find Alex is watching me. He smiles tentatively. I smile back, then return to counting money.

We all wander outside. Harry wraps one arm around Isabella and lazily lodges the other across Marie's shoulders. "See you," he tosses back at the rest of us, and saunters off with them.

We watch them go. After a moment Vanessa says, "Weird night, huh?" and Lawrence leans over to me and whispers, "Aren't you glad we made you come with us?"

I roll my eyes. "Remind me to say I'm busy the next time you ask."

"Aw, come on. Would you really have wanted to miss all that?"

"No, you're right. That was the most excitement I've had since coming here."

We hug good night, and they follow the others back toward campus.

Julia puts her arm through her brother's. "Come on," she says. "Manny and I will take care of you. You coming, Franny?"

I shake my head. "I'm going back to my aunt's— other direction."

They say good-bye and I'm left alone, watching them all go back to the dorm together.

In separate groups, admittedly. The old gang isn't what it used to be.

I turn and head back to Amelia's. The most separate of all.

I've gone about a block when I hear footsteps. It's dark out and it's late and the street is quiet, so I whip my head around pretty quickly. Then I stop and wait for him to catch up.

"Hey," Alex says, as he joins me.

"Hey."

"I didn't think you should walk back by yourself."

"It's not far."

"Still."

"Thanks." *It's Alex,* I think. *Alex. And he's not with Isabella anymore. You've been waiting all summer for this.*

He stands there, tall . . . handsome . . . available. "I feel like I owe you an apology, Franny. I put you in a weird place with Isabella. I didn't mean for that to happen."

"It's fine," I say. "No worries. We had a good talk."

"Really?" He seems a little unnerved by that, but he recovers. "Good. I'm glad." There's a pause. Then he says, "It's over between her and me."

"Yeah. I kind of got that impression."

"Not just because of what she said—it would have been over anyway. I was trying to figure out a way to make that clear to her. That's why I was so out of it tonight."

I don't say anything. I want to believe him. I'm just not sure I do.

He says, "All summer long, I've been thinking about you. A lot." He reaches out for my hand. I let him take it. "I know it took me too long to say something. I didn't want to hurt Isabella. Or you. Or Harry. It's all been so complicated. . . ."

That, I believe. Alex is a nice guy. He wouldn't have wanted to hurt anyone.

It's also possible he wanted to hedge his bets.

I'm not the one playing two girls against each other.

Harry said that last night. I wish he hadn't, because now I can't forget it.

Because it's true.

"Something changed between us last night," Alex says. "You and I both know that. I was just waiting for the right time to say something." I look at our hands, Alex's and mine. His is pulling me closer, winding me in toward him. "You got into my head," he whispers. "I don't know how, but you did. And I couldn't get you out. Even when I tried to, for both our sakes."

I raise my head to say something, but I don't get a chance to. His lips are instantly on mine.

I close my eyes and stretch up into the kiss, summoning the thrill I felt the night before. Trying to summon it, anyway.

Now that we're not rushing, I have time to pay attention, and I have to admit: he's not as good a kisser as Harry.

But that's probably to his credit. A good kisser is sometimes just someone who's practiced a lot more.

God knows how many lips Harry has practiced on.

On the other hand . . . it's nice to be kissed well.

Not that Alex is awful. His lips are firm and warm and he's not trying to eat my tonsils or anything gross like that. It's just that Harry had this way of sending shivers through my body with the slightest flick of his tongue. . . .

A kiss is just a kiss.

I choose you, Pikachu.

I'm not the one playing two girls against each other.

Focus, Franny. You're being kissed. Focus.

The kiss ends. We pull apart and look at each other.

"That was nice," Alex says.

I nod and touch his forearm. Run my fingers lightly down to the wrist, curious. I've wanted to touch him like this for so long I'm amazed I can do it now. I imagine my eighth-grade self watching this, thrilled beyond belief. I wish she were really here. I wish this were happening back when we were both eighth graders and Alex Braverman was the epitome of hot wonderfulness to me.

He understandably takes my caress as an invitation for more contact and leans forward eagerly for another kiss.

I put up my hands, holding him off.

"One week ago," I murmur, a little dazed. "Even just one *day* ago—"

"What?"

"Ever since we got here, all I've wanted was for you to be with me like this," I say. "For us to be alone together."

"Me too," he says softly.

"But now it's too late."

He shakes his head. "No, it's not—we still have a couple of weeks left here. And we live near each other—that's the best part."

"Too late for me, I mean."

He looks surprised. Really surprised. He must have assumed I'd just be there, waiting, available to him whenever he wanted me, if he ever did.

Actually, I'd assumed that too, until today. Which doesn't make me very proud of myself.

"I know I took longer than I should have to let you know how I was feeling," he says. "But I'll make it up to you, I promise."

"It's not that. It's . . ." What is it?

Well, it's him, for one thing. It's the fact that he kept making me think he liked me while he was going out with Isabella, which wasn't fair to either of us. A guy does that kind of thing to you, or even to a friend, and he stops being worth waiting for, no matter how many books he buys you or how warm his smiles are.

But it's not just that, either. I might have thought, *Yeah, he screwed up, but he's still cute and available and we could have fun for a while.* But I'm not thinking anything like that at all.

Because of Harry.

Because of stupid Harry Cartwright. Who horses around like a giddy two-year-old, who flirts with anything that moves, and who's walking back to the dorm right now with his arms slung around two girls who aren't me. Harry, who said to me, "You decided what kind of person I was without even giving me a chance," and who would have stayed by my side if I hadn't pushed him away, if I hadn't said mean, hurtful, unfair things to him because I thought what I wanted was exactly what I'm realizing I don't want at all.

"Sometimes the timing is just off," I say to Alex, a little impatiently. I'm in a hurry for him to go now, and he's just not getting it. I have stuff to do.

"Franny . . ."

"It's okay." I force a smile. He's a nice guy. I don't want to hurt him. I just want to get rid of him. "We're friends, right?"

I think it's the fake smile that finally gets the message across. He bows his head briefly and gives up.

Once we've given each other awkward pecks on the cheek and said good night, he leaves, his shoulders slumping in defeat.

He's had a rough night. Rejection from not one but

two girls. It's all his own fault, but I still feel kind of sorry for him.

I head to campus too, but I take a different route to get there. The last thing I want to do is bump into him again.

I move as fast as I can in heels. My feet are killing me—those shoes weren't meant for this much walking—but I'll survive. My phone buzzes and I grab it, hoping—

But it's just Amelia. *Estimated time of return?*

Wow. She's just asking, not *telling* me what time I have to be back by. Vanessa and Lawrence really did a job on her. I text back, *Don't wait up. I'll be quiet.*

The unexpected freedom from a curfew buoys me up. I'll have time to find Harry and explain. I'm near the dorm when I see Alex approaching it from the other direction. I duck into the shadows until he's safely inside. Through the windows, I can see him heading up the stairs.

Once he disappears completely, I try the front door, but it's locked, of course. And I don't have a key.

"Can't get in?" says a voice behind me.

I turn around and almost groan out loud at my bad luck—it's Marie.

On the plus side, she's not with Harry.

She's holding a Styrofoam takeout cup. Must have needed a warm drink before bed.

Blood, perhaps?

She sidles by with an "*excuse* me," then looks back over her shoulder and says, "Oh, did you want to come in? It's kind of too late, though. We have a curfew." She knows I know that.

"I just needed to ask Vanessa something," I say.

"I'll tell her to come out."

"No, that's okay. I'll text her."

She stares at me. "Why didn't you do that in the first place?"

"I felt like taking a walk."

"Huh." The sound lets me know she doesn't believe me. To be fair, there's no reason why she should, since I'm lying. "Whatever." She pulls the door shut after her.

I take out my phone: I'll have to try sending Harry a text. I'm trying to figure out what I can say after *I'm sorry*, when I hear voices and look up to see Harry and Isabella strolling toward the dorm.

I should have known they'd run out for a smoke alone together before bedtime. Especially after all that's happened tonight: they'd want to rehash it, talk it all out, share their thoughts and feelings. He probably told her she's wonderful and beautiful and kind and deserves someone much better than Alex. She probably told him he deserves someone much better than Marie.

Someone much better than me.

Isabella notices me first. "Franny? What are you doing here?"

"Hi." I wave awkwardly at her. "Can I talk to you for a sec?" I ask Harry.

He hesitates and glances toward Isabella like he's asking her for permission. She studies me thoughtfully for a moment. I give her a pleading look. I know we've never been close friends, but I'm pretty sure we're not enemies anymore.

"I think I hear my mother calling," she says with a shrug, and runs up the steps and disappears inside the door.

Harry settles back against the railing, his hands in his pockets. "What's up?"

I take a deep breath. "I'm an idiot."

There's a pause. "I'm sorry," he says after a moment. "Are you waiting for me to argue?"

"More just hoping you'll forgive me."

"You're an optimist."

"*Hoping,*" I repeat. I'm afraid to look him in the eyes. Talking to Harry was always the easiest thing in the world. Until now.

He shifts, resting the other hip against the railing. "And I should do that because . . . ?"

"Because I want to be with you."

His eyes flicker over me, distant and critical. "And what brought about this change in attitude?"

So he's not going to make it easy on me. I can't exactly blame him. But I wish he'd just open his arms to me. It's the thought of eventually crawling into them that's keeping me going right now. "I hate seeing you with Marie. I don't want to hate it, but I do."

"Oh, that's too bad," he says. "Except for the part where I'm kind of delighted about it."

"You don't really like her," I say. "I know you don't."

"Well, as you'd be the first to point out, it doesn't matter to me. I grab at whoever's near. *Whatever's* near. I'm not picky. Girls, boys, dogs, cats . . ."

"I never said that."

"Didn't you?" He gestures up toward the door. "It's getting late. We done here, Franny?"

I fight rising tears, rising panic. "Did you not even hear me apologize? I said some stupid things. I'm sorry. I was wrong."

"But you believed that stuff you said. Even after all the time we'd spent together. God, Franny—" He cuts himself off. Then he says slowly, "There's the way people look on the outside and the way they really are, and with me you never even saw the difference."

"I do now."

"I meant everything I ever said to you, but you were too busy buying into Alex's good-guy act to realize it." The door suddenly opens right behind him, and we both jump. One of the resident advisors sticks his head out. "Sorry to interrupt," he says, "but it's that time, guys. Got to get up to your rooms."

"Okay." Harry stands up straight. "Thanks for coming by, Franny."

"Please," I say, not even caring that the graduate student is still there. "Please, Harry. I made a mistake. I know I made a mistake. Can't you just—"

"Good night," he says.

He doesn't even look back, just raises a lazy hand in good-bye as he walks through the door.

scene five

So it's back to Aunt Amelia's I go. Alone. The route feels a little creepy now that it's past eleven, and I'm lonely and depressed, so I punch William's number into my phone, and when he answers I say, "Keep me company. I'm all alone on the street."

"Jesus, Franny," he says. "That's not safe at this hour." It occurs to me it's three hours later in New York and I've probably woken him up, but he doesn't complain about that.

"I know. That's why I called you."

"Yeah, and there's so much I can do to help you from a couple thousand miles away." He heaves an exasperated sigh. "Stay on the line with me until you get somewhere safe."

"Okay," I say.

"Couldn't you have found some nice young man to walk you home?" I don't answer, and after a moment he says, "What's that sound? Are you *crying*?"

"Maybe a little."

"Why?"

It's William and he's on my side, so I don't see any reason not to tell him the truth. "You know how I told you that I was going out with Harry but I liked Alex more? Well, I was wrong. Harry's better than Alex, but I said some stupid mean things to him before I realized it, and now he won't even talk to me."

I stop talking because William is cracking up on the other end of the line.

"That's not nice," I say. "I'm crying and you're laughing."

"I'm sorry. It's just not the world's greatest tragedy."

"Shut up. It matters to me."

"I know it does," he says. "I'm sorry. And here's what I think, Franny, for what it's worth. You're my sister and admittedly I'm biased, but I'm guessing the guy you like is just pissed off at you right now and will get over it if you give him a chance. Because you're pretty great, and deep down he's got to know that. So tell him you're sorry and—"

"I already *did*. And he stayed mad."

"He probably just wants to make you suffer a little longer. Try again."

"And if he rejects me again?"

"You'll become a better person for it?" he suggests.

"What doesn't kill us makes us stronger, yada yada yada?"

"All right, fine." I stop and think for a moment. I'm not even halfway home yet. I'm just as close to campus as I am to Amelia's. William is right. I gave up too easily. "Stay on the phone with me a little while longer," I say. "I'm going back in."

I make it to campus safely. The most sinister thing I see is an empty beer bottle someone's left under a bush. I stop to pick it up, then continue on my way.

Once I'm in the theater courtyard, I say good-bye to William, who tells me sternly that I'm not allowed to walk back alone now that it's after eleven, but we both know there's no way for him to actually stop me.

I stay in the shadows around the side of the dorm building so none of the RAs will see me out there, and then I text Harry.

I'm right out front. Please come out. Please. I won't bother you again if you'll just come out now.

His response comes quickly. *It's past curfew.*

Do you really care about that?

He doesn't answer. I wait for a while and nothing happens. It's probably not as long as it feels—but it feels like a *really* long time.

I'm losing hope and about to send another text—but what can I say to make him come if he doesn't want to?—when the door to the dorm opens.

Harry slips out, carefully closing it behind him so it doesn't make a sound. He glances around and I come forward, into view. He shoots me an exasperated look, but he comes all the way down the steps and follows me around to the side of the building, out of view of the front door.

He's changed into sweatpants and a faded red T-shirt. His bare feet are shoved into flip-flops. The back of his hair is messed up, so he was probably lying in bed reading or something when I texted him.

I just want to stare at him for a while.

He came.

He didn't have to. And he did.

But he's still not yielding. "What?" he says, crossing his arms tightly across his chest. "What do you need to say now that you couldn't say before? If I get thrown out of here because of you—"

"I'll tell them it's my fault. That it was an emergency."

"Why are you walking around with that?" he asks, pointing, and I have to look down to remember I'm holding an empty beer bottle.

"I found it on the street."

"Why didn't you throw it out?"

"I needed it," I say, and hurl the bottle down at the cement walkway, where it shatters into a million pieces. I still have my pitcher's arm, I guess.

Harry jumps. "Jesus, Franny! They'll hear that! What are you trying to do?"

"I want to start over," I say, and step toward the smashed bottle. "So I'm going back to the beginning. I'll walk on broken glass and cut my foot and then you can carry me again and we'll start over."

"That's the dumbest thing I've ever heard in my life," he says. "And I should also point out that you're wearing shoes, so you won't actually cut yourself."

"I'll take them off." I raise my right foot behind me, which leaves me perching precariously on one very narrow high heel. I reach down to undo the shoe strap and wobble, losing my balance.

Harry grabs my arm. "Careful! You're going to fall right into the pile of broken glass, you idiot."

I grip his shoulder and raise my head. "I *am* an idiot. That's what I was trying to tell you earlier, but you wouldn't listen. I'm an idiot and I know it."

"I was listening." He hauls me away from the glass and safely onto the grass at the side of the building. "People like you need to stay far away from sharp objects."

"People like you need to rescue people like me."

"It's a full-time job."

"And it doesn't pay very well."

He's still holding on to my arm. He doesn't seem in any rush to let go. He studies my face for a moment, then nods toward the walkway. "You'd really walk

274

barefoot through broken glass for me?"

"I'd *crawl* through broken glass for you."

He shakes his head. "Overkill, Pearson. Now you're getting all hyperbolic." He sounds like himself again. Finally. Like Harry. Like *my* Harry.

I pull his arm tightly around my waist and pin it there. "No," I say. "It's true—I would. If I thought it would work to get you to give me another chance."

"So what?" His voice sounds a little raw, but he's not pulling his arm away. "So now I'm just supposed to be okay with everything? Crush you to my bosom? Say 'all is forgiven, my child'?"

"Yeah, pretty much. Except for the 'my child' part. That's creepy." I butt my forehead against his chest, like a calf. "Harry," I say.

He takes his arm away from my waist, but only to grab my shoulders in both his hands. He shakes me gently, his fingers pressing into the flesh there. "Broken glass all over the cement. You're such a moron."

"I know."

And then he kisses me. It starts out sort of angry, but it ends somewhere else entirely.

Some time goes by. Maybe a lot of time. I don't want to move from that spot, and unless I'm totally misreading the situation—and I'm not—Harry is pretty happy where he is too.

His touch still gives me goose bumps. And his kisses still send tiny little earthquake shock waves through my head and body that leave me vibrating. It's even better now than before, and not just because there's the whole *I thought I'd lost you I'm so glad I didn't* making-up thing, which, believe me, is nice enough in its own right, but also because I was holding back before, not completely believing in the idea of *us*. I thought Harry was some kind of second-place runner-up, someone to distract me while I hoped and waited for Alex to see the light.

Our theme for tonight: Franny is an idiot.

Our moral: the guy who sends smoldering glances your way may turn out to be kind of lame, and the guy who seems like a shallow pretty boy may actually be kind of wonderful.

Also: silky tank tops are an excellent outfit choice if you're planning to make out standing up.

Also: I think I'm in love with Harry Cartwright.

I know—that's not actually a moral.

I just wanted to sneak it in there.

I have no idea what time it is when we stop kissing. Harry walks me back to the apartment, saying that if I could walk through broken glass for him, he can risk a warning slip for me.

It takes me forever to fall asleep.

At some point I do, though, because in the morning I wake up smiling.

Aunt Amelia wants to know how my Very Important and Special Event went. "Best night of my life," I say sincerely.

"You got in awfully late."

"I told you I might."

She can't argue with that.

I walk into the dining hall at breakfast time and look around. There's only one person I want to sit with, and he's already at a table with Isabella and Julia and Manny. Just as I cross to them, Marie sits down next to him and smiles, putting her hand on his arm. His eyes meet mine—he saw me come in—and he kind of looks at me like he's asking a question.

I shake my head. I don't care. He wasn't reaching for her; she was reaching for him. And that's how it's always been, really, except that one time, two nights ago, when I hurt him so badly I can't bear to think of it now, and he wanted to hurt me back.

I get a cup of coffee and a muffin and stroll back to the table. I take the empty seat next to Isabella, who smiles at me more warmly than she ever has before.

So she and Harry must have already talked about us. I'm glad she doesn't hate me. She seems to love Harry almost as much as I love my brother, and I'd hate any girl who hurt William. But maybe Isabella is more forgiving than I am. Or maybe Harry told her to give me a break.

He greets me now with "Looking a little tired there, Pearson. You stay up late last night?"

"You're not looking so fresh yourself, Cartwright."

"That's not what my mirror tells me."

"Yeah? What does it say?"

"That I'm one fine-looking young man."

"God, you're conceited," Marie says, pushing at his arm with a little laugh. But both the gesture and the laugh feel a little desperate. Like she knows something's going on. She turns to me. "I'm really worried about my costume, Franny. The dress is like slipping off my shoulders, and I don't want to be constantly grabbing at it onstage. Can you please tell your aunt she has to fix it?"

"She and I don't have that kind of relationship," I say.

"She's your *aunt*."

"But she's *your* costume designer. I think you'd better give her your alteration notes yourself."

"Thanks for nothing."

"You're welcome!" I say cheerfully.

She looks around to see if anyone's going to back her up. Julia changes the subject, asking which casts are rehearsing in the theater today.

"I think we are," Isabella says. Her eyes fall on Alex, who's sitting at another table with Vanessa and Lawrence and some others. "It should be interesting."

"You mean because you and Alex have to play

opposite each other?" Julia says bluntly. "That happened to me once when I was a sophomore. I was going out with this guy, and then we broke up right before we had to do this huge love scene. It was the most awkward thing in the world."

"We'll be fine," Isabella says. "It's called acting, right?"

"I'm getting a muffin," Marie says, standing up. "Don't let me eat the whole thing, okay?" she tells Harry. "One bite, that's it." She heads off toward the buffet.

Isabella turns to him. "You need to talk to her," she says. "Right now. Or else you're just being mean."

"Who died and made you Jiminy Cricket?"

"Harry . . ."

"I know, I know. Fine." He gets up and goes after Marie.

"Talk to her about what?" Julia asks Isabella.

"Harry and Franny got back together last night," Isabella says with a nod in my direction. "She can fill you in on any details." She stands up with her tray. "I'm going to go over my lines. I'll see you guys later." She leaves.

"Really?" Julia says to me.

I nod sheepishly. Given the last conversation I had with her, when I was insisting I didn't care at all about Harry . . . let's just say this isn't my proudest moment. On the other hand, Harry's got it a lot worse right now.

He's taken Marie off into a corner and they're talking. He looks apologetic. She looks furious.

Julia flings up her hands. "I can't keep up with any of this. Everyone keeps changing partners. Except us. We're the only stable couple." You'd think they'd been going out two years instead of two weeks. She rises to her feet. "Come on, Manny. Let's go somewhere where you can draw me a diagram so I can figure out who's going out with who, because it's all getting way too confusing." She pats my shoulder. "You'll probably regret this, Franny."

"I don't think so."

"It's your life." She and Manny stroll away, leaving me alone at the table.

I sip some coffee and watch Harry and Marie. He holds his hand out—*friends?* She stares at it a moment, swats it away, then turns on her heel and strides rapidly across the floor and out of the dining hall.

Harry comes back to our table. "She changed her mind about the muffin," he says blandly as he sits down.

"Yeah, I saw." We sit in silence a moment. Then I say, "Just out of curiosity—you didn't actually *like* her, did you?"

"Not in any meaningful way."

"So were you just using her to make me jealous?"

"Of course not. That would be wrong." He taps his fingers on the table thoughtfully, then says more seriously, "I don't know . . . I wasn't thinking that was what I was doing—it wasn't deliberate or anything—but

I can't really explain it any other way. She got on my nerves, and I paid her a lot more attention when you were around to see and tried to avoid her whenever you weren't. . . ."

"Yeah, that would be using her to make me jealous."

"Is that bad?"

"Totally morally reprehensible. On the other hand . . . it worked." I shift a little closer to him. "And I'm glad you don't really like her."

"Stay jealous," he says. "I like you that way."

"It's all fun and games until I start boiling bunnies."

"Back where I comes from, we calls that ste-ew," he says.

"Nice accent," I say. "You might want to reconsider the acting career."

"There you go, shooting me down again." He waits a beat. "You know what that means."

"Time for me to build you back up?"

"Past time, I'd say."

"What did you have in mind?"

He considers. "The practice rooms should be empty. We could sneak into one and make out until you have to go to work."

"What kind of girl do you think I am?"

He leans forward and puts the back of his hand against the back of mine. Just kind of presses it there. And he says, "*My* girl?"

"Yeah," I say. "Let's go."

scene six

It's a good thing we grab the chance to be alone that morning, because free time becomes scarce that week. At rehearsal, we're running through the play in its entirety, starting over again as soon as we've finished with the last scene and Charles has given us notes, breaking off only to go to meals or to bed. Time is running out, and Charles's temper is running short. He wants it to be good, and we're all still occasionally flubbing our lines or forgetting the blocking.

I dash back to the workroom during the scenes I'm not in, and, depending on how much time I have until I'm needed again, I either work there until my next scene or bring some hand sewing back to rehearsal.

I have to give Amelia credit: she's working like a madwoman, trying to get all the costumes for all the shows ready by the time performances start in five days, and her output is really impressive. It feels like every time I return to the Sweatshop there's another rack of finished costumes that are neatly labeled and ready for the upcoming dress rehearsals.

So the days are crazy for all of us, but the nights . . . the nights are pretty sweet. When we're done with rehearsal (which gets later with each passing day), Harry and I often walk into town and grab a late-night bite to eat or a cup of tea. Isabella joins us most of the time, and so do Vanessa and Lawrence.

We don't hang out in the common room anymore. Things have gotten too awkward with both Marie and Alex.

For obvious reasons Julia and Manny continue to spend time with Alex, so I don't see them at meals as much, but I see them plenty at rehearsals. They really do seem to be genuinely kind of devoted to each other, which is sweet, and I'm happy for them both, but poor Vanessa isn't so lucky: she has a fling with a fellow cast member that doesn't last long. "He has the worst bad breath," she tells me afterward. "Like something's rotting from the inside."

"That's so poetic."

"Nothing poetic about that smell."

Once the few remaining straight guys know that Isabella is free, she always has someone trailing hopefully after her. Even so, when she's in the Sweatshop trying on her nun's habit for *Measure for Measure*, she looks in the mirror and says grimly, "Suits me. Never knew I was a method actor, but I seem to be living the part."

I get why she's alone: most of the guys there are from small towns and seem way too young for her. She's cursed by her own sophistication.

Lawrence pursues a couple of interesting possibilities but eventually drops them, disappointed. "The good news," he tells me at lunch one day, "is that there are more gay guys in any single room here than in my entire high school. The bad news is that there's still no one I'm all that interested in. Or at least no one who's equally interested in me. I've decided to save myself for Harry. Any signs he might be turning?"

"I'm doing my best for you," I say. "If *I* can't turn a guy off girls, who can?"

"Her," he says, and points to Marie.

Marie.

After Harry broke up with her at breakfast (as gently and apologetically as he could, he swore), she went straight to Charles and told him that she couldn't continue to act opposite Harry because he had made sexually inappropriate advances toward her, and she just wasn't comfortable being in romantic scenes with him anymore.

It was a mistake to use the same unfounded complaint she'd used before, especially since the program had now been running for a few weeks, and Charles had pretty much figured her out. He'd also seen her basically throwing herself on top of Harry just the day before. He told her that he would take her concerns under consideration, and later that day pulled Harry aside to get his side of the story, which Harry said was pretty much "she got pissed off when I picked Franny over her." "That does sum it up nicely," I agreed.

Charles and the other graduate-student directors had a meeting with the head of the program to figure out what to do. They came back to Marie as a group and told her that they had some concerns about the truthfulness of these serious accusations. And they said they all agreed that the safest course of action for all concerned (especially her, since she seemed to be in constant danger of attracting unwanted advances) was to keep some distance between Marie and the other actors. So they were removing her from the cast and giving her a job helping out backstage.

Julia and Vanessa told us later that Marie went ballistic when she heard this, threw a fit, said her parents would sue the entire program, accused all the directors of being sexist and misogynistic (even the females), and said she would go home if they didn't give her her role back. She recounted all this to her roommates that night, alternating between self-pitying sobs and spitting fury.

"Why is everyone out to get me?" she kept wailing.

But when all the dust cleared, she reluctantly agreed to work backstage, and they replaced her as the lead of *Twelfth Night*.

Guess who they got to replace her?

Here's a clue: it's someone who's spent her time at Mansfield quietly working harder than anyone else, someone who hasn't sought any kind of public attention for any of her efforts, but has just done what she's been asked to do, and done it well.

Did you guess?

Madeline Bigelow took over the role of Viola.

Yeah, I didn't really know who she was either.

She'd originally played a bunch of small roles—servants, mostly—and while she had appeared in a lot of scenes, she wasn't a big presence in any of them. Even though we were in the cast together, we'd never really talked, just nodded hello to each other now and then.

Julia was originally upset that she had been passed over—yet again—for a major role, but she calmed down when Charles gave her Madeline's biggest former role. I got an additional role too, as a serving woman, which I didn't have the guts to tell Amelia about, since it would cut down on my sewing time even more.

I figured I'd just sew faster.

Which is what I've been doing: when I'm not actually

onstage, I'm hemming skirts like crazy. I tell Amelia that it's silly for me to keep running back and forth to her workroom so often, that I should just take a bag of work with me when I go to rehearsal and not come back until it's all done.

I sew every second I can, even when I'm at meals. Harry says it's risky trying to put his arms around me, that he gets poked by a needle every time he tries. It's not true. His embraces tend to land very successfully.

Julia goes very quickly from being annoyed she didn't get the lead to freaking out about how many lines she has to memorize in a few days. She's making anyone who has a free second run lines with her.

"I'll never be ready in time," she keeps moaning. And she's not the only one. Everyone's getting more and more anxious and intense as we get closer to performance week.

Except Harry. He's pretty calm. He says he never gets worked up about a performance. "What's the worst that can happen?" he says to me. "I forget a line? I fall off the stage? How bad could that be, really? I've survived being ridiculed and cast out by the woman I love—every other tragedy pales in comparison."

"I never ridiculed you."

"Who said I was talking about you?" He grins wickedly and then kisses me until it's clear that was a joke.

Sometimes at the dining hall I see him walking across the room and I feel sure this guy can't possibly be my boyfriend. He's too good-looking. He's too charming. He's too much the kind of guy a girl like me doesn't get and should probably stay away from. Eyes follow him wherever he goes.

And where he goes is next to me.

Mansfield Mayhem turns out to be the annual party for the actors and directors, to celebrate the end of rehearsals and the beginning of performances. Harry comes by the costume room to pick me up, since I'm trying to squeeze in as much work as I can—there are still some costumes to be altered before the shows tomorrow, and I feel bad leaving Amelia alone working on them.

"I don't know how I'm going to get all this done," she says as we head out.

"I'll come back after the party," I promise.

"It ends at midnight," Harry tells me as we leave the Sweatshop.

"Oh. Well, I'll leave early."

He takes my hand and tucks it under his arm. "You will not. I missed out on dancing with you last time. I'm not going to waste this chance."

"But the costumes—"

"If a few tunics aren't perfectly hemmed, we'll all survive."

"You're a bad influence," I say.

"If you think so now, just wait until I get you alone later tonight."

There's a dinner buffet and a DJ and loud music and dancing. It's like a cheesy bar mitzvah party, but one where you're surrounded only by people you like. Almost everyone is a good dancer—one of the advantages of being in a group of actors—and we've all been working so hard for the last couple of weeks that we're ready to be silly and wild.

Which we are.

Between the loud music and my exhaustion, a lot of the night is a blur, but I can definitely remember dancing every fast dance in a big group of friends and every slow dance curled up against Harry, his arms warm around me, the two of us the only people in the world. I also remember sharing a slice of chocolate cake with Lawrence, our forks clinking against each other as we fought, laughing, for the last bite. And I remember cans of Silly String appearing and everyone spraying everyone and then a long period of time when we were all plucking it out of one another's hair. And I remember a long slow walk back to Amelia's apartment with Harry, our arms so tightly entwined around each other's waists that we could barely walk.

Amelia is still awake when I come in, her home sewing machine gently humming on the kitchen table, unhemmed skirts in a pile on one side of her, hemmed skirts on the other.

She greets me with: "A dozen more to go."

"I'll help as soon as I get changed."

"Go to bed," she says. "You have to perform tomorrow."

"It's okay," I say. "I want to help."

"And I want you to be rested for tomorrow," she says.

"But—"

She swivels around so she can look at me. "I have no desire to spend your performance worrying about whether you're going to be too tired to remember your lines. After all I've put up with to have you be in the show in the first place, I'm not going to risk your success in it for a couple of skirt hems. Now go to bed."

"All right," I say meekly.

When I wake up the next morning, she's already back at work at the sewing machine. Or at least I hope so—I hope she isn't *still* at work.

I brew a cup of some vile herbal tea and bring it over to her, then pull up a chair and work on some last bits of hand sewing for the *Twelfth Night* costumes—we've been wearing the costumes for the last week, but there's some trim that we haven't had time to attach yet.

Amelia found an old-fashioned sailor suit from a production of *HMS Pinafore* for me to wear as Antonia:

it was too big, but since I have to look like I've been shipwrecked in it and the costume was already old and worn, she just shredded the bottoms of both parts and pinned the shirt unevenly and it works. When I play Olivia's maid, my other character, I change into a 1920s-era uniform.

We finish up the final alterations and wrangle the clothing into garment bags, then head over to the theater. Amelia drives us in her car: we don't have time to walk.

I join the other girls, who are putting on makeup in the ladies' dressing room. Julia comes over to me. "Can you help?" she asks in a trembling voice, handing me her eyeliner. "My hands are shaking too much."

"You're going to be great," I say.

"So long as I don't throw up onstage."

Amelia flits around backstage while we change into our costumes, pinning falling hems, tying bows, adjusting hats. . . . She's sharp-tongued and impatient, but she's also everywhere at once, fixing problems faster than they can be discovered. You can tell she's done this before. A lot. And that she's very good at it.

From backstage I peek out at the audience. It's mostly the other students (they're all required to go to one another's shows), the graduate-student directors, the administrators, and staff members. There are a bunch of people I don't recognize out there too—probably family of the local cast members.

Charles gathers us all together ten minutes before showtime and tells us how proud he is of how hard we've worked, singling out Madeline's courage in jumping into a huge role at the last minute and giving a shout-out to me, Julia, and a couple of other cast members who, he says, also stepped up when we needed to. Then he tells us to take our places and we do, but on the way Harry grabs me and gives me a quick crushing hug. "Break a leg," he says.

"Break two," I say, and those are the last words we exchange out of character until after the show.

Julia doesn't throw up onstage and neither, I'm happy to say, does anyone else. I don't forget any of my lines, which is good, and I get a lot of laughs with both my indignation at Viola (whom Antonia mistakes for her friend Sebastian) and my discovery at the end that they're identical when dressed alike. By the time the curtain falls, I'm flying on the high of successful, crowd-pleasing acting.

Madeline and Harry are both amazing. I knew they were good at rehearsals, but the extra adrenaline rush of performing in front of an audience brings them to a whole new level.

I wouldn't have said Madeline was beautiful or dynamic in person—I might even have said the opposite—but she's completely in command on the stage today, arch and sincere by turns, tender when she's falling in love and funny when she's awkwardly fending off the romantic advances of Brianna's Olivia. She's much better in the role than Marie ever was.

But when Harry is onstage, he's all I see. He's so good, so strong and noble and lovable in the role—and so heart-shatteringly handsome in his tux—that afterward I feel shy, like I can't possibly have the right to approach him, let alone claim him as my boyfriend.

But as soon as we finish curtain calls, he turns and looks for me, and when we meet in the center of the stage, he searches my eyes anxiously—for all his swagger and apparent confidence, he's worried about how he did. I tell him he was incredible and that I adore him, and his whole body sags in relief.

Charles congratulates us all and then ushers us out toward the lobby, where the audience is waiting to see us. I stop Madeline to tell her she was great, and I look for Julia, but she's nowhere in sight. I ask Manny where she is and he says uncomfortably, "Um . . . she kind of had to run to the ladies' room."

At least she made it through the show.

Out in the lobby I'm talking to one of Harry's roommates when I spot Marie standing in a corner, silently watching the actors being mobbed by their friends. She looks so separate and alone, I feel sorry for her. I'm about to head over to talk to her—although I have no idea what I'll say and I doubt she's going to welcome me—when someone else calls her name and she turns. It's her boyfriend (former boyfriend? Ex-boyfriend? Once-and-future boyfriend? I have no idea): James Rushport. He's back. Or maybe she never broke up with him and he doesn't even know that she was desperately trying to hook up with someone else for a while.

He calls to her, and she moves into his arms and rests her head on his shoulders, hiding her face from everyone else. They walk to the door like that, and, as they go by, he spots me and says, "Hey! Franny, right?" I wave, and he calls out, "Your foot all better?" I give him a lame thumbs-up by way of a response, and he smiles and nods and they make their way, entwined, out the door.

I feel a tap on my arm and turn. Amelia is waiting there. She says, "You were very good, Franny."

"Thanks."

"I mean it. Very good."

I thank her again, and we stand together in awkward silence for a moment.

"Well," she says then, "I have a lot to do." And she turns to go. But then she stops and says, "I'm glad you did this." And then she walks away.

Once we've changed into our street clothes and hung up our costumes (but left on our stage makeup, because it's totally a badge of honor), a bunch of us go out to dinner together in town—big plates of pasta, we're all starving—and then head right back to the theater to watch the first performance of *A Midsummer Night's Dream*. I go backstage to help Amelia with all the last-minute costume tweaking, but then slip back out to join Harry in the audience for the show.

Vanessa and Lawrence both blow me away. He's a perfect Puck, graceful, small, mischievous, and sprite-like in his earth-colored tunic and leggings, and she *owns* the role of Titania, queen of the fairies. I know she wanted to be Bottom originally, but this is definitely the right role for her. There's always been something regal about Vanessa, and she taps into it for Titania. She wears her hair loose and unfettered, so it springs out in a wild mass of curls that almost look like they're alive. Amelia made a sky-blue robe for her embroidered with glittering silver thread in star patterns. It's really stunning.

My palms are red-hot and my voice is hoarse when I'm done cheering for them during the curtain calls, and afterward, when I see them in the lobby, the three of us throw our arms around each other and just stay like that for a while.

Then we all go out for ice cream.

Then I go back to the apartment and sleep the sleep of the dead.

I'm pretty tense when we go to see *Measure for Measure* the next afternoon. I can feel Harry watching me whenever Alex is onstage, and I try to keep my expression as neutral as possible. But Alex is really good as the duke, and he looks great in his period robes. His character falls in love with Isabella's about halfway through the (wildly shortened) play, and if they feel awkward about acting opposite each other, neither of them shows it.

It's a strange play, though: the duke is supposed to be the good character, the hero of the piece, and yet he does all these hateful things, like let poor Isabella think that her beloved brother is dead when he's actually still alive.

"*I* wouldn't marry him," I say to Harry when the curtain falls on former nun Isabella accepting the duke's hand in marriage.

He narrows his eyes. "Okay, but would you *date* him? Pine after him if he fell in love with someone else? Let him keep you dangling around, waiting for him to change his mind?"

"You sure we're talking about the duke here?" I ask.

"You're avoiding the question."

"There's only one 'the duke' for me," I say.

"You better mean that."

Backstage he instantly heads for Isabella. He puts his arms around her and she bursts into tears. "It's okay," she says to me between sobs. "I always do this after a performance."

"Yes, she does," Harry says fondly as he pats her

back and murmurs little soothing sounds.

"Too much emotion," she weeps.

"Too little perspective," he says fondly.

A couple of nights earlier, after he came back from a smoke-filled tête-à-tête with Isabella, I asked him if I should be jealous of how much they love each other.

He raised his eyebrows. "You once said I'd never be able to make you jealous."

"I thought we'd proven you already have. Anyway, I'm serious. You guys are so close—"

He shook his head. "Isabella is my sister, my mother, and my best friend all rolled up in one. But I'd rather gouge out my eyes than ever go out with her."

"I don't understand why. You love being with her—"

"Would *you* want to go out with your sister, mother, and best friend?"

"Maybe not all at *once* . . ."

"Well, there you go. Anyway, she's too much work for a girlfriend. She's too needy."

"*I'm* needy," I said, reaching for him.

"Only in the best ways," he said.

"They're mostly physical," I agreed, and we moved on from there.

Still, watching them all folded up together now, after the show, I feel a tiny stab of jealousy. They have so much history together. And their lives are entwined in a million different ways—school, theater, geography, social circles . . . Even their parents are friends.

But I reject my own jealousy. I actually *like* that Harry can care about a friend as much as he does about her. It's part of what I've come to value about him: he seems to skim along the surface of relationships, but now I know that once he commits to caring about someone, he cares deeply. And once you're one of the people he cares deeply about, you don't ever want to lose that.

I turn away, letting them have their moment, and look for other people to congratulate. And there's Alex. Julia's got her arms around his neck and she's telling him he was great.

I move closer to them, and when he sees me standing there, I smile and say, "You were great. I wish I'd brought a flower."

"Just steal one," he says, detaching himself from his sister. "Preferably from her." He holds out his arms and we hug awkwardly and briefly. "I wish I'd given you the whole bouquet back then," he says with a small smile. "Might have helped me out this summer."

"Poor old Alex," his sister says affectionately. "You kind of got burned. But don't worry. Pretty soon we'll be back at school, where all my friends are madly in love with you."

"Yeah," he says without much enthusiasm, and I see his glance flicker over to where Isabella and Harry are talking. So it's not just *me* he's feeling wistful about.

Of course, it was never just me he felt anything about this summer. And never just her, either, I guess. That was the problem.

Across the lobby, Isabella's roommates are descending on her, so Harry leaves her to them and comes over to join us. "Good job," he tells Alex with a brusque nod.

"Thanks."

Harry takes my hand and tucks it under his arm. It's a small gesture, but I have to hide my smile, because its message is so obvious.

She's mine.

He doesn't have to worry. I think I've made that pretty clear in every way a girl can make these things clear.

That night we lie together on one of the practice-room sofas. We've discovered that no one uses those rooms at night, and it's especially quiet right now since everyone else is either in the cast or the audience of *A Winter's Tale*. Harry and I are supposed to be there too, but we'll have another chance to see it, so we're playing hooky. We're starting to realize our time together is slipping away.

The sofa is pretty narrow, but we're comfortable, my head on his chest, my legs curled up on top of his. There are worse ways to spend an evening.

"Three more days," I say, a little sleepily, because I'm cozy and warm. "And then I don't get to see you again."

"Of course you will. We'll visit each other."

"Will we?"

He tugs my hair, making me raise my head so I'm looking at him. "Are you kidding me? Phoenix to L.A. is an easy flight."

"I know, but . . ." I hesitate.

"Then I'll come to you. I can drive there."

I push myself up into a sitting position. "Oh, sorry," I say, because I accidentally leaned on his stomach and he made an *oof* sound. I lean back into the cushions and regard him seriously. "We come from really different worlds, Harry. It doesn't matter so much here—a little bit but not so much—but you have no idea how awkward my real life is. My mom and I live in this pathetic little apartment—I'd be embarrassed to have you come visit there. And I don't know if I could deal with seeing your huge estate of a home and all your servants and your pool and your Porsche. . . ."

He sits up, swinging his feet down and onto the floor, and regards me somberly. "First of all, I don't really have a Porsche. Second of all, I never knew you were such a snob, Franny."

"A snob? Harry, it's the opposite. Your house would be way too nice. I'd be overwhelmed. And I'd feel like I was trying to fit in where I didn't belong."

"Total snob. Letting the difference in our families' wealth influence you." He crosses his arms. "If I were poorer than you, would you say all that stuff about how different our houses are and how you don't even want to come visit me because of it?"

"No, but it's not the same thing. I *wish* you were poorer. I would love that."

"Well, I'm sorry, but I can't arrange that." He gives a sarcastic shrug. "So maybe we should just break up."

"You know I don't mean that." I take his hand and crush it in mine. "I want to be with you all the time, Harry, but I want to be with you *here*, in this stupid little practice room, where it doesn't matter how different our lives and families are. Or at college. Or some other neutral place. I'm scared of letting you see the way we live and I'm even more scared of seeing the way *you* live."

He squeezes my hand back. "Don't you think I'm terrified about it too? We've been in a safe little bubble here, and it's always agonizing to expose your life to someone else, especially someone you care about. You don't have the monopoly on embarrassing family situations, you know. In fact, I bet I beat you." He runs the fingers of his other hand through his hair, making it stick up. "We may have money, but we're a pathetic bunch. There are things I haven't even told you because they're too humiliating. My dad hits on my female friends. Just ask Isabella. And my mom dresses like she's fourteen and is basically the poster child for plastic surgery gone wrong. It sucks, and if I could lock them away in a base-ment until I move out, I probably would." He presses his knee hard against mine. "But I can't, and I want you to come and visit anyway because I want you to be a part of my life, even with all its horrors. And I kind of assumed you felt the same way. But I guess maybe I was hoping for too much, because if you think I wouldn't be able to deal with the stuff that embarrasses *you*, then I guess that means you don't want to deal with the stuff that embarrasses *me*, and so maybe—"

I put my hand across his mouth. Sometimes it's the only way to shut Harry up. "Shhh. You're right. I'm sorry. Please stop talking."

He pulls my hand away. "You've hurt my feelings," he says with a mock sniff. "All that racist talk—"

"*Racist*? I'm pretty sure you're not using that word right."

"Wealthist, then." He curls up in a fetal position against the sofa arm. "Whatever. I'm all bitter and unhappy and worked up now, thanks to you."

I lean over him and pat his arm. "Poor baby."

"Poor baby is right. I think you'd better make it up to me."

"How can I do that?"

"Honestly, Franny, have you learned nothing from our time together?" He stretches back out on the sofa and looks at me from under heavy-lidded eyes.

I figure out a way to make it up to him. One that works out nicely for both of us.

Each cast performs one more time over the next two days. Our second performance is strong for the first half but gets a little messy toward the end, as it hits us that this is it—we won't get to do this ever again.

There's a big going-away party on the last night, but first the casts meet in separate rooms so the directors can make speeches about each of the actors. I'm worried I'll be late, because Amelia and I have to organize all the costumes, separating out the ones that will go to the cleaners and pressing, labeling, and hanging the rest, but I make it just in time.

Charles makes a funny speech about how worried he was when he first met his cast, how he was convinced he could never pull Shakespeare off in five weeks with such a motley crew, but he did, and we did, and it was amazing . . . and then his speech turns sentimental, so that by the end we've all stopped laughing and are in tears. "I'm proud of each and every one of you," he says, and holds out his arms, and we all jump to our feet and come together in a giant soppy group hug. Madeline reaches out for Marie, who's standing back a little bit, and pulls her in close with the rest of us, and I'm glad she does.

For dinner we head to the dining hall, where we

join up with the other casts and the administrators and staff of the program, including Amelia, who's changed into a long black dress and pulled her hair up on the top of her head in a severe topknot. She's sitting at the center table with the program director. I've seen him make some speeches before, but this is the first time I've seen him up close, and I remember that he's Alex and Julia's uncle. He's pudgy and bald, and at first I think he doesn't look anything like them, but when I come over to their table to say hi to Amelia, I see that his eyes are the same light blue as theirs.

Once we're all seated, he stands up and makes a speech about how this was the most talented group of summer students they've ever had at Mansfield.

I'm guessing he makes that speech every year.

He congratulates and thanks all the people who worked hard to make the summer go smoothly, and we clap after each name. When he singles out Amelia for her hard work and terrific costumes, I jump to my feet, cheering, and all my friends follow suit, so Amelia gets the biggest round of applause of anyone there. She bobs her head awkwardly, flushes, and flaps her hands with a "shush" in my direction, but I see her hide a smile, and I know she's pleased.

After the speeches we eat dinner. This is a calm, contained, civilized party—nothing like Mansfield Mayhem. We're all subdued tonight, partially because the adults are there, but also because we know it's our last time to be together. We're celebrating, but we're also mourning.

Once the official dinner is officially over, Harry, Vanessa, Lawrence, Julia, Manny, and I find a couple of sofas in the common room that aren't taken. We curl up together and talk, sometimes in pairs, sometimes in one big group. Harry and I are always next to each other. Even when I'm talking quietly with someone else, I can feel his leg warm against mine. I don't ever want to stop feeling that.

The graduate students don't make us go to bed. They come through a couple of times just to check on us, but they don't scold us and they don't tell us it's curfew. Ted and Charles even join us on the sofas for a little while around two in the morning. Charles tells me he's never been so blown away by an actor so quickly. "You said three lines and I knew I wanted you in my play."

I store that compliment so I can take it out later, when I have time to think about it. "I want to act more," I tell him, and I realize it's true as I say it. "I'm going to try out for the school play this year."

"You should also look at colleges with good drama programs," he says. "I'm not saying it has to be your career, but theater should always be a part of your life."

The older guys eventually leave and the rest of us keep talking, lazily, dreamily, sleepily. . . . At some point I doze off on Harry's shoulder. I wake up and look around, and ask Vanessa where Lawrence has disappeared to, but she says it's his secret to tell.

At some point Harry dozes off on *my* shoulder. When he wakes up, he asks what time it is. I tell him it's almost five, and he says, "Let's all go watch the sunrise together."

So we struggle up off the sofas and up the stairs to the rooms to grab quilts off the beds; then we go out into the courtyard and wrap ourselves up and lie together in one big heap, on our backs, our heads propped up on one another's legs, all of us gazing up at the sky, which gradually grows lighter until we can see the first arc of the sun poking above the trees that surround us.

And then we all doze off.

I wake up first and it's seven and I panic because my flight is at noon and that means I only have a few hours left to be with everyone. I wake the others up, and we agree to meet in the dining hall in half an hour. I go up to Julia and Vanessa's room so I can use the bathroom and wash my face. Marie is asleep, her already packed bags on the floor next to her. Julia and Vanessa want to change their clothes, but I have only the dress I was wearing the night before and I don't want to waste any time waiting for them, so I leave them behind and head over to the dining hall by myself.

The first person I spot in there is Lawrence, who's

sitting at a table by himself, staring off into space.

"You okay?" I ask as I approach him.

He startles and looks at me. "Hey, Franny. I'm so tired I think I'm having an out-of-body experience." He rubs his eyes. "I didn't get any sleep last night."

"I got like an hour at most. What happened to you? I fell asleep for a few minutes and when I woke up, you were gone. Where'd you disappear to?"

"I was just hanging out . . . ," he says with a little smile. And at that moment one of the actors I only know slightly, a guy named Kevin who was in the *Midsummer Night's Dream* cast with Lawrence, comes over with a couple of cups of coffee and I realize that Lawrence isn't *really* sitting alone. He was just waiting for Kevin to return. I catch his eye and bob my head questioningly in Kevin's direction, and Lawrence smiles again and nods his answer, and I know who he was with for the second half of last night.

They found each other . . . just in time to say good-bye. It sucks, but we're all facing tough partings.

I hug Lawrence and make him promise not to leave without telling me. "Are you kidding me?" he says. "There will be tears. Many tears. Prepare yourself."

It's the beginning of an endless morning of emotional good-byes. People are running back and forth between the tables, exchanging emails, cell phone numbers, memories. The early morning sunlight streams through the windows, catching dust motes in every beam—it looks like movie lighting. It's melodramatic. Clichéd. Magical. It *feels* like the last morning of something.

Harry comes in with his roommates, gets himself a cup of coffee and a bowl of cereal, and joins me at the table where I've settled with Vanessa and Julia, who came in together a few minutes earlier, and Manny, who's just arrived.

Alex and Isabella show up a little while later, and to everyone's surprise they walk through the buffet line together. When they emerge, they exchange a glance and then join us at the table. Harry looks at Isabella, and she gives a slightly embarrassed shrug, which I think means that she and Alex hooked up at some point last night. But they still seem awkward and uncomfortable around each other—the conversation doesn't exactly flow from either of them—so I think it was more of a nostalgic last fling than any kind of new beginning.

Marie never shows up at the dining hall. She's either still asleep or gone.

Vanessa has to leave breakfast first, because she's getting picked up by a relative who's taking her to the airport. Her hugs are tight and enthusiastic and she orders every one of us to stay in touch and come visit her in New York. "Most people would kill to have a place to stay right in the city," she points out. "You guys are nuts if you don't take advantage of it. And I can show you around NYU and Columbia if you're interested in either."

Lawrence decides to walk out with her so they can have some time alone together while she's packing, so I have to say good-bye to him too.

"You will video-chat with me at least once a week," he says during our last hug. "Do you hear me? Repeat that so I know you heard me."

I repeat it. Through my tears.

A little while later, I'm the one who has to leave. I stand up, setting off another round of hugs.

Julia and I agree that we'll make a point of getting together a *lot* back home, now that we've reconnected, and I tell Alex I'm including him in that plan.

Isabella kisses me on the cheek. "Come to L.A.," she says.

"Why?" I say with a grin. "What's in L.A.?"

Harry doesn't bother getting up. "Bye," he says, glancing up briefly. "See you around, babe."

"Yeah, okay. Later." I head toward the dining-hall door.

He catches up with me as I'm crossing the threshold. "Hold on," he says. "We should probably shake hands good-bye, don't you think?"

"Don't get all mushy on me, Cartwright."

But the joke is over. We stand, facing each other, in the damp heat. The sun has gone behind some heavy clouds. The sky can't make up its mind what it wants to be.

Neither of us says anything for a minute.

He breaks the silence. "How long is the drive from L.A. to Phoenix?"

"Six hours, maybe?"

"That's not so bad."

"I don't have a car."

"I do."

"Then come," I say. "Soon. And often. All the time." I'm done worrying about our ugly little apartment. The only way I can bear to say good-bye right now is if I know I'll see him again soon.

"You have to come visit me, too," he says. "Just so you know what I'm talking about when I talk about my crazy family. And I want to show you around L.A. It's crass and materialistic and fake—you'll love it."

"Yes," I say. "You know how much I adore things— and people—that are crass and materialistic and fake." I snake my fingers between his. "Okay, so you have, what, a three o'clock flight this afternoon? And then it's like a couple of hours to L.A.?"

"Something like that."

"And then you have to get home from the airport . . . and you should probably say hi to your parents, maybe have an early dinner with them, so they don't feel hurt . . . so let's say it's seven, maybe eight p.m. before you can hit the road? You could be at my place by, like, two in the morning. If you drive fast and don't stop."

"Make it three. I'll need to drink a lot of coffee to stay awake."

"I'm joking," I say.

"I'm not."

"Then that's a first."

Harry rocks back on his heels. "You still don't think I'm capable of being sincere, do you?"

I start to answer, then give up on the idea of talking and just throw my arms around his neck and hold him tight like I'm drowning. Because I trust him and believe him. Completely. And I don't want to joke around anymore.

"Come as soon as you can," I whisper in his ear.

"As soon as I can," he promises.

Amelia drives me to the airport, and when I get out of the car, she gets out too and embraces me and tells me that she's loved having me there, that I'm a wonderful niece and a semidecent seamstress and she'll miss me horribly. I'm stunned by her sudden warmth. She hasn't shown me much over the course of the summer, but maybe the affection has been there all along, just hidden behind all the anxiety and judgment.

When I hear my name being called at the baggage carousel, I'm so exhausted that for a second I look around to see where Amelia is and wonder how she ended up in Phoenix, but then I realize it's my mother. I'd never noticed before how similar their voices are. Their features, too—my mother's a softer, sweeter, prettier version of her sister. A *better* version. I'm happy to be with her again, happy that she's my mom and Amelia's just my aunt, happy that she can say "I've missed you, Franny" and "I love you" without discomfort or uncertainty—and happy that I can say both things back to her and mean them.

Mom helps me bring my bags in, pours me a glass of iced tea, then sits me down at the kitchen table and orders me to keep her company while she bustles around making dinner—it's early, but she's making lasagna since that's my favorite and it takes hours. She's so happy I'm back she's practically shimmering with joy.

"Your dad is coming by later to see you," she tells me, as she chops an onion at the counter a foot away from where I'm sitting, her back vibrating slightly with each *snick-snick* of the knife. "And William said you should call as soon as you get home. But I want you for a little longer all to myself. If you call him, you'll tell all your stories and then you won't want to tell me." She turns, knife in her hand, to look at me over her shoulder. "I've loved your texts and phone calls, but I know there's a lot you didn't get around to telling me. So tell."

"Yeah, you're right." I take a sip of iced tea and

lean back comfortably against the familiar curve of the wooden kitchen chair. "I wanted to tell you in person, like this. Because there was this guy—oh, and there was this other guy too." I think for a moment. "But mostly? There was this guy. . . ."

Turn the page to read the first chapter of
Claire LaZebnik's

one

The front office wasn't as crazy as you'd expect on the first day of school, which seemed to confirm Coral Tree Prep's reputation as "a well-oiled machine."

That was a direct quote from the Private School Confidential website I had stumbled across when I first Googled Coral Tree—right after my parents told me and my three sisters we'd be transferring there in the fall. Since it was on the other side of the country from where we'd been living—from where I'd lived my entire life—I couldn't exactly check it myself, and I was desperate for more information.

A well-oiled machine didn't sound too bad. But I was less thrilled to read that Coral Tree was "basically a country club masquerading as a school." The same anonymous writer added, "I've yet to see a student drive a car onto campus that's not a Porsche or a BMW. And even an AP math student would lose count of the

Louboutins on the girls here." Yuck.

But while I was clicking around that site, I learned about another private school in L.A. that had a "condom tree"—kids allegedly tossed their used condoms up into its branches—so I guess my parents could have done worse than, you know, *Coral* Tree.

True to the school's reputation, the administrator in the office was brisk and efficient and had quickly printed up and handed me and Juliana each a class list and a map of the school.

"You okay?" I asked Juliana, as she stared at the map like it was written in some foreign language. She started and looked up at me, slightly panicked. Juliana's a year older than me, but she sometimes seems younger—mostly because she's the opposite of cynical and I'm the opposite of the opposite of cynical.

Because we're so close in age, people frequently ask if the two of us are twins. It's lucky for me we're not, because if we *were*, Juliana would be The Pretty One. She and I do look a lot alike, but there are infinitesimal differences—her eyes are just a touch wider apart, her hair a bit silkier, her lips fuller—and all these little changes add up to her being truly beautiful and my being reasonably cute. On a good day. When the light hits me right.

I put my head closer to hers and lowered my voice. "Did you *see* the girls in the hallway? How much makeup they're all wearing? And their hair is perfect, like they spent hours on it. How is that possible?" Mine was in a ponytail. It wasn't even all that clean because our fourteen-year-old sister, Layla, had hogged the bathroom that morning and I'd barely had time to brush my teeth, let alone take a shower.

"It'll all be fine," Juliana said faintly.

"Yeah," I said, with no more conviction. "Anyway, I'd better run. My first class is on the other side of the building." I squinted at the map. "I think."

She squeezed my arm. "Good luck."

"Find me at lunch, okay? I'll be the one sitting by herself."

"You'll make friends, Elise," she said. "I know you will."

"Just *find* me." I took a deep breath and plunged out of the office and into the hallway—and instantly hit someone with the door. "Sorry!" I said, cringing.

The girl I'd hit turned, rubbing her hip. She wore an incredibly short miniskirt, tight black boots that came up almost to her knees, and a spaghetti-strap tank top. It was an outfit more suited for a nightclub than a day of classes, but I had to admit she had the right body for it. Her blond hair was beautifully cut, highlighted, and styled, and the makeup she wore really played up her pretty blue eyes and perfect little nose. Which was scrunched up now in disdain as she surveyed me and bleated out a loud and annoyed "FAIL!"

The girl standing with her said, "Oh my God, are you okay?" in pretty much the tone you'd use if someone you cared about had just been hit by a speeding pickup truck right in front of you.

It hadn't been *that* hard a bump, but I held my hands up apologetically. "Epic fail. I know. Sorry."

The girl I'd hit raised an eyebrow. "At least you're honest."

"At least," I agreed. "Hey, do you happen to know where room twenty-three is? I have English there in, like, two minutes and I don't know my way around. I'm new here."

The other girl said, "I'm in that class, too." Her hair was brown instead of blond and her eyes hazel instead of blue, but the two girls' long, choppy manes and skinny bodies had been cast from the same basic mold. She was wearing a narrow, silky turquoise tank top over snug boot-cut jeans and a bunch of multicolored bangles on her slender wrist. "You can follow me. See you later, Chels."

"Yeah—wait, hold on a sec." Chels—or whatever her name was—pulled her friend toward her and whispered something in her ear. Her friend's eyes darted toward me briefly, but long enough to make me glance down at my old straight-leg jeans and my THIS IS

WHAT A FEMINIST LOOKS LIKE T-shirt and feel like I shouldn't have worn either.

The two girls giggled and broke apart.

"I know, right?" the friend said. "See you," she said to Chels and immediately headed down the hallway, calling brusquely over her shoulder, "Hurry up. It's on the other side of the building and you *don't* want to be late for Ms. Phillips's class."

"She scary?" I asked, scuttling to keep up.

"She just gets off on handing out EMDs."

"EMDs?" I repeated.

"Early morning detentions. You have to come in at, like, seven in the morning and help clean up and stuff like that. Sucks. Most of the teachers here are pretty mellow if you're a couple of minutes late, but not Phillips. She's got major control issues."

"What's your name?" I asked, dodging a group of girls in cheerleader outfits.

"Gifford." *Really? Gifford?* "And that was Chelsea you hit with the door. You really should be more careful."

Too late for that advice—in my efforts to avoid bumping into a cheerleader, I had just whammed my shoulder on the edge of a locker. I yelped in pain. Gifford rolled her eyes and kept moving.

I caught up again. "I'm Elise," I said, even though

5

she hadn't asked. "You guys in eleventh grade, too?"

"Yeah. So you're new, huh? Where're you from?"

"Amherst, Mass."

She actually showed some interest. "That near Harvard?"

"No. But Amherst College is there. And UMass."

She dismissed that with an uninterested wave. "You get snow there?"

"It's Massachusetts," I said. "Of course we do. Did."

"So do you ski?"

"Not much." My parents didn't, and the one time they tried to take us it was so expensive that they never repeated the experiment.

"We go to Park City every Christmas break," Gifford said. "But this year my mother thought maybe we should try Vail. Or maybe Austria. Just for a change, you know?"

I didn't know. But I nodded like I did.

"You see the same people at Park City every year," she said. "I get sick of it. It's like Maui at Christmas, you know?"

I wished she'd stop saying "You know?"

Fortunately, we had reached room 23. "In here," said Gifford. She opened the door and went in, successfully communicating that her mentoring ended at the room's threshold.

* * *

6

Over the course of the next four hours, I discovered that:

1. Classes at Coral Tree Prep were really small. When we got to English, I was worried that half the class would get EMDs or whatever they were called because there were fewer than a dozen kids in the room. But when Ms. Phillips came in, she said, "Good—everyone's here, let's get started," and I realized that *was* the class.

2. The campus grounds were unbelievably green and seemed to stretch on for acres. I kept gazing out the window, wishing I could escape and go rolling down the grassy hills that lined the fields.

3. Teachers at Coral Tree Prep didn't like you to stare out the window and would tell you so in front of the entire class who would then all turn and stare at The New Girl Who Wasn't Paying Attention.

4. Everyone at Coral Tree Prep was good-looking. Really. Everyone. I didn't see a single fat or ugly kid all morning. Maybe they just locked them up at registration and didn't let them out again until graduation.

5. Girls here wore every kind of footwear imaginable, from flip-flops to spike-heeled mules to UGG boots (despite the sunny, 80-degree weather), EXCEPT for sneakers. I guess those marked you as fashion-impaired.

6. I was wearing sneakers.

two

There are all these clichés about what it's like to be the new kid at school, like in movies, when you see people playing pranks on them or ostracizing them or publicly ridiculing them. I had no previous experience at being new: I had gone to only one public elementary school, which fed into my middle school, which fed into my old high school. So I don't know what I had been expecting, but the reality was more boring than anything else.

People were all willing to acknowledge me, ask me if I was new and what my name was, welcome me to the school (literally, several kids said, "Welcome to Coral Tree!"), and then they lost interest and went back to talking to their friends. I was isolated but not ostracized, ignored but not abused.

Still, it was stressful sitting alone and trying to look like I was fascinated by the posters on the various classroom walls whenever the other kids were chatting, so I was *very* happy to spot Juliana waiting in the cafeteria line when lunch break finally rolled around.

"Hey, you!" I ran over and just barely restrained myself from hugging her.

"Hey, yourself," she said calmly.

"How's it going? No one's talking to me. Is anyone talking to you?"

"Actually," she said, "people have been really nice."

"That's great." I wanted to be happy for her, but I had been looking forward to sharing the misery. "So what are you going to eat?"

"I don't know." She gave a vague look around. "Salad maybe? I'm not that hungry."

"You're not? I'm starving." It wasn't until I had grabbed a huge turkey sub and Juliana was balancing a dainty little green salad on her tray that it occurred to me there was something weird about Juliana's not being hungry. Usually she had a pretty healthy appetite. The only other time I could remember her not wanting to eat (when she wasn't sick) was the year before, when she had a crush on a guy in her Health and Human Fitness class. That had not ended well—the guy turned out to be a total tool.

As I moved through the cafeteria line, I saw raw tuna sushi. And pomegranate seeds. And tamales. And

Nutrisystem shakes. And sausage sticks made out of ostrich meat.

We definitely weren't in Massachusetts anymore.

I passed by a guy grabbing a can of soda out of the cold case. He was at least six feet tall, broad-shouldered, dark-haired, and way cuter than any guy at my old school, which had been full of highly cerebral and physically underdeveloped faculty brats. (To give you an idea: we had both a varsity and junior varsity debate team, but only enough recruits for a single basketball team.) While Juliana and I waited in line to pay, I glanced over my shoulder at him again—I'm not usually a gawker, but I'd had a tough morning and deserved a little pleasure.

I balanced my tray against my hip, checked the line—still a few people ahead of us—and stole another glance at Handsome Guy.

Whose gorgeous eyes met mine as he turned around, soda in hand. He gave me a vaguely annoyed and weary look—a look that said, *I'm so done with people staring at me*—and turned on his heel. Guess I wasn't as subtle as I thought. Blushing furiously, I turned back to the cashier before I embarrassed myself any more.

After we'd paid, Juliana led the way out of the cafeteria to the picnic tables scattered around the school courtyard.

"Outside tables?" I said. "What do they do when it rains?"

"It's L.A.," Juliana said absently, turning her head from side to side like she was searching for something. "It doesn't rain."

"That's got to be an exaggeration. How about there?" I pointed to an empty table. I just wanted to be alone with Jules, have a few minutes to relax before starting all over again with the afternoon classes.

But she was on the move, marching deliberately toward one of the tables—

Where some guy was rising to his feet and exuberantly waving her over, then gesturing down at the empty space next to him, like he'd been expecting her.

And she was going right toward him.

Suddenly, her loss of appetite made sense.

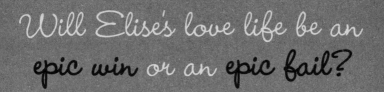